HER COWBOY BILLIONAIRE BEAST

CHRISTMAS AT WHISKEY MOUNTAIN LODGE, A HAMMOND BROTHERS NOVEL, BOOK 4

LIZ ISAACSON

ISBN-13:978-1-63876-169-3

CHAPTER 1

Cy Hammond stayed close to his parents and grandmother while people seemed to be moving in every direction. The lodge was a massive building, with plenty of high-end finishes, and it fit in this mountain landscape perfectly.

The Whittakers knew how to put on a good holiday party, that was for sure. Simply keeping track of everyone that would be at the lodge for the Christmas Eve tree lighting and ensuring they'd have a stocking with gifts was a huge feat.

He knew exactly who'd taken care of it, because Cy was low-profile enough here to blend into the background, with the racing thoughts that kept him looking from person to person, watching them.

Observant, he liked to think about himself.

Patsy Foxhill was the one who directed everything here at the lodge. She talked to several other women, as well as

Beau Whittaker, and the whole system ran without a hitch. If she didn't do that, everything would fall apart.

Cy knew, because he had a guy at his motorcycle shop who did the same thing. Wade knew every little thing that happened at Rev for Vets, but he wasn't the public face of the operation. In that situation, Cy *was* the high-profile one, and he always knew everyone was watching him.

Beau had just announced that Cy's shop would be open by spring, and it would be. The building was coming along great, especially now that the walls and roof were done. For a couple of weeks there, he'd thought the weather would prevent him from getting the shop back up and running before next Christmas.

He'd called Wade last week, just to make sure he couldn't relocate. He'd offered him the job the moment he'd spoken to Patsy and gotten confirmation on an asking price for the twenty acres of apple orchard he now owned.

Wade had said no, for the third time, which meant that Cy had no manager for his shop. He knew who he wanted, and the blonde came into the living room, those pretty blue eyes obviously searching for someone.

"Graham," she said, spotting him. "We need you in the kitchen."

The tall cowboy went with her, and Cy wondered if she felt any spark for him at all. His skin and muscles still vibrated with the electricity from her touch, and it had happened months ago. He had her number, but he'd only communicated with her about professional things, and once the contract was signed, there was nothing else for them to talk about.

Cy had rented an old house on the north side of town, and he was planning to build himself a house on some of the twenty acres he now owned. The shop took up four in the back corner of the lot, and Cy had actually considered adding a third floor to the building design and simply living above everything.

In the end, he didn't want his whole life wrapped up in one place, and he'd hired an architect to start designing him a house that would be lavish and comfortable, but wouldn't require the removal of too many apple trees.

Cy didn't even really like apples—he couldn't remember the last time he'd eaten one—but the orchard meant a great deal to Patsy. And for some reason he could not name, he wanted her to be happy with the decisions he made with her orchard.

Your orchard, he reminded himself as a dinging sound filled the air. He glanced toward the front door, but no one else seemed to be looking that way. "All right," Patsy said over the intercom system in the lodge. "We're gathering in the dining room. Dinner will be served in two minutes."

Cy's heartbeat filled the back of his throat at the sound of Patsy's voice. It carried a sense of authority he liked, as well as the kindness that spoke of her femininity. She didn't hide behind her hair, and she accented it with big earrings and the perfect amount of makeup. Tonight, she'd been wearing a skin-tight pair of black jeans with a bright yellow sweater with a white star in the middle of it.

People started moving into the kitchen, and Cy reached for Grams. "Stay with me, Grams," he said. "I'll get you a good seat." He turned toward the doorway, and his eyes finally met Patsy's. They'd been dancing around one another all afternoon and evening, and now he stood face-to-face with her.

"Hello, Cy," she said easily, giving nothing away.

"Hey, Patsy." He gave her what he hoped was a bright smile. It felt good on his face, and her mouth curved upward too, so maybe it had worked. "Merry Christmas."

"Merry Christmas." She looked at Grams. "I have a spot for you, Opal." She reached for her, and Cy passed his ninety-eight-year-old grandmother to Patsy's care.

He felt like he couldn't breathe, and he stepped through the doorway and let his parents go in front of him too. He lost sight of Patsy behind the width of his father's shoulders, and he ducked down a side hall that had a door at the end of it.

He didn't go all the way outside, because without a coat, doing so would be a death wish. He cracked the door and took a slow, deep drag of the fresh air, the temperature difference between inside and outside probably a hundred degrees.

"What am I going to do about a supervisor?" he asked. "You led me here, Lord. I need help." He'd managed to get McCall to agree to come to Coral Canyon in March, as well as two other mechanics. Winslow and Dom from his custom design team had agreed to come, and his secretary, Marissa.

He'd employed a lot more people, but in the past six months, they'd all gotten different jobs. McCall and Winslow had too, but they'd been willing to quit when Cy had called with his job offer, which included a moving package.

"A lot more help," he added to his verbal dialog with the Lord. He reached over and flipped the rubber band on his wrist, the *thwap* comforting him. Outside, the wind blew, rattling the ajar door.

He quickly reached for the knob to make sure it didn't get stolen off its hinges. Lightning flashed, and only two seconds later, thunder grumbled through the sky. Loud thunder.

Cy pulled the door closed and locked it, peering through the glass as hail started to pummel the ground. He flipped the rubber band again. Then again.

"Why do you do that?"

He flinched and turned toward the very woman who'd been in his head in some form since she'd almost run over him in that giant Hummer of her brother's. Cy looked at Patsy, wishing he could be as verbal with her as he was with the Lord.

His thoughts moved in and out of his head so fast, he couldn't grasp onto them. He'd just prayed for a solution to his supervisor problem, and Patsy had appeared.

Without giving it too much thought, he asked, "Would you come run my motorcycle shop?"

Patsy blinked at him, the surprise laid out in her eyes. He saw doubt as it moved quickly across her expression, and then her rejection. "I have a job," she said.

"Yeah, but you're bored in it." He walked away from her, foolishness streaming through him. He didn't know her. He shouldn't have said that.

"Hey," she said, her voice angry behind him.

He stopped near the corner and turned around to face her again. "Sorry," he said, holding up one hand. "I'm sorry."

Patsy once again looked like he'd thrown cold water in her face. She marched toward him, her face broadcasting anger. She paused a couple of feet from him. "How did you know I'm bored in the job?" she asked. "Not that I'm bored in the job. This place is a zoo most of the time."

"They need two people to do what you do by yourself," he said. "Anyone can see it. Why haven't you told… whoever your boss is?"

"Graham," she supplied. "And I don't know."

"Have Wes do it. I think he's still consulting with them."

Patsy sighed as she looked past him. "He is." She shook her head and reached up to brush her short bangs off her forehead. They weren't long enough to tuck or stay back with her other hair, and they just fell back into place. "I'm not going to ask him to say anything."

"I shouldn't have said anything either," Cy said. "Moment of desperation." He'd had a lot of them lately, and he really needed to school his mouth during those moments.

She dropped her eyes, and she looked soft and beautiful in that moment. She was organized and knowledgeable, and to an untrained eye, she came across as cold. Cy had thought that the first time he'd met her too.

"Apology accepted," she murmured.

The next thing he knew, her fingers touched his, and he

sucked in a breath involuntarily. She heard it, and she lifted her eyes to his. That electricity that pulsed through the sky and then called down thunder now coursed between the two of them.

As she looked down again, her fingertip ran along the thick rubber band on his wrist. "It helps you focus, right?"

"Yes," he said, his voice much lower than normal. He told himself in a very stern mental voice not to clear his throat. *Don't do it*, he thought, easily switching it to a prayer. *Please don't let me clear my throat.*

He backed up a step when she met his eyes again. His back bumped into the wall behind him, and he stilled.

"My brother used to wear one," she said, finally dropping his hand.

Cy's fingers immediately started rubbing the area of his wrist around the rubber band where she'd been touching. He shifted to the left a little, his shoulder blade running into a box there.

A rousing round of laughter erupted from around the corner, but Cy didn't even look in that direction. He didn't care what was happening in the dining room. He only wanted this moment to continue.

"Would you like to go out with me?" he asked, and he was so deep inside the moment, he heard the words echoing outside his head. It took a moment for him to realize they actually had echoed through the house.

He glanced up at the ceiling as if it held the answer to his confusion. "What's...?" He heard that piping through the speaker system too, and horror filled him.

Colton appeared around the corner, taking in Cy and

Patsy standing there, facing off. He knocked on the wall a couple of times as pure glee filled his expression. "You might, uh, wanna turn that off before she answers." His grin was the size of Texas, and he disappeared as quickly as he'd appeared.

Cy pressed his eyes closed and stepped to the other side of the hall. When he turned and opened his eyes, he saw the box on the wall and the speaker embedded into the wall above it, where Patsy had spoken the announcement for dinner.

CHAPTER 2

Patsy Foxhill traded places with Cy Hammond, her pulse pounding dangerously loud in her ears. She hadn't heard the dinging that always preceded an announcement through the public address system at the lodge. The laughter in the dining room had covered it.

They'd all heard him ask her to go out with him, though, and Patsy honestly had no idea how to answer him. The truth was, she'd very much like to go out with Cy Hammond. He'd worn a regular pair of slacks to the lodge tonight, and with the bright blue dress shirt and paisley bow tie, he was downright handsome.

He ducked his head, his black cowboy hat cutting off their connection. Across the hall, she heard the distinct sound of his rubber band slapping against his skin.

Without obsessing any longer about his question, she twisted back to the wall, leaned forward, and said, "Yes."

The word filled the lodge, and she had enough time to

turn and face him before a roar in the dining room filled the air.

Cy's head jerked up, and Patsy reached to brush at her bangs again. She really needed to stop doing that, because it accomplished nothing, and it revealed her nerves.

"Patsy?"

Patsy spun toward the child's voice to find Ronnie and Averie standing there. "Yes?" She took a couple of steps toward them. "I'm coming. Did you guys save me any of those meatballs?" She put her arms around each of them and didn't dare glance over her shoulder to see what Cy was doing.

In the kitchen, she found trays and pans of food, a lot of it taken already. Averie asked for another roll, and Patsy got it for the seven-year-old. Ronnie wanted pie, but Patsy could tell it wasn't time yet. "You'll have to ask Celia," she said. "Or your mother."

"No pie," Laney said from the other side of the counter. "We're still eating, bud. Come sit down."

With the extra table in the dining area, there was hardly room to move around. Patsy kept her eyes down as she put mashed potatoes and meatballs and gravy on her plate. Celia had made her fancy lemon-garlic peas, and Patsy noticed there were plenty of those left.

She felt a lot of eyes on her, and trepidation accompanied her as she picked up a red plastic cup of punch and finally allowed herself to look up.

Sure enough, everyone in the dining room was looking at her. Heat filled her face, and she didn't know what to say.

"There's a seat over here," Elise said. "I saved for you." She glanced out into the hallway and back to Patsy.

Patsy went that way, and thankfully, one of the triplets chose that moment to spill their juice, which caused a commotion and offered the ice-breaker everyone needed to move back to their own conversations and lives.

Patsy put her plate down, as well as her drink, and took the seat beside Sophia on one side and Todd Christopherson on the other. She glanced at him, hoping he didn't care about her love life.

He flashed a grin at her and then turned back to his twins. "Did you hear, Patsy?"

"Hear what?" she asked.

"Vi and I are expecting another baby."

"You are?" Patsy looked past him to Vi. "That's so great. Congratulations." Happiness filled her, and she pushed against the thread of jealousy as it threatened to stitch her lungs too tight.

"Thanks," Vi said, reaching for a napkin and using it to wipe Mary's face. "Hey, let me clean you up. Stop it." She got the job done, and Patsy went back to her dinner.

Sophia leaned toward her. "Did you really just say you'd go out with Cy Hammond?"

Patsy nodded as she cut a meatball in half and scooped up a bite of meat, potatoes, and gravy. Celia's onion brown gravy was the stuff dreams were made of, and Patsy realized how hungry she was. She couldn't remember if she'd eaten lunch, and she knew she'd only had a protein shake for breakfast.

There was always so much to do at the lodge for this

evening, and Patsy worked a lot during the holidays when others didn't. As soon as dinner ended, she'd slip out the front door and head down the canyon to her father's house. She'd invited him up to the lodge over and over, but he'd never wanted to come.

Betty was making dinner tonight at the house where they'd grown up, and Patsy had promised to be there in time for dessert. She loved spending time with her nieces, and Joe had started coming back to the land of the living after his divorce had been finalized just after Halloween. He'd bring his son and daughter tonight, and his ex-wife would have them tomorrow.

"How did this happen?" Sophia asked, her voice still a hiss in Patsy's ear. "What happens if you fall in love with him? You realize these Hammonds are taking over this lodge, right?"

"They are?" Patsy asked. "None of them live here." She turned toward Sophia and searched her best friend's and roommate's eyes. Sophia possessed a bit of a salty streak, and her chocolate-brown eyes held plenty of it right now.

"They've taken three of our friends," Sophia said as if Patsy didn't know.

"He bought half of my dad's orchard," Patsy said. She hadn't told anyone that, even Sophia. The two of them shared a cabin in the corner of the back yard, and they'd grown close in the last three years since they'd been working here at Whiskey Mountain Lodge. "So I met him a few months ago."

She glanced around to see if Cy had come in. He hadn't. A blip of betrayal slid through her veins with every beat of her heart. He'd left her to face the whole crowd—people she knew way better than him—by herself.

Maybe she shouldn't have said yes to his dinner invitation so quickly. Patsy didn't normally let her hormones dictate what she did, and she certainly didn't date men like Cy Hammond.

"Have you been talking to him since he bought the orchard?" Sophia asked.

"Sophia, I'm not going to fall in love with him."

Sophia shrugged one shoulder and said, "You might."

Patsy didn't argue further, because she didn't need to get into her personal insecurities at the Whittaker family dinner on Christmas Eve.

The truth was, Sophia was right. She might very well fall in love with Cy Hammond, but Sophia didn't need to worry about one of the Hammond brothers "taking" her from the lodge.

Even if she fell for him, no one she ever dated had ever fallen in love with her. Her last boyfriend hadn't even noticed when she'd cut off ten inches of her hair.

Cy noticed your hair at the orchard, she thought, and Patsy really hated that she remembered that from months ago.

She finished eating and started cleaning up, picking up dishes children had left behind. About the time the ice cream came out of the freezer and the Everett sisters brought their guitars out of the master bedroom, Patsy slipped into her coat and out the door to go to her father's.

"Oh," she said when she encountered a cowboy on the front steps. "It's cold out here, Cy. What are you doing?"

He looked up at her. "Thinking." He stood up and shuffled a couple of steps back. "Sorry about that in there."

Patsy's annoyance flared. "Which part?"

Cy blinked and cocked his head, the same way her father's dog did when she talked to him in a high-pitched voice. "I...don't know."

"Why didn't you come eat?" she asked. "You threw me to the wolves." She hitched her purse higher on her shoulder, unable to stay for much longer. "I have to go. I'm late."

"Where are you going?"

"My father's," she said as she walked away.

"You didn't have to use the intercom to say yes," he called after her.

Patsy had half a mind to spin around and march back to him to really give him a piece of her mind. Instead, she turned and walked backward as she said, "I take it back, then. I don't want to go out with you."

She waved and continued to her car, surprised Cy didn't say anything else. She got behind the wheel, her heart pounding. She had no idea what had just happened in the last hour. She'd asked him a very personal question, which he'd answered. He'd made an innocent mistake pressing the public address system, but he had asked her out.

She liked that he'd asked her out, but she had zero confidence in her ability to hold a man's attention for longer than a few minutes. And now she'd taken back her acceptance.

A sigh filled the car as it left her mouth, and she looked

into her own eyes in the rear-view mirror. She hardly recognized herself, and that only added another layer of unrest to her already weary soul.

"Help me get through tonight," she whispered as she fitted the key into the ignition. As she backed out of her parking space and headed for the exit, she added, "And what just happened with Cy Hammond? Can You give me a little more direction there, please? Would that be so hard?"

It obviously was, because Patsy's mind ran around and around the long-haired Hammond brother all the way to her father's house, which sat in the middle of thirty acres of apple trees.

Joe's Hummer sat closest to the garage, which meant he'd been here the longest. His children were eight and five, and he was probably exhausted. He didn't have them very often, because literally the day after his wife had filed for divorce, Joe had lost his job. He'd picked up a new one driving the new bus around town, and since it was a new system, he worked a lot.

He seemed to like it though, and the last Patsy had heard, his boss liked him and had told him he was a smart guy who had management potential.

His ex-wife, Kathy, still lived in town, but she'd moved to a house across the street from her parents, and the kids spent a lot of time over there. Patsy actually missed her. No one had ever talked about what happened to the extended family in a divorce, and Patsy felt like she'd lost a friend she'd known for fifteen years.

Betty's minivan was parked behind Joe's truck, and it

looked like it had been driven through a mud field to get to their father's. It probably had been. Betty and Cory lived on a farm on a muddy piece of land off a dirt road about halfway to Dog Valley. They had four teenage girls, and Patsy sat in her car for a few extra minutes, trying to gear herself up to go inside.

It would be loud, she knew, and she'd just come from somewhere with the same pulsing energy she'd find behind the front door.

When her phone chimed and the curtains on the front window fluttered, Patsy knew she'd been spotted. Betty probably wanted to know why she was sitting in her car when she could be inside with the family.

Patsy sighed as she got out of the car and hurried to the safety of the covered front porch. The hail had stopped, thankfully, but the sky looked like it could easily start to dump more. She opened the door to the wall of noise she'd been expecting, but it actually made her smile.

"I knew that was you," Betty said from her spot next to the window. She stood taller than Patsy, and she'd never had her blonde hair cut above her shoulders. In fact, when Patsy had shown up to their father's for dinner one week and Betty had seen her hair, she'd been downright dumbfounded at what had "possessed" Patsy to cut her hair so short.

Betty had curves Patsy didn't, due to carrying and giving birth to four children, but her eyes were just as bright blue, and her skin freckled in the summer, just like Patsy's.

"Who else would it be?" Patsy worked hard not to roll

her eyes. She stepped around the couch while she unzipped her coat. She tossed it on the back of the couch and hugged her sister. Betty was a dozen years older than Patsy, and she'd met and married Cory when she was only twenty-four, and their first child had come along only a year later.

"Aunt Patsy," Laura said, coming around the corner from the dining room, where all of the noise came from. She wore the hugest smile, and she hugged Patsy too. She was seventeen, and trim, with beautiful blonde hair and blue eyes. Apparently, she had a lot of boys interested in her, and Betty had "lost so much sleep" worrying about her eldest daughter. Patsy knew Betty liked the drama of literally everything, and she'd actually been encouraging her girls to have boyfriends since the time they turned thirteen.

"I'll tell Gramps we can have pie now." Laura stepped back, her smile still in place. "And I wanted to show you that new program I coded. Do you think you have time to see it?"

"Sorry I held you up," Patsy said, refusing to look at her sister. "I'm sure I have time to see it. I can't wait."

"You didn't hold us up," Laura said. "Gramps wants to eat pie twenty-four-seven." She laughed as she went back into the kitchen and dining area that was one big area. Her father also had another set of couches back here, with the television and his beloved record player. He spent almost all of his time in this one room that served different purposes, and Patsy tried to tell how he was feeling just by looking.

He sported a lot of color in his face today, and he was grinning at Betty's youngest daughter, Jessica, while she acted out something. Everyone else shouted at her, and Patsy had no idea how Jess would even be able to tell if someone got it right.

She detoured over to her father and bent down to hug him. "Merry Christmas, Daddy." She took in a deep draw of his distinct smell, which was the perpetual scent of apples and leather, a unique blend that he'd accomplished early in his life from his mutual love of two things: horseback riding and growing apple trees.

"Hello, darling," he said, his voice raspy. He should probably be on his oxygen, but Patsy couldn't even see the tank out here. He'd probably left it in the bedroom, as if the grandkids didn't know he had it.

"Yes!" Jess squealed, and she pointed at Wendy. "It was a monkey riding a bike."

The noise lessened after that, and Joe said, "Aunt Patsy's here, so we can have pie." He grinned at her, and his five-year-old daughter slid off his knee and ran to Patsy.

She giggled as she scooped Angie into her arms. "Howdy, partner," she said to the girl. Patsy had been taking Angie to ride ponies since she was old enough to walk, and they had a standing date every September for the western festival in Dog Valley. They wandered around and ate candied apples, threw horseshoes, and once, they'd gotten one of those black and white old west photos taken.

Betty had followed her into the kitchen, and Patsy

turned to watch her sister and her oldest daughter slice the pies, get out quarts of ice cream, and lay out spoons next to the bowls. "Okay," Betty said, always confident in the leadership role. Patsy had a word for her sister that wasn't all that nice, but Betty really could be bossy sometimes.

She supposed with four girls, she had to be.

"We're ready for dessert," she said. "Dad, what do you want?" She glared Jess back a few steps, and even Joe held his spot in the living room on the couch.

"Pecan," their dad rasped, and Betty handed the bowl to Laura.

"With lots of ice cream," she said to her. "Okay, we're going to go in age order. Oldest to youngest, so that makes my husband next."

Patsy rolled her eyes, because that was just like Betty. Serve her father and then her husband. After that, Joe got his treat, and Betty deviated from the declared plan again by giving his children what they wanted too. Patsy thought she could just as easily take a piece of pie from a plate as Betty could, but she helped get Angie situated at the large table in front of the back door, and she waited her turn.

She wasn't the youngest, but Betty went ahead and let her girls go next, so Patsy ended up getting her pie last.

There was plenty of apple, the kind she liked best. It would almost be a crime if the Foxhills couldn't make the best apple pie on the planet, so it was a good thing Betty could. Patsy could too. She just didn't have as many opportunities as Betty did to show off her baking skills.

The conversation was easy as they talked about what

they hoped to get for Christmas and what they'd be doing for the next week until school started again. Angie told Patsy all about the Christmas around the world stuff she'd done in kindergarten, and Patsy enjoyed the sense of family she felt here.

"I want hairspray," Michelle said, glaring at Laura.

"Hairspray?" Patsy asked, glancing at the girls. "Your mom doesn't get that for you? It's like, two dollars a can."

"Hey," Betty said. "Don't judge me. Hairspray is a real commodity around our house." She glared at Michelle and Laura. "We get enough every month. Some people just need to learn how to conserve it."

"Yeah," Michelle said. "And keep their sticky fingers out of other people's bathrooms if they run out of their own hairspray."

"I told you, I didn't—"

"Girls," Betty said with a sigh. "Do we have to argue about this on Christmas Eve?" She looked like she was poor, picked-on Betty, and Patsy hated her oldest sister's act. Since she lived up the canyon, she ordered a lot of her supplies online, and she could easily ship Michelle an extra can of hairspray once a month. Betty would never side with the younger girl, and everyone knew it. Laura, the oldest, was definitely Betty's favorite, and she probably *had* stolen her younger sister's hairspray and gotten away with it.

She helped clean up and helped her father back to his recliner. "How's the lodge?" he asked, reaching over to pat her hand.

"Good," she said. She came down to visit him alone

sometimes, because it was easier to have a real conversation with him when Betty and her entourage weren't around. "How are you doing, Daddy?"

"Good," he said. "This last round of chemo wasn't bad. I think they might have found the right combination."

"That's great," Patsy said. "I can take you to the doctor this week."

"Oh, Betty's going to do it," Dad said, and Patsy pursed her lips and nodded. She needed to get going back to the lodge, but she decided to stay for just five more minutes.

"Hey," Betty said from the formal living room in the front of the house. "There's a big truck here."

Patsy didn't move, because no one would come here looking for her. No one had called or texted, and she watched Joe's kids set up a checkerboard on the floor in front of her. Alan, the eight-year-old, was definitely the one with all the bossy Foxhill genes, but Angie let him claim the black checkers and put them on the squares just-so.

"Patsy," Betty said, appearing in the doorway, her face flushed. "It's for you."

"What's for me?" She let go of her father's hand and stood up, confusion furrowing her brow.

"The door," Betty said, her eyes wide and astonished.

Patsy hadn't even heard the doorbell ring. Of course, Betty stood at the window like she expected a burglar to be creeping through the front yard. "Who is it?" Patsy started toward the only doorway leading into the front of the house.

Betty turned sideways to let her pass, and Patsy saw Cy standing just inside the front door, a delicious cowboy hat on his head, covering his long hair.

"What in the world are you doing here?" Patsy demanded, her steps slowing to a near-stop.

"Can I talk to you for a sec?" He didn't wait for her to answer before he turned and went out the front door. Laura looked at Patsy, and she could feel Betty's eyes on her back too.

So she followed Cy, wondering how in the world he'd even figured out where her father lived.

CHAPTER 3

C y marched across the deck and down the steps, his annoyance with himself and his brothers and Patsy and the whole wide world foaming inside him. He finally heard the slamming of the door behind him when he touched the sidewalk with his cowboy boots.

He wasn't even sure what he was doing here, only that the Lord had directed him to come. Cy had argued with Him the whole way down the canyon, but sometimes his feelings wouldn't be put to rest.

"What is going on?" Patsy hissed from behind him. "How did you even find this place?"

"Uh, I own the twenty acres on the other side of the highway?" His voice came out too sarcastic, and he knew it. "You said your father lived on this side. It wasn't that hard, Patsy."

He'd wished it had been. He'd been perfectly happy sitting in his truck too, and if the other blonde woman hadn't come out onto the porch, her arms folded, and her frown so disapproving, Cy would *still* be sitting in his truck.

It felt like the whole world was conspiring against him today.

"Well, what are you doing here?" She darted up beside him, her short legs doing a good job of keeping up.

"I just wanted to—I really do think you should come work for me."

"What?" She shook her head as if trying to get the words to line up right. "You drove down here after me to badger me about a job?"

"I'm not badgering you."

"You interrupted my family Christmas Eve party."

He reached for the door, but she threw her hand out and put hers on the handle, preventing him from opening the door. He finally allowed himself to look at her, which was a big mistake. Lightning and blue fire danced in those eyes, and when Cy's blood warmed, he realized what a horrible error he'd made. He shouldn't be attracted to the tongue-lashing he was about to get, but oddly, he was.

"This has nothing to do with a job that doesn't even start until March," she said. "You're here to soothe your broken ego."

"Don't flatter yourself," he said, though pushing her further away was the last thing he wanted to do. "I can get a date any night of the week." Just because he and his couch had gotten really close the last year or so didn't mean he couldn't find someone to share a meal with.

Your brothers don't count, he scolded himself. *Neither do your parents. And Grams is ninety-eight.*

"You're being a beast," she said, removing her hand from the handle. "You make one little mistake and hide like a child. You don't apologize when I call you on your behavior. And then you *stalk* me to my father's to say I need to work for you?" She shook her head, the lower half of her jaw starting to shake. "What a joke."

He opened the door, because he couldn't argue with her. "Come sit in here," he said. "It's warm." Cy watched her look back to the house, clearly torn. It must've been pretty bad in there for her to even consider staying out here with him, especially after what she'd just said.

Patsy's whole body shivered then, and Cy said, "Up you go, Patsy. You're turning blue."

She did as he said then, and Cy followed her into the truck. She slid over and over until she met the other side of the bench seat, and he turned on the engine and got the heater blowing.

"What are you really doing here?" she asked, her voice much quieter now. She didn't fold her arms like the woman inside, and she kept her eyes out the passenger window.

Cy looked around at all the dormant apple trees on his side of the truck. A sigh pulled through his whole body, but he did not let it out of his mouth. He'd had some real disappointments in his life too, and he knew how to cage the emotions and keep them captive until later.

"I don't know," he finally said. "I just felt like I should come."

"Really? Why?" She did look at him then, and Cy found her vulnerability absolutely charming. He liked her fire too, and he liked that they didn't get along like kibbles and bits.

Cy shrugged. "The Lord doesn't always make everything ultra clear for me."

Patsy gaped at him, and Cy realized she might not be as religious as he was. "But anyway," he said. "I was standing there, watching you drive away, and I just thought...." He shrugged again. "And I did go back into the lodge, I'll have you know. I ate dessert and took a good ribbing from my brothers." He ducked his head, glad he'd stuffed the cowboy hat from the back seat on his head before going up to the front door.

"I do still want to go out with you," he said. "I'm sorry I threw you to the wolves. That was not my intent." He hadn't even known he'd done it. He'd simply needed a few minutes alone to clear his head. He hadn't asked anyone out in a very long time, and he hadn't even wanted to. Not since Mikaela, who he could barely recall when faced with Patsy Foxhill.

"I'm sorry I said I wouldn't go," she said. "I'm just... flustered today." She turned back to the window. "Frustrated."

"You work a lot," he remarked. "You run a tight ship at that lodge, and that is not easy. Trust me, I know. It takes a huge mental toll on a person that they carry around all the time."

"Mm," Patsy said, neither confirming nor denying what he'd said.

Cy didn't know what else to say, and he started a prayer in his mind. *Gotta help me out here, Lord. I don't know why I'm here.*

"I do think you should at least consider coming to work for me," he said. "You can come see the building, and I'll give you a tour, go over the job, all of it. I pay really well, and you wouldn't have to do anything much different than you do now."

Patsy scoffed, but it didn't carry nearly the attitude of some of the other things she'd said. "I believe you were the one who said motorcycles and horses weren't even on the same planet."

"And you said they co-exist just fine," he threw back at her.

A couple of seconds passed and then Patsy started to giggle. It grew into a laugh, and Cy basked in the warm happiness of it. He ended up laughing with her, and that sure did heal something inside him he hadn't known had been knocked loose. He had the strong urge to reach over and take her hand in his.

Before he could, she gasped and said, "Oh, you've *got* to be kidding me," and launched herself out of the truck.

"Patsy—what?" He searched the orchard on her side of the truck, where she'd been focused.

It didn't take long to spot the horses grazing openly, and Patsy waving her arms, trying to get them back where they belonged.

With utmost clarity, Cy knew why he'd been prompted to make the forty-minute drive down the canyon to Patsy's father's house. He expected to see her siblings and maybe those older teenage girls he'd seen in the house to come spilling out the front and back doors to help her.

No one came.

Cy didn't even take time to turn off his truck.

He went to help, thanking the Lord for the opportunity to show Patsy he wasn't, in fact, a beast.

By the time they had the four horses her father owned back in the stable where they belonged, the door fixed, and the situation diffused, Cy was covered in mud and chilled to the bone. Patsy had run inside to get her coat at one point, and still no one had come out to help the two of them wrangle the horses.

He remembered the first time he'd met her, and how frustrated she'd been with her family then. He could see why, though he worked not to judge them. After all, he didn't like it when people passed judgment on him because of the type of pants he wore, his method of transportation, or the length of his hair.

"Thank you, Cy," Patsy said, finally looking at him. She too had taken on plenty of mud during the scuffle. "Those horses are like toddlers."

Cy thought that fit really well for horses, and he smiled. "Well, at least now I know why I came."

She nodded and started a slow walk back to his truck. They reached it, and she said, "I'm headed home, I guess." She threw another look to the house, but this time, the overbearing sister wasn't standing in the window. "Thanks again."

"Sure," he said easily. "And about that dinner…."

Patsy smiled and shook her head. "I suppose we can still go to dinner."

"Great," Cy said. "I have your number, and I'll call you to set something up."

"Sounds good." She didn't move, and the moment turned awkward. Cy had always known what to do with women. As a teenager, he'd had the most girlfriends, because he was the one willing to anger their father.

He felt a bit rusty though, as if Mikaela had left him out in the rain to freeze up every time he felt a spark of attraction for someone. Eventually, he stutter-stepped toward Patsy and took her into a very awkward embrace, patting her lamely on the back.

He cleared his throat and said, "Okay, bye." He got in his truck, muttering to himself about the throat-clearing and the ridiculous good-bye. He flipped the rubber band on his wrist, which sent a sting of pain up his arm.

Focus.

He should've done that before he'd practically lunged at her and hugged her like she had a contagious disease he didn't want to catch.

"Uncle Cy, what's a five-letter word that means a 'word with duty or pride'?" Hunter looked up from his crossword puzzle, his expression open and innocent.

Cy stirred his coffee, his mind whirring. "Let's see," he said. "Do you have any other letters?"

"Not yet." Hunter looked back at his puzzle. "I've had this clue before, but I can't remember."

"Civic," Cy said. "Try that."

Hunter put the letters in and looked at another clue. "I think that's it. Thanks." He continued to scratch his pencil over the puzzle, and Cy marveled at the twelve-year-old. Cy had never wanted to sit at a table and do puzzles when he was Hunter's age. He always wanted to be outside, doing something. Hiking, fishing, riding a dirt bike, building something, literally doing anything but being trapped inside.

"Knock, knock," Wes said as he came through the front door of Colton's house. "Merry Christmas." He carried a red sack slung over his shoulder, and he wore the biggest smile Cy had ever seen.

He thought he'd seen Wes happy before, but it was nothing like the man now. He seemed so free now that he wasn't the CEO, and he sent out beams of joy as he hugged Colton and then Ames. He went around the couch and embraced their parents, then Grams, and then he came over to Hunter and Cy.

"Guess what I brought for you, Hunt?"

Hunter put down his pencil and stood up. "Merry Christmas, Uncle Wes." He hugged him tight, clapping him on the back, and Cy realized how tall Hunter had become. "What's in the bag?"

"Oh, your dad is going to *hate* it." Wes sounded absolutely gleeful about that, and Cy chuckled.

"They're only going to be gone for a week," Cy said. "Better be something Hunt can use up in that amount of time." He stood up and gave Wes a healthy hug too, casting his eyes over to his mother, who now held the newest member of the Hammond family.

Well, Cy supposed Elise was the newest member of the family, but baby Michael was definitely the cutest. Because both Bree and Wes had dark features, so did their son, and Cy watched his mother slide her fingers through his downy soft hair, a blissful smile on her face.

He looked away, his thoughts moving to Patsy for a reason he couldn't name. He hadn't called her last night after leaving the orchard, and he wondered what her holiday plans were. Surely there wasn't work to do at the lodge on Christmas Day, but he knew Whiskey Mountain Lodge never slept.

Even if there were no guests, there would be work to do. Colton had said the Whittaker family had activities every day, all day, during their stay at the lodge, and while Cy had enjoyed being with his family the past few Christ-mases, he didn't want two weeks with everyone under the same roof.

"No way!" Hunter yelled, and Cy clued back into the happenings in the kitchen. "Uncle Wes, this is the best fishing pole there is. The *best*."

"I know," Wes said, grinning. "Well, I didn't know, but I do now, and now, it's yours."

"I wish we could go fishing right now," he said, admiring the pole. "Do you think they do ice fishing here?"

"Only for those who want to die," Colton said, joining them in the kitchen. "You got him a fishing pole?"

"The best fishing pole there is," Wes said, glancing at Colton.

"Why will Gray hate that?" Cy asked, looking between Colt and Wes.

"Because he doesn't have it," Wes said with a wolfish grin.

"Or maybe because he'd like to be the one to buy his son the best fishing pole on the planet." Colton cocked his eyebrows at Wes, whose smile stayed right on his face.

"Either way." Wes shrugged and started digging in his Santa sack again.

"Are we opening gifts then?" Ames asked. "I didn't realize. My stuff's in the bedroom." He went back upstairs, and Cy figured he better get his gifts out too. He'd put his in the pantry, and he got up and took out the candy he'd bought for everyone. Gray wouldn't like the giant bag of gummy bears Cy had bought for Hunter either, but he believed in his nephew's ability to consume them all before his father came home.

Annie turned on some festive music, and everyone gathered in the living room, where Colton had two large couches. They all fit just fine, and Cy liked watching everyone open their gifts, and expressing their gratitude, all while the scent of bacon filled the air.

"Okay," Annie said. "Breakfast will be ready in a few minutes." She went into the kitchen, and Colton joined her. They worked so well together, and something pinched in Cy's chest.

He wanted what Colton had found. He looked at Wes

and Bree, sitting side-by-side on the couch, the tiny infant in the crook of Wes's arm. Cy wanted that life too.

He wanted it all, and he always had. He'd gotten the motorcycle shop—almost. He'd thought he'd found the woman of his dreams, but he'd been wrong. And not just once, but twice. Once with Jen, and then with Mikaela. At least he hadn't made it all the way to the altar with Mikaela.

His thoughts wandered to Patsy, and he was seriously considering calling her when Ames sat down beside him and said, "So, when are you and Patsy going out?" He wore such a look of teasing that Cy didn't want to answer.

He lifted his chin and glared at his twin. "Nothing's been decided."

"Oh, I see."

"You see what?"

Ames sobered a little bit. "Nothing."

"Are you seeing anyone?" Cy challenged.

"No." Ames looked away, his eyes landing on Bree, Wes, and Michael too. "I hate that you moved here too." His voice had dropped in volume considerably.

Cy's heartbeat bounced in his chest. "I know, Ames. I'm sorry. There wasn't anything in Denver."

Ames nodded, but his jaw muscle jumped, and Cy couldn't admit he hadn't looked very hard. The commercial land market in Denver was exceedingly expensive; it was the reason Cy had relocated to California the first time. Surely Ames understood that.

"You should just move up here too," he said.

"Mom and Dad live in Ivory Peaks," he said. "Hammonds back five generations hail from Colorado. With everyone else gone, I don't know. I feel responsible to carry on that legacy."

"Gray and Hunter can carry on that legacy," Cy said. "You should be able to do what you want."

"I've been on the force in Littleton for fifteen years. I can't just leave now. It takes a long time to work up the ranks on a force."

Since Ames didn't need the money, all that was left to earn was status. Cy understood that, as he held the least in terms of status among the Hammond brothers. No college degree. No certifications. No graduations past high school.

He could only nod, and then he looked at Ames again. "Would I be too bold if I called Patsy this morning? Maybe she'd have some free time today."

"And you'd do…what, exactly?" Ames asked.

Cy shrugged, his fingers moving to the rubber band on his wrist. He didn't flip it though, just ran his fingertip along the edge of it. "I don't know. Hang out?"

"You aren't sixteen," Ames said gently. "Or in California anymore. If you want to see her, you need a plan for a *date*." He hit the T in the last word with the force Cy expected from a seasoned cop.

"Then be a good twin brother and help me come up with a plan for a date."

CHAPTER 4

P atsy spent Christmas morning at the lodge, watching all the children open presents, play with their toys, and run around in their new pajamas. Celia and Sophia served a huge breakfast, and Patsy had eaten far too many of the pancake sausage rolls that Celia was famous for.

She'd left when Eli Whittaker had gone over the public address system to say they were starting morning movies in the basement. She was welcome to stay, she knew. But Sophia would be in the kitchen cleaning up for a while, and she liked hanging out with Vi and Rose, holding Andrew's kids on her lap, and making afternoon cookies.

Patsy felt like she needed a break from all the peopling. She normally handled it just fine—thrived on it even—but the last few days at the lodge had been particularly stressful with the double wedding and the threat of snow.

As she climbed the front steps of the cabin in the corner

of the yard behind the lodge, Patsy knew her exhaustion and short fuse had nothing to do with the weddings, the Whittakers, or the white stuff that had been predicted but hadn't made an appearance yet.

Yesterday at her father's had taken a huge toll on Patsy, physically and mentally. Not even her brother had come out to help with the horses, and if Cy hadn't been there, Patsy felt sure she'd still be wandering through the apple trees, clicking her tongue, and wondering if anyone would notice if she froze to death.

She frowned at herself as she went inside the cabin, where a rush of warm air greeted her. Winter in Wyoming was no joke, as Patsy knew. She'd lived here her whole life, except for a few years in college. Even then, she'd only gone to Utah, where the winters weren't as bad, but they weren't a picnic on the beach either.

Patsy would like a picnic on the beach right now, if only because it meant she'd be somewhere warm. She certainly wasn't hungry.

A dog barked, and Patsy flinched. "Oh, Jonas," she said to the black and white dog who came trotting out of the kitchen. "You scared me." She bent down to give the mutt a pat. She'd completely forgotten that Sophia had picked up another foster dog. Ruff Rescue had called, and Sophia had a problem saying no, especially to a dog under thirty pounds, and Jonas was only twenty-four.

All of her fosters slept in her bed and usually went everywhere with her. Christmas at the lodge was crazy, and perhaps she'd intended to come back and get him. As if on cue, Patsy's phone chimed and Sophia's name sat at the top.

I forgot about Jonas! Can you let him out and bring him over?

I can keep him, Patsy sent back. *Unless you want him there.*

No, keep him, Sophia said. *Thank you, Patsy.*

"Yeah," Patsy said to herself. "Come on, boy," she said to the dog. "Let's go out, and then I think we can lay in bed and watch a movie." She returned to the front door and opened it for Jonas, who preceded her out of the cabin. She stood on the top step, her hands tucked in her pockets, while he sniffed around and finally found the right spot.

He came waddling back up the steps, and Patsy could admit he was one of the cuter foster dogs. Sometimes the pups took a shine to her, and she'd end up with them following her around all day, snoozing on her feet in the office, or trotting beside her as she went back and forth from the cabin to the lodge.

Sometimes the foster dogs had big personalities, and sometimes they wanted to sleep all day. Since there was always something going on at the lodge, they all got a lot of time around people, horses, and nature.

Ten minutes later, Patsy had shed her coat, made hot chocolate, and put on her thickest, fluffiest pair of socks. "Come on," she said to Jonas. "Let's relax." She didn't get much time off, and while a pinprick of guilt moved through her for not going down the canyon to her father's on Christmas Day, it didn't stay long.

Betty would be there, as she always was. Her father wasn't alone. Joe had taken his kids to his ex-wife's house, and he'd said he wanted to go visit some friends in Dog Valley. Patsy hadn't said anything. When her father had finally asked her about her plans, she'd just said, "Oh, there's a lot going on at the lodge. Since it's supposed to snow in the afternoon, I'm just going to stay there."

She accentuated every refusal to do something or be somewhere with a smile, and no one had said anything else. No one knew how terribly lonely she was, though she was surrounded by people all the time. No one knew how hard it was for her to paint that smile onto her mouth, keep it there, and not crack.

Right now, she didn't have to be strong. She didn't have to hold the lodge together, manage bookings, deal with unhappy guests, or late employees. She didn't have to speak to Graham and wonder if he found her incompetent. She didn't have to sit in on a meeting with Wes Hammond and all the Whittaker brothers to discuss how they could improve the lodge.

In her mind, there was nothing to improve. The lodge operated at full capacity ninety-seven percent of the time. Last year, they'd only had eleven nights where a room went empty, and five of those had only had one empty room.

The brothers didn't need money; they were on the quest to be the best they could be. Provide the best service. Give the best experience to families who came to the Tetons. Simply be the best.

Patsy had tried to emulate that for the first year she'd been at Whiskey Mountain Lodge. She'd dang near ended up in the hospital, one breath away from a mental and physical breakdown.

Again, she found herself attaching blame to a situation that wasn't entirely true. Yes, she'd worked too hard that first year. She'd set unreasonable expectations for herself and everyone at the lodge. She hadn't been happy.

She had come down with pneumonia that had taken her to the hospital.

But the real reason—or at least a very strong contributing factor—for her near breakdown was Carter Lewis.

Oh, how she'd loved him.

Too bad he didn't love her back.

Patsy pushed the maddening, gorgeous, cocky cowboy from her mind as she peeled back her covers and set her hot chocolate on her nightstand. The cabin only had one bedroom that she and Sophia had put a dressing panel down the middle of. They shared a bathroom too, and Patsy literally had to go sit in her car if she truly wanted to be alone. So her loneliness made no sense. Yet, it lingered in her soul.

"Come on, buddy," she said to the little dog, and she scooped him up and put him on the bed. "There you go. You can snuggle with me." She smiled at him, and it wasn't hard. Patsy thought maybe she should get a whole family of dogs to take care of. She could mother them as well as human children, couldn't she?

She set up her tablet and pulled her covers up to her waist, then reached for her hot chocolate. She'd just gotten hooked into her favorite murder mystery show when her phone rang.

Patsy sighed, but she didn't have the right kind of genes to ignore a phone call. She dug in the blankets to find her phone, finally touching the hard plastic case. She lifted it to see Cy's name on the screen.

She immediately dropped the phone, her heartbeat booming like a big, bass drum. She muttered as she grabbed the phone again, but she'd taken too long--the call went to voicemail. She watched as the screen darkened, wondering what he wanted on Christmas Day.

Should she call him back? Let him leave a message and then wait an episode so she didn't seem desperate?

Patsy wasn't desperate for another man in her life. Since Carter, she'd dated three or four men, and every one of them had turned out to be a loser. She somehow had a magnet for them, and she didn't have high hopes for her and Cy either.

He was easily the most handsome man she'd ever laid eyes on, though…

"And he doesn't need your money, your sister didn't date him, he's not unemployed, and he didn't cheat on you with your best friend."

Patsy paused for a moment, thinking through her last few single years. Yep, all of those had been true. She no longer had the best friend, or the cheater. She didn't have to "compare notes" with Betty, nor did she have to try to figure out what to do with expensive gifts from an out-of-work man who then wanted to borrow what he'd given her.

Her phone bleeped and the voicemail icon popped up at the top of her screen. Patsy had forgotten about the murder mystery, the real-life drama playing out in her life so much better. She swiped and tapped, and a few moments later, the line rang. She held the phone in front of her, the ringing coming through the speaker.

"You have one message," a cool, clinical voice said.

"Hey, Patsy," Cy said. "It's Cy Hammond. I know it's Christmas Day and all that, but my family is done with all the celebrations, and I wondered if yours was too." Something scuffled on his end of the line, and Patsy giggled when she imagined the cowboy billionaire dropping his phone.

She couldn't believe he'd called already. Honestly, with how they bickered, she was a little surprised he'd called at all. Surely he knew they didn't get along the greatest. At the same time, the fire between them certainly was hot, and Patsy had been attracted to other men, but none quite so much as Cy Hammond.

He finally added, "If you're free, I'd love to see you today. My brother says there's great snowshoeing round here, and I figured you being a local and all, you could show me the best spots. Okay, well, you can give me a call if you want…bye."

The call ended, and the voicemail operator started talking again. Patsy sighed and leaned back against her headboard.

Snowshoeing had not been on her list of things to do that day. But if she could see Cy…. She did know a lot of great trails around Coral Canyon.

She sat up and tapped again, her pulse positively panicking in her veins while his phone rang.

"Patsy, hi," he said, sounding a bit breathless. Something whirred in the background, and Patsy tried to figure out what at the same time her brain told her to say hello.

"What are you doing?" came out instead, and she pressed her eyes closed. Had she sounded accusatory? Probably.

"Oh, I got on the treadmill," Cy said. "I have this nervous energy…." He let the words hang there, and Patsy could see him doing that. Gray Hammond, Cy's brother, had run the canyon sometimes this past summer, and since all the Hammonds were tall, broad-shouldered, and beautiful, she felt like she knew exactly what Cy running on a treadmill looked like.

"Listen," she said, to which he immediately said, "Uh, oh."

"What?"

"Anytime someone starts a sentence with 'listen,' it's bad."

Patsy smiled, because the teasing quality of her voice landed loudly in her ears. "This might not be so bad," she said.

"Lay it on me, Pats."

Patsy blinked, surprised into silence for a moment. Then she pealed out a string of laughter, the joy overcoming her hitting her hard and fast. Cy chuckled with her, and when they quieted, he said, "Sorry. I don't know where that came from."

"It's okay," she said. "I actually hate my name."

"You do?"

"Yeah."

"Why's that?"

"How many Patsy's have you met in your life?" she asked, cocking her head as if he were there.

"Well, I don't know. I'm sure some."

"I'm sure you haven't," she said. "Unless you spend a lot of time in retirement homes, Cy." She giggled again, though she really disliked her name. "It's an old lady name. My sister is Betty. She hates it too. We're not ninety-five-years-old."

Cy remained quiet for a moment. "What about Patty?"

"How is Patty better than Patsy?" she challenged, plenty of her own teasing in her voice. "Besides, that's not a nickname for Patsy; it's a whole new name."

"Yeah, I see that," he said.

"Is Cy your whole name?"

"Yes, ma'am," he said. "Two letters is all I got."

"Oh, I think you have more than that," she said. "Must be a family name."

"How did you know that?" he asked.

"Lucky guess," she said, smiling as she threw her covers off. "So listen, Cy. It's freezing outside. Not sure if you're aware of what state you're in and what the thermometer actually says." She stood in front of the window in the bedroom and looked outside. As if taking sides, Mother Nature sent a gust of wind across the back fence, sending snow flying up into the air.

"It's supposed to snow this afternoon," she said. "And

it looks like it's getting started." She swallowed, suddenly needing something to drink.

"So another time," Cy said, his tone turning dark.

"Well, I was wondering if you could stand to stay inside," she said. "You could run a couple of miles, shower, and come up to my cabin. I have stuff to make pizza, and we could make dinner together, and light a fire, and put on a movie." The idea sounded ridiculous to her own ears as she spoke it.

Make pizza?

This wasn't a high school dance.

"What kind of pizza?"

"I have pepperoni, olives—"

"I'm kidding, Patsy," he said, chuckling. A sliver of embarrassment moved through her, and she didn't know what to say.

"You live at the lodge?"

"There's a cabin behind it," she said. "If you park way down at the far south side of the lot, you can see it behind the lodge. I'll make sure the lights are on in the living room and bathroom. They're on that side of the cabin."

"I'm on my way," he said.

"You're not going to run?" She thought of that rubber band he wore around his wrist. Did he wear it all the time? Would he snap it when he was with her?

"I don't need to now," he said. "See in you a few."

The call ended, and Patsy looked at the screen as the number showed, along with how long they'd been talking. Eight minutes. It had felt a lot shorter and a lot longer than that.

"Come on, Jonas," she said. "We have work to do." She hurried into the bathroom and made sure there was toilet paper and quickly used a cleaning wipe to disinfect the countertop, door handles, and toilet.

In the kitchen, she loaded the dirty dishes into the dishwasher, and she picked up her and Sophia's boots from beside the front door. She stood there, surveying the rest of the cabin, realizing the small, intimate space she'd just invited the big, bold, boisterous Cy Hammond to share with her.

Her heartbeat flew into a frenzy, but her mind still got enough blood to tell her to warn Sophia. Patsy almost dropped her phone as she tried to get it out of her pocket. With it firmly in hand, she sent a quick text to her roommate.

I invited Cy Hammond to the cabin. Maybe I'm insane? We're going to make pizza and—

Her mind snapped.

"Did I really said we could *light a fire*?" Horror snaked through her, because oh, yes. She had.

Light a fire.

Was that an activity couples did on dates?

Was this a date? She looked down at her comfortable elastic-waisted pants and long-sleeved sweater. Should she change her clothes if this was a date?

She shook her head, trying to get the self-doubt and questions to stop. She'd met Cy several times now. Sure, he had charisma oozing from him. He was gorgeous. He called to her as much as he annoyed her, and Patsy returned to her text.

I'm definitely insane. Tell me this is a bad idea.

Not a bad idea, Sophia said a few seconds later. *And I'll stay here through dinner. Have fun! Can't wait to hear all about it.*

Patsy let her phone drop to her side, her fingers barely holding onto it.

CHAPTER 5

"Y ou're going to get stuck at that lodge," Cy told himself as he aimed the truck up and into the storm. *Into* it. Anyone with half a brain would know driving on this road in this direction was a bad idea.

And yet, he couldn't get himself to turn around.

"Okay, talk to me, Lord," he said. "Up or down?" Cy was having a very hard time deciphering which promptings were coming from God and which were his own desires to see Patsy that day.

He and Ames had sat on the couch for a solid hour, brainstorming things Cy could say to Patsy. It had been Colton who'd finally said, "She's a local, you guys. Ask her to take you to do something locally."

"Like what?" Ames had asked.

"I don't know," Colton said. "Wes made Bree take him hiking." That had gotten everyone involved, which was exactly what Cy hadn't wanted.

"I didn't *make* her take me hiking," Wes said, offended. "I asked her to show me her favorite trails."

"There you go," Ames said. "Hiking trails."

"It's ten below freezing," Wes said. "You want her to take you skiing or snowshoeing." He'd stood at that point as his baby had started to fuss.

"Patsy likes snowshoeing," Bree had said, smiling at Cy.

After that, the plan to get a Christmas date with Patsy had come together. Cy didn't want to believe that God had put everything together so perfectly, only to have the weather ruin what he hoped would be an amazing afternoon.

So he kept driving.

He wasn't sure what about Patsy spoke to his soul so strongly, only that he dang near craved her presence. He wanted to run his fingers through her short hair and see if he could hold onto it while he kissed her.

He blinked rapidly, trying to regain control of his thoughts. He scoffed at the idea of kissing Patsy. They were a long way from that, and he shouldn't even be thinking about it.

His truck shook with a particularly violent gust of wind, and Cy started praying that he'd make it to the lodge at all. Eventually, he saw the lights shining from the windows, and he pulled into the parking lot.

It wasn't anywhere close to nightfall yet, but the gray storm clouds certainly made it feel like it. He'd just put his truck in park when the first flakes of snow landed on the windshield, and Cy killed the ignition and got out, already looking for the cabin behind the lodge.

Three rectangles of light beckoned to him, and Cy wasted no time in getting to the cabin. A wide porch extended from the front of the cabin, and it was covered, thankfully. But a covered deck didn't protect from the subzero temperatures or the wind, and Cy quickly rang the doorbell.

"Coming," Patsy called from within, and a few seconds later, the lock unlatched and the petite, pretty blonde woman stood in front of him.

Cy smiled at her, wondering what she thought of him driving into the center of the storm just to see her. It reeked of desperation, but Cy couldn't go back in time now, turn around, and save himself some humiliation.

"Come in," Patsy said, falling back a couple of steps.

Cy did, nodding his cowboy hat at her. "Hey, Patsy," he said when he realized he hadn't even greeted her yet. So he could add creepy, silent staring to his list of blunders.

Honestly, he felt like he'd never been out with a woman before. He reminded himself that he had as he closed the door behind him, sealing them in the cozy cabin together. "This is nice," he said.

"It functions," Patsy said. "And this is all there is, so this is the grand tour." She gestured to the couch as if she were game show host displaying a luxurious prize. "This is the living room. As you can see, we have *two* couches in a shade of gray that matches the rug and the curtains." She turned slightly and pointed into the kitchen. "The kitchen is where we're going to start today, and we recently upgraded to these fingerprint-resistant, stainless steel appliances when our fridge went out."

She grinned and walked into the kitchen. Cy stayed where he was, basking in the good energy she put out. She wore a loose pair of black pants that could've been slacks or lounge pants, and they looked great on her. A blue, long-sleeved shirt completed her ensemble, and the color brought out the dazzling azure of her eyes.

"I ate a ton for breakfast," she said, which spurred Cy into motion, and he followed her into the kitchen. She glanced at him as he joined her at the butcher block in the center of the room. "So I skipped lunch. Are you hungry?"

"Not even a little bit," he said. "We had a huge breakfast, brunch, thing only a few hours ago."

Patsy looked down at the dry ingredients she'd gathered—flour, sugar, salt, yeast. "Maybe we should wait a little bit to make dinner."

"Well, it's only two-thirty," he said. "So we have time." He grinned at her and nudged her playfully with his elbow. "Unless you have the dining habits of someone you share your name with, and you eat dinner at four o'clock."

She looked at him like he'd just spoken another language, and Cy cursed himself for trying to be funny about her name. Then, all at once, a smile spread those very pink lips, and she shook her head. "I shouldn't have told you about my name."

"No, I liked it," he said. "I can see what you mean."

"So who were you named after?" She turned toward him and leaned her hip into the butcher block. With her facing him, and her makeup done just-so, and her hair styled perfectly, and all that blue getting absorbed into her eyes, Cy was struck dumb by her beauty.

"Ah, must've been a black sheep in the family," Patsy teased, breaking Cy from his trance.

"You know what?" Cy asked. "He was, and I'm definitely the outsider in my family."

"Are you?"

"Oh-ho, yeah," he said, half chuckling. "You've met my brothers. Tell me I'm like them."

Patsy tilted her head, never looking away from him. "You own your own business."

"Yes, well, Wes was born and groomed to be a CEO. The letters flow in his blood. Gray, the next oldest, argued cases for fun in high school. My mother sometimes joked that he'd come home from the hospital in a suit and tie."

Cy shook his head. "Colton is the fun-loving one. The one everyone gets along with. Each of us thinks we're his best friend, when really he's best friends with all of us. He's the glue between the two older brothers—the perfect Hammonds—and me and Ames—the oddball twins."

He grinned at her, his words the truest he'd spoken in years. She looked like she didn't believe him, though her smile remained.

"Hey," she said. "You're wearing jeans today, so I don't think you're that odd."

Cy burst out laughing, his hand sliding easily along her waist as he put his arm around her. She giggled too and barely reacted to his touch. He wasn't sure if he was happy about that or not. Sparks popped through him, and the motion had felt so natural. Almost like he'd touched Patsy this way before, like they were old friends, and he could lean down and press his mouth to hers, and it wouldn't even be weird.

The moment broke, and Cy eased away from her. "So I stopped for marshmallows." He looked toward the front door. "But I forgot them in the truck." The thought of going back out into the storm didn't appeal to him, and he glanced back at Patsy. "I thought we could start a fire and have indoor s'mores."

"We have fondue forks," she said, opening a drawer. She took out a few long forks and lifted them up.

"I'll go grab the stuff," he said. He zipped up his coat again and walked toward the door.

"Don't die out there," she said. "And when you get back, you have to tell me about your name. You still haven't said who you're named after."

"All right," he said over his shoulder, and he braved the wind and snow to make the trek to his truck and back. He didn't bother knocking when he returned, because his hand that carried the groceries was going to be lost to frostbite.

He stomped his feet just inside the door while he wrestled it closed and turned to find Patsy kneeling in front of the fireplace. She'd started to build the embers into a flame, and Cy shrugged out of his coat and hung it on a hook by the door, took his groceries into the kitchen, and joined her.

He held his hands out in front of the baby flame, a sigh leaking from his mouth. "It's *freezing* out there." He rubbed his hands together. "I'm not going to make it down the canyon tonight."

Patsy looked up at him, alarm on her face. "Really?"

"No way." He held her gaze for several long seconds. "Is there room at the lodge? Aren't just the Whittakers there?"

"Yeah, but they fill the place."

"Colton said he stayed there once."

"Annie's family came for the wedding," Patsy said. She stood up, the fire forgotten. "Let me see what I can figure out." She took out her phone and nodded to the hearth. "Will you keep feeding that?"

"Sure." Cy crouched down to tend to the fledgling flame, stoking it with small sticks and then another piece of wadded paper. "So I'm named after my great-grandfather. His name was Cornelius Cy Hammond, and he's the chemist who actually invented the polyethylene plastic in the early twentieth century that took our family company into the stratosphere."

Patsy didn't respond for a moment, her attention on her phone. "He doesn't sound like a black sheep, Cy."

"Oh, he was," Cy said, adding another piece of wood. "He went against his father's wishes when he married my great-grandmother. He refused to become a lawyer. He wore these ridiculous trench coats." Cy shook his head, the black and white photographs of the man he was named after right there in his mind's eye. "I'm a lot the same way."

"You went against your dad's wishes?"

"Oh, my parents were disappointed from my birth," Cy

said, picking up a bigger chunk of wood. He carefully laid it over the teepee she'd built, hoping he wouldn't smother the fire. It started to lick the wood, and he watched it dance and play. "My mother wanted a baby girl so badly."

Cy had carried the weight of his gender for a while, but his therapist had helped him let go of that guilt. He added another piece of wood, and then a third, satisfied the fire would continue, and stood up.

Patsy was looking at him, and he asked, "What?"

"So you're the black sheep because you're a boy?"

"Felt like it for a while." He shrugged, the words crowding in his mouth refusing to be held back. But he didn't want to reveal too much. "After my last girlfriend broke up with me, I went to see a counselor." He cleared his throat. "It was a very hard break up for me."

Patsy's expression turned compassionate, and she tucked her phone away, all of her attention on him now.

He wasn't sure if he liked that or not. "Anyway, he helped me get over the whole girl thing. My mother doesn't even know I felt bad about it." He drew in a deep breath and held it. "And I never went to college—a great disappointment to all Hammonds, stretching back generations."

He put a smile on his face, but wow, he was speaking hard truths right now. How had he come to this conversation topic with Patsy? Today was supposed to be fun. Making pizza and cuddling on the couch.

He reached up and removed the cowboy hat, his long hair brushing against his knuckles. "Ames at least became a local hero. Colton has two degrees and worked on a project that has impacted mankind for the better. Gray's the lawyer. Wes the CEO. I just liked motorcycles." He shrugged again, because he didn't know how much Patsy knew about his family.

"Anyway," he said. "Let's have s'mores."

Her phone chimed as he moved into the kitchen, and when he retuned, she grinned. "You can stay in Elise's cabin. She and Bree used to live up here, and it's empty."

"Perfect," he said.

"We should get over there and make sure the heat is on, though," Patsy said, looking toward the window. "Go now, or have a snack, and then go?"

"Go now," Cy said, putting the bag with marshmallows and graham crackers on the couch. "I know I won't want to go later."

"Okay."

They put on their coats, and Patsy added a hat and gloves to her arsenal. Outside, the snow fell down in a beautiful arrangement of flakes. Cy stopped at the top of the steps. "It is beautiful, isn't it?"

"I love the snow," Patsy said at his side.

"I don't hate it," he said. "Though it was nice to never have to deal with it in California."

"You started your shop there, right?" She tucked her hands in her pockets and stepped out from underneath the protection of the roof.

"Yes," he said, following her.

"Why there?"

"Uh, let's see." Cy blew out his breath, which created a white cloud in front of his face. "Following a dream?

Wanted something different? Needed to get away from the perfection of four older brothers in Colorado?" He thought for a moment. "Yeah, all of those work for reasons why."

Patsy glanced at him. "You know, all of you Hammonds are pretty dang-near perfect."

Cy burst out laughing, sure she was kidding. She didn't join him though, and Cy wasn't sure what to make of it. What did she see in him?

"And you're not the only one who feels like they don't belong in their family."

"You?" he asked, thinking of the stern, non-smiling woman who'd come out onto the porch yesterday. "Why don't you fit?"

"I have the same perfect older siblings you do," she said. "Especially my sister. She got married young, and had all these beautiful daughters, and she's just so perky and wonderful and everything." Patsy spoke with a bit of bitterness in her tone that Cy had certainly felt way down deep in his soul many times.

"I think you mentioned your frustration with them the first time we met," he said, trying to be casual so he didn't press the wrong button for her.

"Yeah." She led him up a slight rise, and a stable appeared on her left. Two men came out of the huge doors, and Patsy called to them. Cy lifted his hand in greeting to Beau and Graham, and he and Patsy continued down the sidewalk. He wasn't sure how much farther it was, and he hoped they could find their way back.

"I did everything I could to get some of my father's attention," she said. "I learned to paint, because he loves watercolors. I went to school and learned business, human resources, and administration management, all with the hopes that he'd let me run the orchard. Nope."

Cy reached over and linked his arm through hers, though he didn't wear gloves. She didn't break stride or look at him, but comfort bled through him at the simple connection. He knew he needed human connection—probably more than any of his other brothers—and he'd been isolated for so long.

"I taught horseback riding lessons, because Betty's kids wanted to take them. I took a finance class at the community center here. I learned to cut hair." She shook her head. "None of it mattered. None of it was enough. I stopped trying."

"I'm sorry, Patsy," Cy said, his voice muted in the snow.

"There it is," she said, and a vague outline of a cabin came into view. They picked up the pace, and before long, Cy stood in another cabin, this one bigger than the one where Patsy lived. It was fully furnished and ready to be lived in, and he wondered who was going to live here. For some reason, *he* wanted to live there.

"Who owns this place?" he asked, lifting his cowboy hat off his head to shake the snow from it.

"Laney Whittaker," Patsy said. "Graham's wife. This is actually on her ranch, which borders the lodge."

"No one lives here?"

"Well, Elise did, but...no." Patsy looked at him as she nudged up the central heat. "It's on seventy-six now." She turned toward the fireplace. "And there's wood here, so you can build a fire too."

He nodded, still looking around. "Would Laney let me live here?"

"You want to live up here?" Patsy gaped at him. "Why? Your shop is at least forty minutes from here."

Cy shrugged. "It won't be done for another few months." Longer, if this snow kept up.

"Where are you living now?"

"I rented a place," he said, not wanting to say he'd chosen the house on the north side of town because it was ten minutes to the shop. "I'm going to build a house in the orchard." He looked at her then to judge her reaction.

Surprise filled her whole face. "Wow."

Cy felt her slipping away from him, and he had no idea why. He'd bought the land; he could do what he wanted with it.

"Would you cut my hair?" he asked, the question just there.

"What?"

"My hair." He ran his hand through it. "It's way too long, and I need a change. You just said you learned to cut hair, and I'm asking you to cut mine."

"Today?"

"Yeah, when we get back," he said. "We can make s'mores, and you can cut my hair, and then maybe we'll start getting hungry enough to make pizza." He smiled at her, hoping to draw her back to him.

It seemed to work, because she relaxed, and a hint of a

smile even lifted the corners of her mouth. "I haven't cut anyone's hair in a while. It could be a hack job."

"I'm willing to take the risk," Cy said seriously. Those words could've applied to so much more between him and Patsy, and he wondered if she knew it as keenly as he did.

"Okay," she said, and Cy smiled. He extended his hand toward her, a moment of truth, and prayed with everything in him that she'd put her hand in his.

CHAPTER 6

Patsy couldn't look away from Cy's deep, dark eyes. He was so mysterious, and so different than she'd first assumed when she'd met him at the orchard. She knew she'd been emotional then, and dealing with a lot of stress, and he'd only added to it.

But now, he was helping to relieve it.

She put her hand in his, and a stream 0f fire shot up her arm. A shiver shook her shoulders, and Cy said, "We should get back to the cabin with the roaring fire." He tugged her gently toward the exit. "Let's go."

Outside, he released her hand, and she pulled her glove back on. He tucked his hands in his coat pockets and bent his head into the wind. Patsy did the same, and while the weather had intensified, she wasn't nearly as chilled on the walk back. Cy's touch had electrified her, and Patsy couldn't ignore the attraction running through her.

Back at her cabin, they hung up their wet clothes and

stood in front of the fire for a few minutes. "When you go tonight," she said. "You'll have to text me when you get to that cabin so I know you made it."

"Good idea," he said. "I was just thinking about making that walk alone, and I'm not sure I can do it." He reached up and pushed his hair back, the tips of it wet from the snow.

Patsy tore her gaze away and cleared her throat. "S'mores first?"

"Let's do this." Cy turned and pulled out the groceries while Patsy went to get the fondue forks. She stood in the kitchen for a moment and watched him rip open the bag of marshmallows and put one straight into his mouth.

That simple act filled her with joy for some reason. It reminded her of a simpler time in her childhood, where getting a treat from her mother had lit her whole world with joy.

"My mother loved marshmallows and pretzels together," Patsy said as she returned to the living room.

Cy looked up, his expression open and vulnerable. "Yeah?" He handed her the bag of marshmallows. "I love these things." He grinned at her, and Patsy took one out of the bag.

"She kept them in a high cupboard," she said, the memories she'd kept carefully boxed now streaming through her mind. "Above the microwave. We only got them on special occasions. The last time was on my birthday when I turned sixteen."

"That long ago?" Cy stilled in his work of opening the

package of crackers. "I mean, where is your mom? You've not said anything about her."

"She's somewhere in Minnesota," Patsy said, expecting something in her chest to tighten. Her voice stayed even though, and she wondered if she'd finally come to terms with her mother's decisions. "She left my dad, oh, right after I graduated from high school. It was like she was just waiting for me to be an adult, so she could leave."

She gazed down at the marshmallows, the little pillows bringing back so many good memories. She took one out of the bag and stuck it in her mouth. "Mm." She smiled, and Cy went back to work unwrapping the chocolate and the grahams.

"Do you talk to your mom?" he asked.

"Every now and then," Patsy said. "She'll call, or I'll call her."

He nodded and reached for a fork. She handed it to him, and they put marshmallows on and held them over the flames. She felt him watching her, and she deliberately kept her eyes on her marshmallow to make sure it didn't start to turn black.

Some people liked lighting theirs on fire, but Patsy wasn't one of them. She liked a toasty, golden brown marshmallow, and that took a great amount of patience and care. Constant watching and turning. She simply couldn't look at Cy right now.

"So," she said, barely looking at him out of the corner of her eye. "If you weren't running a motorcycle shop, what would you be doing?"

"What do you mean?"

"I mean, if you had unlimited resources and time to learn something, what would it be? What do you want to know more about? What do you wish you knew how to do?"

"Patsy," he said quietly, slowly rotating his own marshmallow. Because the forks weren't very long, and the fireplace not very big, he sat right beside her, his shoulder touching hers. "You know I *do* have unlimited resources and time, right?"

"Yeah," Patsy said. "I know." She pulled her marshmallow back and turned fully toward him. Their eyes caught, and lightning could've struck and it wouldn't be as hot as the chemistry between them.

Patsy barely knew what to do with it, because it filled her lungs and pushed out the air. It made her muscles tighten and stay that way. Then he smiled, and everything released. Relief filled her, and she ducked her head with a light laugh.

He possessed a stunning smile, with straight, white teeth, and Patsy hoped she could see the vision of his face as she fell asleep that night.

"So what would you do?" she asked, observing her marshmallow again. It was almost done, and then she could make her s'mores sandwich.

"Do I have to commit to doing it?"

"Nope." She removed her marshmallow from the heat of the fire and reached for a graham cracker. She broke it in half and put a couple of squares of chocolate on one piece. Then she used the two graham crackers like mitts to slide the marshmallow from the hot fork.

She looked at Cy, who had watched her do all of that. "Nothing?" she asked. "You've got nothing?" She took a bite of her s'mores sandwich, the chocolate the strongest flavor. She loved the crunchy cracker, the gooey marshmallow, and the in-between chocolate. Whoever had put this combination together should get a medal in heaven.

"I need some time to think about it," he said. He started making a s'more too, his chin dipped down. "What about you?"

"What would I do if I had unlimited time and resources?" she asked. "Besides the painting, the finance class, the horseback riding, and the hair-cutting?" She popped the last bite of her snack into her mouth to give herself a couple of seconds of thought. "I think I'd like to learn to ride a motorcycle."

Cy jerked his head up, his eyes widening. A moment later, he said, "Oh, you're teasing me."

"Kind of?" she guessed. "You said riding a horse and riding a motorcycle weren't the same at all, and I'd like to know if that's really true."

"You know I can make that happen, right?"

"I know you had a motorcycle in the fall," she said. "And that there's no way you're riding one in this weather."

"So we'll have to wait until spring," he mused.

Patsy hadn't realized that until he'd said it, but yes. Hopefully, there would still be this electric attraction between them once the snow melted.

He finished his s'more, and Patsy stood up. "I'll get my clippers and scissors."

"All right." Cy picked up the bag of marshmallows and popped another one in his mouth. "I'll think about what I want to learn how to do."

Patsy took the few steps down the hall to the bathroom and closed the door so she could open the cupboard behind it. She didn't use her hair-cutting supplies very often, but she found the clear, plastic bin with her black drape, her clippers, several combs, and a pair of scissors in it.

She pulled it down and turned around. She looked into her own eyes, wondering what Cy saw when he looked into them. She knew they were very bright blue—something she'd inherited from her father. One of her previous boyfriends had told her he'd never seen eyes like hers, and Patsy had liked that.

She finger-combed her hair, as some of it had started to drift in a different direction, and she focused on herself again. "You don't have to tell him anything else," she whispered. She'd already said too much about her family, and she told herself to focus on simple things. How he named his custom shop. What he'd eat for his birthday meal. If he'd prefer a dog or a cat for a pet.

Taking a steeling breath, she opened the door and took her kit into the kitchen. "All right, cowboy. Over here."

Cy turned away from the window, where he'd been standing, watching the snow fall while he held Jonas in his arms. "Cowboy?"

"You do know what kind of hat you're wearing, right?" She started unpacking the bin.

"Yeah, seems like that's what you do when you live in Wyoming."

"You said you knew how to ride a horse," she said. "Grew up on a farm." She picked up the drape and checked the snaps on the back. The cells in her body vibrated, because she was going to be very close to Cy. Cutting hair was an intimate experience, even if it wasn't sexual. The person in the chair had to trust her, and she had to press in close, touch his neck and ears….

She started praying that she'd be able to deliver a good haircut for him, and that he'd like it. Her fingers shook, and she really needed them to stop. She didn't want him to find her nervous, and the only person she'd ever been worried about cutting their hair had been her sister. Betty was so critical, and she'd said she was "pleasantly surprised" with Patsy's haircut. Betty was the queen of backhanded compliments, but Patsy took what she could get from her sister.

Patsy tapped the barstool as Cy approached. "Right here."

"Motorcycles aren't like horses," he said, pausing before he sat down.

"You've said that."

"But I have ridden horses, and I did grow up on a farm."

Patsy slid the drape around him and snapped it at the back of his neck. She ran her fingers through his hair, desire popping through her. "You have a lot of hair."

"Yeah." He reached up and pushed his hand through it too. "My mother is going to be thrilled." He chuckled and took a deep breath. "I grew it out in California, and I don't live in California anymore. It's time for a change."

"The cowboy hat will fit better," she said, reaching to plug in the clippers. "What are you thinking? How short are we talking?"

"Have you seen Gray?"

Patsy plugged in her clippers and stood back. "You are not going to a military-slash-lawyer cut like Gray."

"No? Why not?" Cy twisted to look at her.

Patsy just shook her head. "It's not you."

"What is me, then?"

She stepped to the side, so he could see her better without that twist in his spine. They looked at one another, and Patsy lost her voice for a moment. Then she asked, "Do you trust me?"

"One hundred percent," he said.

A slow smile crossed her face, and for the first time in a long time, Patsy felt truly happy. The feeling sparkled inside her, and she wanted to trap it and keep it with her. Just like she wanted to do with Cy Hammond.

"All right," she said. "Now sit up straight and look down for me." She looked through her attachments and found the largest one, snapped it into place, and clicked on the clippers. Buzzing filled the kitchen, and Cy tensed as Patsy ran her fingers along the side of his neck and then placed the small appliance against the nape of his neck.

The dark hair fell to the floor in soft curls, and Patsy said, "Oh, boy. This is a lot, Cy."

"It's fine," he said, his voice calm and reassuring.

She continued up the back of his head and around his

ears. She shaved up the sides, and then stopped. Cutting hair was like riding a bike, and her fingers knew exactly what to do. She picked up the scissors and started trimming the top, leaving it long enough to style to the side. She'd never cut one of her boyfriend's hair before, and she wondered why.

"Let's say it's your birthday," she said.

"It's in May," he said.

"Okay," she said. "It's May, and it's your birthday. Two questions: One, how old would you be, and two, what would you want for your birthday meal?"

"My birthday meal?"

"Yeah. When I had a birthday growing up, my mom made us a birthday meal. All of our favorite things. When we turned twelve, we got to choose a restaurant, which was a big deal. We never went out to eat."

Snip, snip, snip. Patsy moved around to the other side and started evening things out.

"And the whole family didn't even go. Just one parent and the birthday kid. My mom took the girls. My dad took Joe."

"Just when you turned twelve, huh?"

"Yep." She brushed the hair off his shoulders where it had collected. "My mom made dinner every night. Meat and potatoes and some sort of vegetable. The meat was always dry. *Always* overcooked." Patsy giggled and shook her head, still working around the crown of his head. "But she made great scalloped potatoes. And dessert. We always had an apple dessert."

"I bet you did," he said.

Patsy told herself to stop talking. Why did her mouth run away from her like this? Hadn't she just told herself she didn't have to tell him anything else about herself or her family?

Yes, yes, she had.

"I had to share a birthday with Ames," Cy said. "I still do, I guess." He chuckled, and Patsy wondered if he was nervous. "Anyway, as a kid, I wanted boxed macaroni and cheese. Always. Ames has never appreciated the simple things in life, and our dad spoiled him with steak and seafood from the age of three. So he wanted stuff like steak sandwiches and shrimp scampi."

"I don't even know what shrimp scampi is," Patsy said.

"Right?" Cy laughed, his shoulders shaking. She liked the sound of it, and she liked how easy it was to be here with him, cutting his hair and talking. "Ames has always been the diva of the family."

"And Colton's the best friend. Wes is the CEO. Gray's the stuffy lawyer. You're the…free-loving, surfing, motor-cycle guy?"

"That's way too many descriptors," he said.

"Narrow it for me." She stepped back and looked at her work. She put on a shorter attachment and started to blend the lower half of his hair into the upper half.

"I'm the fun one," he said. "Simple."

"The fun one." She made sure everything looked uniform and even, laughing to herself. "That is simpler."

She finally took the attachment off and shaved his neck, unsnapped the drape, shook the hair from it, and said, "You're done."

Cy groaned as he stood up, and he faced her. "Thank you, Patsy."

"Yeah, sure." She looked down at the ground, and he did too.

"Wow," he said, bending to grab a chunk of his hair. "This *is* a lot." He reached up with the other hand and ran his fingers through his hair. "Holy cow, it hasn't been this short in years."

"Bathroom right down the hall. Go look."

He held her gaze for another few seconds, and then he turned and went down the hall. Patsy drew in a deep breath, getting the scent of his cologne and his skin. He'd permeated her cabin now, and Patsy really liked it.

She just hoped he liked his haircut too. *Please, dear Lord,* she thought. *I really like this man. Help me not to make a mess of this relationship. Just this once. Okay?*

"Holy cow," Cy called from down the hall, and Patsy's heart leapt into the back of her throat.

CHAPTER 7

Cy stared at himself in the mirror, stunned at the pretty boy haircut he now sported.

"You hate it," Patsy said, pausing in the doorway.

"No," he said slowly. He reached up and pushed his fingers through the top—which still had some decent length—and moved it to the left. "This side?" He honestly wasn't sure how to wear it. "Or this way?" He combed it to the right. "Nope."

He moved it back to the left and ran his palm down the back of his head. His hair was *short*.

"I'd do that side, yes," she said. "And you can put some product in it, and it'll be amazing."

He met her eye in the mirror, and he felt like she was pretty dang amazing. "Thank you," he said, turning and easily taking her into his arms. "I really like it."

"Are you just saying that?" she asked, her voice slightly muffled against his shoulder.

"No." He released her and stepped back. He couldn't help glancing at himself in the mirror again, and he felt like he'd been completely reborn. New town. New building. New haircut.

New girlfriend?

He let Patsy go down the short hall to the kitchen, where she started sweeping up his hair. "I'm going to preheat the oven for the pizzas," she said, and he finally pulled his attention from his reflection.

"Okay." He took the few steps down the hall. "Would you take my picture? I want to send it to Ames and the other brothers."

"Sure." Patsy leaned the broom against the counter and took his phone. "All right." She held it up and pointed it at him, and Cy struck a pose.

Patsy burst out laughing, and Cy couldn't help doing the same, dropping his stance. She shook her head and said through her giggles, "Not like that. You seriously looked like you were going to attack me."

Cy chuckled and self-consciously ran his hands through his hair, swooping it to the left.

"Just smile," she said, and since he already was, he kept the happiness on his face while she tapped on his phone. "Perfect." She handed the device back and returned to her cleaning. He looked at the photos, and he actually really liked them.

He looked clean-cut, but not military. His hair was darker than he'd thought, and he didn't have a stitch of gray anywhere. Thankfully. He wasn't even forty yet, and he'd lived a fairly easy lifestyle in California.

The past few months had been stressful, but they obviously hadn't taken their toll yet. Construction on his new shop would continue as soon as the New Year started and the weather allowed.

He'd have Rev for Vets open by the end of March, and they had to stick to a pretty regimented schedule to do it. His house would come after that, and a touch of foolishness bumped out with his next heartbeat over the way he'd asked about living in the other cabin here at the lodge.

It made no sense for him to move up here. He had one reason and one reason only: the gorgeous blonde now tapping buttons on the oven to get it preheating.

He looked away from her just as she turned around, and he put his new photo in the brothers text with the words, *Patsy cut my hair. What do you think?*

He hoped he'd get a favorable response, and if he wasn't with Patsy, Ames would probably call. His strait-laced, no-nonsense, police officer brother got twitchy if his hair grew longer than two inches, that was for sure.

Wow! Colton said. *It's amazing, Cy.*

Looks great, brother, Wes said.

Ames's message came in only a moment later. *Totally suits you. You look like you could run a business now.*

"Gee, thanks," Cy muttered, though he wasn't really annoyed with his twin. He'd just slipped his phone in his back pocket when another message came in. He pulled it out to find Gray's commentary.

I really like it, Cy. Looks amazing.

And not two seconds later: *Patsy? Like the Patsy who works at the lodge?*

He'd been in the lodge when Cy had asked her out over the PA system. He probably just thought Cy wouldn't actually follow through.

Yeah, they're dating now, Colton said, and Cy's lungs stuck together.

Whoa, whoa, he typed out quickly. *No, we're not.*

You're on a date with her, Ames said.

"No," he said out loud, typing the two letters. *I'm just spending the afternoon with her.*

In her cabin, Wes added. *They're making dinner and cuddling by firelight.*

Sounds like a date, Gray said.

Cy's irritation grew, and he needed to get out of this brothers text. Fast. *I'm out,* he said. *Talk amongst yourselves. But we're not datING.*

Did you or did you not ask me to help you make a plan for a DATE?

Cy ignored Ames's text and shoved his phone in his back pocket.

"Everything okay?" Patsy asked, and he focused on her.

"I have four brothers," he said. "Who all think they know better than I do."

She nodded, a knowing glint in her eye. "But did they like the hair?"

He grinned at her and looked at the ingredients she'd gotten out while he'd been texting. "Yeah, they did."

She grinned back at him, and said, "Okay, so this is

what we've got. Put on anything you want," and Cy took in his options.

"What are you going to put on yours?" he asked.

She placed a ball of dough in front of him. "I like green peppers, pepperoni, and olives," she said.

"A woman after my own heart," he said, and he unwrapped his ball of dough.

"Really?" she asked. "I pegged you for an all-meat type of pizza eater."

"That's good too."

"White sauce or red?"

"Either," he said. "I like the white sauce with bacon and ham and pineapple."

"Okay, no." Patsy kneaded her dough liked she'd done it countless times before. She probably had. "Pineapple has no place on a pizza."

"You're kidding, right?"

"I am not kidding." She gave him a pointed look. "You'll notice there are no fruits here to choose from."

Cy scanned the ingredients again. "I see that." He couldn't help the glow of happiness moving through him. "You obviously like apples. So what's the deal with pineapples?"

"No deal," she said. "They just shouldn't be eaten warm."

Cy pressed his dough into a round disc. "My mother makes an amazing pineapple upside-down cake. That's got warm pineapple." He reached for a spoon. "With ice cream, it's not bad."

"So you don't like warm pineapple either."

"Sure I do," he said. "There are no rules when it comes to pineapple."

"That's where you're wrong." Patsy smiled at him and added, "And you never did say what you'd like for your birthday meal."

"Sure I did," he said.

"Oh, come on," she said, tossing him an exasperated look. "I'm not going to make boxed mac and cheese for your birthday."

Cy ducked his head, once again glad for the cowboy hat. She was already planning to make him a meal for his birthday, and he found himself looking forward to that though it was five months away.

"Oh, all right," he said. "If I were going to get anything I wanted for my birthday meal, I suppose it would be fried chicken, mashed potatoes and gravy, and this creamed corn my mother makes. It's amazing."

"What kind of gravy?"

"Brown." He sprinkled cheese over his sauce and glanced at her. Everything about the last couple of hours appealed to Cy, and he vowed not to leave her cabin that day without another date on the horizon.

––––––––

THE NEXT MORNING, CY OPENED THE FRONT DOOR OF THE cabin where he'd stayed the night, the sunlight bouncing off the fresh snow blinding him. He pressed his eyes closed and threw up one hand to shield them while Sophia's little dog trotted out like he didn't even realize the world now carried another foot of snow.

"You're going to get buried, bud," he said to the pup, but Jonas bounded happily down the steps, disappearing into the drifts but popping right back up again.

Cy had stayed at Patsy's until well past dark. Sophia had come back, and they'd all enjoyed more s'mores. Finally, he'd had to admit he couldn't sleep on their couch, and when he'd gone out, Jonas had come with him.

He'd asked if he could take the dog with him, and Sophia had been more than happy to oblige. His truck was still parked up at the lot by Patsy's cabin anyway, so it wasn't a problem to take the dog back.

Cy simply couldn't get himself to leave the porch and trudge through the snow.

In the distance, a humming started, which grew to a buzz. Finally, he realized what he was hearing—a snowmobile. Sure enough, only a few seconds later, the machine came over the rise in the hill that led to the stables, and Cy could only stare when he realized it was Patsy manning that thing.

"Wow," he said to himself. "Would you look at that?" She was easily the sexiest woman he'd ever met, and he couldn't wait until they could spend more time alone together. She'd said she needed to work for the next couple of days, as they did a deep clean on the lodge while there were extra hands to help.

Not only that, but that giant tree that they'd set up and decorated had to be taken down and all the pine needles cleaned up. Patsy said they usually started un-decorating the tree only a couple of days after Christmas, and the tree left the lodge the day after New Year's. The family left very soon after that, and then it was back to business as usual.

"Thought you could use a ride," Patsy said as she brought the snowmobile to a stop at the bottom of the steps. "Where's Jonas?"

"Out there somewhere," Cy said, and the little dog popped his head up.

"Come on, Jonas," Patsy said, and the black pup hop, hop, hopped over to her. He got right on the back of the snowmobile, and Cy shook his head as he tromped down the steps.

"I think you're in my seat, bud," he said, throwing his leg over the back of the snowmobile. The dog pressed into Patsy's back, and Cy picked him up and settled him on his lap as he situated his feet.

"Ready?

"Yes, ma'am," he said.

"Okay, hold on." She took off like she was trying to win a race, and Cy yelped as he got thrown backward. He leaned forward and grabbed onto Patsy, not worrying about squishing Jonas between them. The dog would be safer if he did.

Patsy didn't pull any punches, and she handled the big snowmobile flawlessly. She took him all the way to the edge of the parking lot, which had already been cleared.

"Wow," Cy said. "You guys are efficient around here."

"We know how to deal with snow," Patsy said.

Cy got off the snowmobile with Jonas in his arms and turned back to put the dog back on the seat. "Thanks for the ride," he said. "And thanks for yesterday. It was an amazing Christmas for me."

"Me too," Patsy said, smiling at him. "I'll call you in a couple of days?"

"Can't wait," Cy said, and he tapped two fingers to the brim of his hat. He forced himself to walk away before he forced another awkward exchange, and he didn't look back when the buzzing of the machine started up again.

He had a house to go home to, but he didn't want to be alone. He'd forgotten to put the rubber band on his wrist after breakfast yesterday, and he felt on the edge of rest-lessness. He needed something to get this energy out, and Colton had a treadmill at his place.

Ames's truck sat in the driveway too, and Cy knew he'd have to talk about his "date" with Patsy. Surprisingly, he wasn't dreading it, though he was planning to make sure his brothers knew going on one date and dating were two different things.

They'd continued texting yesterday without him, and by the time he'd gotten back to the cabin and was alone, he'd missed over a hundred texts.

"Knock, knock," he said at the same time he opened the door. The scent of maple syrup met his nose, as did a chorus of "He's back," and "Hey, Cy," and "Do you want to eat?"

"I always want to eat," he called, taking a few seconds

to step out of his boots and hang up his coat. Once he went into the kitchen, he found Colton scooting over to make room for him at the table, and he wondered if he really was the black sheep of the family or not.

He was definitely different from the others, but that didn't mean he didn't fit in with them. "Wow," he said. "Belgian waffles. Looks great." He picked up a plate from the counter and put a waffle on it before joining his brothers at the table.

No one said anything, though Cy suspected Ames and Colton were dying inside. They'd probably scripted the questions, and Cy wasn't going to open the door for them.

"Cy, dear," his mother said. "I heard a rumor that you spent the afternoon and evening with a woman."

Colton snorted, the smile on his face filling the whole thing. Ames wore a stone mask, and Cy kept his in place too. "That's right, Mother," he said. "You know Patsy. She helped Grams at lunch yesterday."

"Blonde?" Grams asked. "She has a kind voice." It took her so long to say a single sentence, and while she did, Cy buttered and syruped his waffle.

"She sure does, Grams." Cy smiled at his grandmother and looked around at the rest of his family. Colton grinned like the Cheshire Cat, and Cy rolled his eyes.

"Tell us about her," his mom said.

"She's nice," Cy said.

"Pretty," Ames added.

"Smart," Colton said.

"Yeah, all of that," Cy said, determined not to say any

more. "I came here instead of going home, because I was hoping I could use your treadmill, Colt."

"Oh, sure," he said. "Anytime."

"Great." Cy met Ames's eyes, and they had a whole conversation in that one moment. "Now, Grams, what did you do yesterday afternoon?"

CHAPTER 8

Patsy laid the vacuum cleaner all the way flat and pushed it under the bed. Annie, who was in charge of housekeeping at the lodge, had put together a chore schedule for everyone in the family. Patsy had accepted her role in the Whittaker family, which Graham had said was the GO: General Overseer.

Andrew had said they'd be dead in the water without Patsy, and she'd enjoyed her life and job at the lodge. She did oversee everything, and everyone, and such a thing fit her personality to a T.

After she finished vacuuming, she needed to go through Celia's receipts with her, review Sophia's schedule with her for the next month, as her mother had fallen last week and needed extra help, and put in an order for the toiletries and supplies they needed for the guest rooms.

Sometimes her task list overwhelmed her, but today Patsy simply hummed a hymn her mom had taught her.

She'd been a clean freak, and she'd designed games and songs to make tidying up the house in the orchard more fun.

Singing had been one of those things, and Patsy had loved the days they all learned a new song the most. Her mom had a beautiful alto singing voice, and Betty had inherited that. Patsy's voice was quite a bit higher, and she'd always learned the soprano parts.

She finished up in the Princess Diana Suite—they'd named all the rooms this fall at Wes's suggestion—and unplugged the vacuum, Cy on her mind.

It seemed the man never left her mind, as Patsy had fallen asleep with him there for the past two nights, and he'd been in the forefront of her thoughts the moment she woke.

They did text at night, and Patsy supposed that was why he lingered with her until she fell asleep. New relationships were always exciting, and Patsy knew that would fade.

Her voice quieted as she considered that possibility.

Perhaps that was the problem. Shouldn't the excitement remain in a relationship? Shouldn't she be chomping at the bit to see Cy, hold his hand, get to the altar with him?

She thought of Bree and Wes and how they'd gotten married the very night they'd arrived in Hawaii. Elise had given up her job and business here to move to Colorado to be with Gray. Annie and Colton had fallen in love over a Christmas just like this one, with lots of snow and holiday spirit.

Patsy had never had the fairytale romance. Never had a man come into her life and sweep her off her feet. Never even had a boyfriend who'd fallen in love with her.

She'd been in love before, and the result of that had been painful and trying, and Patsy really didn't want to go through that again. At the same time, she'd seen her sister and her friends find their true love, and she knew it could be beautiful and rewarding.

She thought of Joe, and how his marriage had ended a few months ago. She remembered the day her father had called to say Mom had left. Even when people did try to make a life together, sometimes things fell apart. There were no guarantees in life, that was for sure.

Husbands and fathers, wives and mothers, went to war. They died in car accidents. They got sick.

Patsy's stomach tightened, and the feeling moved immediately into her chest, then her throat. She swallowed, trying to work through this negativity.

"You don't want to be alone forever," she told herself. And she didn't. Even if she ended up divorced, even if her husband died young, even if things fell apart, Patsy wanted to find someone to spend her life with. As much of it as possible.

"So don't give up," she murmured as she put the vacuum in the cleaning closet upstairs. Not every romance had to be the fairytale kind, and Patsy was okay with that.

She ran her hand through her short hair as she went down the magnificent staircase in the lodge to the main floor.

Stockton and Bailey, the two oldest Whittaker children,

worked in the living room, removing ornaments from the tree. Bailey stood on a ladder and passed a gold ball the size of her head to Stockton, who placed it in the plastic casing and slid that in the box.

Many more boxes lined the wall separating this main room from the kitchen behind it, and Patsy was glad she hadn't been assigned the task of getting those out or putting them away.

"Hey, guys," she said with a smile.

"Hi Patsy," they said together, and she continued past the long couches.

"Oh, Patsy," Bailey said. "My mom wanted me to ask you if you'd come down to the ranch today."

Patsy paused in front of the fireplace. A couple of years ago, when the power had gone out, they'd used it to keep warm, as well as brew coffee.

"Sure, I can," Patsy said. "What for?" She'd grown up in Coral Canyon, same as Laney McAllister—now a Whittaker—but she was at least a decade younger.

"She said she had some pictures for you." Bailey passed another ball to Stockton. "She said she can bring them up if you're too busy."

"Pictures?"

"Of the orchard," Bailey said. "I guess you guys did a big thing when she was younger?" Bailey continued working while she talked, and Patsy did enjoy the girl. She was a hard worker, she got excellent grades in school, and she was responsible. A lot like Laney, actually.

"She has all these pictures at the orchard with one of her school classes." Bailey stood on her tiptoes to reach the next ornament. "She thought you might like them, since they're a piece of your history."

"Sure," Patsy said, her curiosity piqued. "I'll text her."

"Ronnie's sick today," Bailey said. "So she said you could come anytime. She's not leaving the house."

"Okay."

Patsy did have access to a four-wheel-drive vehicle, and she'd take one of the trucks down to the ranch once she finished a few other things today.

Celia poked her head around the corner. "I thought I heard your voice," she said. "Are you ready for me?"

"Yes," Patsy said, glancing at her. "Thanks, Bay. Good job on the tree you guys." She stepped in front of Celia and went down the hall away from the kitchen and dining room that served as the heart of the lodge.

When there was something going on, either with the family or with their guests, it happened in the kitchen and dining room. Wes had suggested getting a bigger table and expanding this part of the house, though it was already quite big.

But with thirteen rooms at the lodge and more and more people joining the family every Christmas, he'd thought expanding the hub of the lodge would be wise.

Graham took everything Wes said seriously, and he'd brought a general contractor to the lodge, and plans had started to be made to add on to the house. A room that would double the size of the dining room would fit behind the garage, and Patsy had sat in on the meeting with the four Whittaker brothers and Wes Hammond while they went over designs and timelines and budgets.

Then they'd handed the project to Patsy to "oversee."

The folder sat on the corner of her desk, because she also needed to get to that in the next several days.

She'd been on the phone for the past couple of weeks, talking to construction managers, the interior designer, and a carpenter that did custom, high-end furniture.

She was meeting with Noah on January second, in fact, as he sourced wood locally and needed time to find what they were looking for.

He'd take it from the property where it would live, if he could, and Patsy looked out the window of her office as if she could see the forest that bordered the back of the lodge.

It sat on twenty-one acres, and they used the land the most in the summer months, though they had plenty of guests who enjoyed snowmobiling and snowshoeing parties in the winter too.

Patsy sighed as she sat behind her desk. She probably needed to go over next week's guest list and see what activities they'd signed up for.

Losing Bree had been hard—beyond hard. A catastrophe was what it was. She managed all of the events at the lodge. She organized them, she ran a crew in the stables, she led some of the horseback riding expeditions, she sent the emails and texts to guests, she put up the whiteboard announcing that day's activities. All of it.

Patsy had been doing it for the past month since Bree had had her baby, but she knew she couldn't keep doing it. She needed to hire someone very soon.

She picked up her pen and scrawled, *job board - new*

events coordinator on her notepad. One more thing on her list.

"All right," she said, looking up and smiling at Celia. "Let's do your receipts."

Celia was very good at keeping track of what she bought for meals here at the lodge, and she kept everything in a neat zipper pouch Andrew's oldest daughter had made for her.

She unzipped it, and Patsy tapped to get her spreadsheet open.

They did this once a month, and they had a system in place. Celia read the numbers; Patsy typed them in. She totaled it, wrote Celia a check, and put all of that in the expense report she emailed to all of the brothers once a month.

Graham and Andrew were still heavily involved in their father's energy company, and if there was a problem, Patsy almost always spoke with Beau or Eli.

As Celia read her last receipt and said, "That's it," Patsy's phone rang.

Cy's name sat on the screen, and the bubbling excitement started in her stomach. She swiped on the call and tapped the speaker button. "You're on with me and Celia," she said.

"Oh, okay," he said, and he sounded cheerful. Patsy smiled as she started the formula in her spreadsheet. "I suppose I can ask you this in front of her, since I did announce my feelings in front of the whole crew." He chuckled, though Patsy knew he'd been embarrassed. "I was hoping I might be able to see you today. What are the possibilities of that?"

Warmth filled Patsy as she dragged up the column of numbers. She wanted to blurt out yes, of course. Then she remembered the long list of things she had going on—and how she'd literally added two more items in the past fifteen minutes.

"Um," she said. "Maybe tonight? I thought I'd be free by mid-afternoon, but I just learned I need to go down to the ranch and look at some pictures."

"What kind of pictures?" Cy asked.

Patsy pulled out the business checkbook as she said, "I guess Laney has some photos of the orchard from years ago. She thought I might like them."

"Maybe I could come look at the pictures with you," he said.

Patsy looked at Celia, her eyebrows raised. Celia was already smiling and nodding. "You have time to see him," she said quietly. "It's Christmas, Patsy. Take some time off."

Patsy's first impulse was to resist that suggestion. She never took time off unless she was so sick she couldn't physically work. She *liked* working; she always had.

"Patsy?" Cy asked.

"Yes," she said, deciding right then and there to go against her natural impulse. She wanted to see him. "Come up to the lodge, and we can go look at the pictures together." She maintained eye contact with Celia who mimed applauding her. Patsy grinned and shook her head, though the excitement popping through her testified that she'd done the right thing.

"What time?" he asked.

"Whenever," Patsy said.

"All right," Cy said. "See you later."

The call ended, and Patsy dropped her eyes to the checkbook. "Okay, so it's six hundred and—"

"Good for you, Patsy," Celia said. "That seemed hard for you."

Patsy had been working with Celia for a few years now, and they were good friends. So Patsy didn't mind the comment, and she didn't mind admitting, "It was. But…." She signed her name on the check and ripped it off. She met Celia's eye as she handed her the money. "I really like him."

It felt good to admit it out loud, though a dose of worry ate at her too. "I just hope I don't mess it up."

Celia's smile slipped. "Why would you?"

"I don't know." Patsy leaned back in her chair. "It just seems like the last few men I've been out with…I've made a mess of things."

"I don't think that's true at all," Celia said. She carried something in her voice that made Patsy perk up.

"You have more to say," she said.

"I don't want to hurt your feelings."

"You won't."

Celia took a breath, her eyes harboring a bit of nervousness. "Well, from my perspective, Patsy, it's not you that's made a mess of things, other than who you choose to go out with."

"Who I choose to go out with?"

"They've all been…." Celia cleared her throat. "I never say this. I don't judge people."

"Just say it," Patsy said, her pulse bobbing a little too high in her chest now.

"Losers," Celia said. "They've all been losers, Patsy. It's not you; it's them, and they just make you *feel* like it's you."

Patsy just blinked at her, her mind running through everyone she'd dated in the past few years since coming to Whiskey Mountain Lodge.

"I'm sorry," Celia said, standing. She came around the desk, and Patsy rose to meet her embrace. "But it's true. You're an amazing woman, Patsy, and you shouldn't think of yourself as the one who messes up. It's not you." Celia stepped back and nodded like that was that. She'd declared it and it was true.

She left the office, and Patsy sat back down, wondering if what she'd said was true.

"Hey," Sophia said, entering the office. "You ready for me?"

"Yes," Patsy said, reaching to save her spreadsheet and open her calendar. "Let's do this." She looked at Sophia as she took the seat Celia had just been in. "First, how's your mother?"

A moment passed, and then Sophia burst into tears.

"Oh, no." Patsy jumped back to her feet and went to comfort her best friend and roommate. She had a feeling this meeting had just gotten a lot longer, which meant her to-do list had as well.

"Hey, it's okay," she said as she crouched in front of Sophia. "Let's say a prayer together, okay? Would that help?"

"Yes," Sophia said, her voice high and nasally. "Thank you, Patsy."

"Sure," she said, closing her eyes as she took Sophia's hands in hers. "Dear Lord...."

CHAPTER 9

Cy pulled up to the lodge, his anxiety at an all-time high. He reached for the rubber band, which he'd remembered to put on that morning. Actually, he hadn't taken it off last night, so he'd slept with it in place and woken with the constant pressure around his wrist.

Better there than squeezing the life out of his chest.

He'd forced himself to stop by the building in the orchard before coming up the canyon to the lodge. He'd been dressed and ready to go when he'd called Patsy, and while he didn't want to seem too desperate to see her, he couldn't stand to sit around his house for another minute either.

So he'd gone by the building to see how it had fared in the Christmas Day storm. The crew had been there, cleaning things up and moving forward with the project, and Cy had spoken to Chris, the construction manager over the whole thing.

That had taken about half an hour, because Cy went by the building every day. He had nothing else to do, and he couldn't take his motorcycle out right now. So he'd filled his days with running and hanging out with Wes and Colton and stopping by the building to see how it was going.

As he gazed at the huge piles of snow that had been cleared from the parking lot at Whiskey Mountain Lodge, he had serious doubts about his decision to move his shop to Wyoming.

This was a normal winter, not something out of the ordinary. And all that snow wouldn't melt anytime soon, though the sun had been out in full force for the past two days.

If anything, such a clear, bright day only made the temperatures colder in Coral Canyon.

Cy stayed in the truck, working up the courage to go inside. He knew Patsy was busy. She'd told him last night that she'd been doing Bree's job for the past month, as well as her own. Sophia's mother had gotten injured. The Whittakers were doing a lodge addition.

He liked talking to Patsy and learning about her life, as well as life at Whiskey Mountain Lodge. But he wanted to see her. He wanted to hold her hand, and see what color her sweater was today. He'd learned she loved sweaters and wore them year-round. When he'd asked her how many she owned, she said there was no way to count.

He'd laughed then, sitting on the couch in his rented house. In that moment, he'd realized he couldn't go another day without being in the same physical space as her. He'd barely slept last night, because he'd been stewing about how to see her without causing more stress for her.

When Ames had shown up at the gym, Cy had been there for twenty minutes already. "Oh, boy," Ames had said, tossing his towel over the bar. "You're already in a lather."

"I don't want to talk about it." Cy had kept running, and Ames had just gotten on the treadmill next to him and started. When Cy finished, Ames glanced at him.

"Breakfast tomorrow," he said. "Just you and me."

Cy had nodded, and he'd never been more grateful for his twin. In fact, he pulled out his phone and sent a text to Ames. *Thanks for not making me talk this morning. Tomorrow, though, get ready.*

I'm always ready, Ames said, and he was a very good listener. Colton had told him he should go into counseling, because Ames had a way of listening and absorbing, thinking through problems, and offering support without ever passing judgment. It was why he made such a good cop and why he'd advanced up the ranks in Littleton so quickly.

At the same time, Cy knew Ames felt stymied in his job. He had no chance of becoming Chief there, at least not for another fifteen years at least. The city had just hired a new Chief four years ago, and Ames hadn't been ready then. He hadn't had the experience and the qualifications he had now.

His phone vibrated, and Cy looked at it. Ames had added, *Now go inside the lodge.*

A grin crossed Cy's face. Of course his brother would know he was hesitating out in the parking lot.

Cy flipped the rubber band on his wrist and turned off his truck. The cold would permeate the cab quickly, and he wouldn't be able to loiter in the truck.

He didn't want to either, and he told himself he'd feel better the moment he saw Patsy. He knew he would, and that actually scared him a little bit.

He didn't want to be alone, but he didn't want to attach himself to the wrong woman again. He had to be sure before he let himself truly fall for Patsy Foxhill. Because when Cy fell, he fell fast and hard, and if things didn't work out, the aftermath of that was not pretty.

He'd been living in that aftermath for a year and a half now, and he was so ready to move on.

He wasn't sure if he should knock on the front door or what. He didn't see a doorbell, and he ended up standing there, staring at the fine craftsmanship on the covered porch of the lodge.

Before he could do anything, the door actually opened and a man pulled up short. "Oh, hey, Cy."

"Hello, Beau," he said, putting a smile on his face. "I was just trying to figure out what to do to get inside."

Beau grinned at him and fell back a step to welcome him in. "You just come in, Cy. The door's always open here."

"Thanks." Cy entered the lodge and looked around. This place did hold a particular brand of magic that Cy couldn't identify, but he could definitely feel.

"I think Patsy is in the office," Beau said, reaching to

pull the door closed behind him. Cy watched it click into place, and then he faced the living room.

He had no idea where the office was, but he figured it wouldn't be upstairs. He knew where the kitchen was, and he'd stood down the hall leading to the back yard when he'd asked Patsy out in front of everyone.

He went into the hall that led to the kitchen and looked both ways.

He turned back to the kitchen, wondering what sat down this way. He had a strong inclination this was where the basement steps were, and sure enough, right across from the dining room sat a doorway with stairs that led down. He turned and surveyed the dining room, which had a huge table with a lone coffee cup on it, leftover from breakfast.

Cy thought the lodge sure did seem quiet for how many people were supposed to be there. He continued down the hall, but the boots on the floor and hooks on the wall told him this door led outside.

He opened the door anyway, only to be met with the garage.

"Cy?"

He turned around, his heart leaping in a strange way. It settled instantly when he saw Sophia, not Patsy. "Hey," he said, moving toward her. "Beau said Patsy was in her office, but well, I don't know where her office is." He chuckled, mostly to stop himself from reaching for that rubber band.

"It's this way," Sophia said, spinning away from him

and striding back down the hall. He wasn't sure what he'd done to upset her; Beau had let him into the lodge.

He followed her past the dining room and kitchen, past the hall that led outside, and past another guest bathroom. Finally, she indicated a room on the right-hand side of the hall, and Cy heard Patsy say, "Sophia? Is everything okay?" before he reached the doorway.

His eyes met hers, and everything in the world stopped. Cy didn't know what to make of it. He'd just been faced with Sophia, and nothing like this had happened. Nothing even close.

What does that mean? he thought. *Lord, if you could tell me what that means, I'd appreciate it.*

The Lord did not tell him anything, but Sophia said, "Excuse me," and squeezed past him to go back the way she'd come.

He stepped into the office, wanting to close the door and whisper how he felt about Patsy. Did she feel the same thing? Had she ever felt it before?

"Hey," he said. "Sorry, I'm sure I'm really early, but I didn't have anything else to do today."

"It's okay." Patsy looked down at the things on her desk—papers, a checkbook, a couple of folders. She glanced at her computer, and then her eyes traveled back to his. "Let's go down to Laney's."

"Right now?" He took in the office, as everything in this lodge was made of the very best. Her desk took up the spot in front of the window, and it would easily fit two more computer screens. Big ones, too.

To the right of that was a built-in bookcase, but it

wasn't filled with volumes. Instead, all of the shelves held pictures, and Cy gestured to it. "I can just look at those while you finish what you need to finish."

"I'm never going to finish what I need to finish," she said. "The work here never ends."

"I bet," Cy said, walking over to the bookcase anyway. "Some of these people I recognize." He saw Graham Whittaker and his wife and two kids. Eli and his family. Andrew and his, and Beau and his. Then all four of them together, with all of their children.

"These look recent."

"This fall," she said, joining him. She pointed to the biggest one. "That's all of us."

"Oh, yeah," he said as he found Patsy in the picture. It wasn't hard, because she seemed to have an angelic glow about her he couldn't look away from.

"We really can go," she said. "I just have to put a quitting time on my day. There's always more to do."

"I understand." Cy didn't make a move to leave the office, though. "That's how things are at the shop when we're running. Sometimes I felt chained to the place."

"Yes," she said. "Chained."

Cy reached out, and he didn't have to go far to find Patsy's hand. It was surprisingly easy to slip his fingers between hers and hold on, and wow, he thought he could die right then and float away on clouds of joy.

A thrill shot from the top of his head to his fingertips, which seemed to be crackling with energy.

He looked at her, and she took a moment to continue studying the pictures before she turned her head toward him too. "Tell me you feel it," he said, his voice quiet. "Or maybe I don't want to know I'm the only one who feels like I come alive when I'm with you."

He was used to saying exactly what he thought, and he'd never had to hide how he felt from anyone before. But surprise lifted Patsy's eyebrows.

She squeezed his hand, and Cy thought that was probably some sort of code for *I feel it too.*

She had to. God wouldn't be cruel enough to play a joke on him like this.

He nodded toward the pictures again, breaking eye contact with her. "Who are the rest of the people?"

"You know Celia and Zach," she said. "Those are her daughters, and his kids." She indicated a grouping of several pictures on another shelf. "Some of these are recurring guests. People who book their next trip for the next year when they leave. This is the Everett family. Jack and Fran—the Everett sisters. They all met their spouses right here at Whiskey Mountain Lodge and live in Coral Canyon now."

"Wow," Cy said. "Guests at the lodge?"

"The lodge has only been available for guests for about four years now. That's when I started up here. All of the Whittaker brothers lived here at one point. When Lily Everett came, she fell in love with Beau." She pointed to their family picture.

"And her sisters came, and they each fell in love with a cowboy here too. They all live here now."

Her words rang in Cy's ears. It seemed like what had happened with the Everetts was slowly happening to his family too. Four of them had homes in Coral Canyon now. Only Ames and their parents still lived full-time in Ivory Peaks.

"This lodge has a real family atmosphere," he said, finally landing on what made Whiskey Mountain Lodge so special. "Everyone who comes here feels like they belong."

"That's the goal," Patsy said. Behind them, on the desk, her phone chimed, but she ignored it.

"I bet you work hard to make that happen," he said.

"I try."

"Hmm." Cy tore his eyes away from the big group picture that had everyone in it. He saw Bree and Elise next to Patsy, and they all looked so happy. Like they really did belong.

He wanted to build that at Rev for Vets too, and he knew he needed someone like Patsy to make it happen. He opened his mouth to ask her to come work for him again when the question froze in his mouth.

It wasn't the right thing to do, and Cy turned toward her to see if she'd noticed that he'd literally gone mute.

She looked at him too, and the only thing he could think of in that moment was kissing her. He shifted so he faced her more fully and leaned toward her. Her eyes drifted closed, and Cy took that as a big-time yes for him to do what he wanted to do.

"Patsy?"

She jumped away from him so fast Cy wasn't even sure she'd been beside him at all. He turned as she said, "Rose, what can I do for you?"

"Sorry to interrupt." Rose looked past her to Cy and

flashed an apologetic smile. "But there's a delivery guy here, and he says he needs to talk to you."

"Thanks," Patsy said, reaching for one of the folders on her desk. "I'll be right behind you."

Rose left, and Patsy took her time finding a pen on her desktop. Then she turned and looked at Cy and asked, "Can we pick that up later?"

"Definitely," he said.

"Okay." She gave him a smile, and those bright, bright blue eyes fanned flames in his direction. "Because you're definitely not the only one who feels this…thing between us."

With that, she left him standing in the office, a smile spreading across his face and through his whole soul.

CHAPTER 10

Patsy sat through the brief meeting with Eli and Beau, her mind down the hall in her office. She clasped her own hands together and nodded, as if she'd been listening to the brothers. She hadn't been. A buzzing had started in her head about the time Cy had walked through the door of her office, and it had only intensified as she stood beside him, when he held her hand, and as he'd leaned toward her.

She'd actually closed her eyes as if she would kiss him. She cleared her throat and shifted in her seat. Oh, yes, she wanted to kiss him.

She disliked these little impromptu meetings anyway. The brothers never seemed to have a schedule for their day, but Patsy sure did. She frowned as she listened to Eli talk about putting in new flooring when they did the dining room remodel. "I think we have the budget for that, based on this sheet Carole gave us." He laid a single sheet of paper on the table, but Patsy didn't even look at it.

"It's probably a good idea," Beau said. "Things can start to look a little ragged with so many people in and out."

"Right, so flooring on the entire main floor, and leading upstairs to the second level." Eli pointed to a number on the sheet that made Patsy's head swim. It took a moment for her to even realize if she was looking at tens of thousands or hundreds of thousands.

Neither of the brothers blinked. "All right." Beau picked up the paper and slid it to Patsy. "What else?"

"That's it," Eli said.

"Good," Beau said. "Because we've got our Everett family dinner in a few minutes." He stood up just as Lily, his wife, came into the dining room. "I'm coming," he said. "Sorry, we're done here."

Patsy stood too, catching the disgruntled look on Eli's face as his brother walked away. She knew the Whittakers mixed in a lot of business over the holidays, because otherwise, it was hard to get them all together in the same room at the same time. Only Andrew worked full time anymore, and Beau and his family were set to leave for the South in a couple of days, to do a whole tour of where Lily had grown up and visit her extended family.

Patsy took the sheet down the hall to her office and found Cy still standing in front of the bookcase. She put the paper on top of the blue folder with all of the other information about this lodge remodel, determined not to think about it until tomorrow. There wasn't anything she could do today.

"Should we go down to the ranch?" she asked, and Cy turned.

"Sure." He gave her a gorgeous smile, and Patsy wanted to tuck it away in her pocket to experience later.

"Do you still like your hair?" she asked, eyeing his cowboy hat.

"Sure," he said, sweeping the hat off his head. "And I got some styling products, and I think it looks pretty good." He paused in front of her, only a couple of feet away.

She reached up and stood on her tiptoes to brush her hand along his hair, pushing it to the side. "Good," she said. "I'm glad you like it."

He cleared his throat and settled the hat back on his head. "So we're going down to a ranch?"

"It's just a mile down the road," Patsy said. "Laney said she found some pictures."

"Let's go see them." Cy tucked his hands in his coat pockets, thankfully, because while Patsy sure did like holding his hand and she really did want to kiss him, she didn't want to do it as a display for anyone.

She turned and left the office in favor of the hallway that went out to the back yard. She took her coat from the hook, and Cy was right there to help her put it on. "Thanks," she said, smoothing down her short hair. Since she'd cut her hair a while ago, she'd stopped the old habit of reaching to pull her hair out from underneath her collar, but it seemed she couldn't just put on a coat anymore. She always had to touch her hair.

"You can drive, right?" she asked.

"Sure thing." He led the way back through the lodge to the front door and out to his truck. He held her door for her, and when Patsy sat in the passenger seat, she was reminded of him coming down to her father's orchard because he'd felt like he should.

She glanced at him as he got behind the wheel. "How do you know what you should or shouldn't do?" she asked.

Cy looked at her, surprise in his eyes, as he pressed the button to start the truck. "What do you mean?"

"The other day, when you came down to the orchard, you said you did because you felt like you should."

"Oh, well, that's just a feeling I get," he said. "I've learned not to ignore those in my life."

"Do you think it's God telling you what to do?"

"Yes," he said simply. "Sometimes it's a really strong feeling, and sometimes it's more like a thought I can't let go of." He looked at her, a new kind of vulnerability on his face. "Don't you get those feelings?"

"Every now and then," Patsy hedged. "They don't sound as strong as yours."

"Everyone is different," he said, his voice light and casual. "Left here, I'm assuming?"

"Yes," Patsy said. "It's the only other house out here. Can't miss it."

Cy took them down the plowed road to the ranch, and he pulled in the driveway beside Graham's big, boxy, luxury SUV. They got out of the truck and went up to the front door. Patsy knocked and threw a nervous smile at Cy.

"What are these pictures of?" he asked.

"Supposedly the orchard," Patsy said. "I don't know what they are. Laney just thought I might like them."

The door opened, and Laney backed up with a smile. "Hello, Patsy." She glanced at Cy. "Cy Hammond, what a pleasure. C'mon in." She kept her gaze locked on Patsy's as she entered, but Patsy ignored her.

She knew Laney, but they weren't best friends. If Sophia asked about Cy, Patsy would tell her. She trusted Sophia explicitly, and she knew her best friend wouldn't be all over town gossiping about her. Laney wouldn't either, but Patsy still wasn't going to say anything.

"When I was in ninth grade," Laney said, coming up behind them as they moved through the hallway and into the kitchen and living room in the back. "We did this science unit on the life cycle of plants. Our teacher took us to the orchard, and we got to see trees in various stages of growth, and we learned what it takes for an apple tree to actually produce apples."

Patsy stopped at the kitchen table, where Laney had spread out the photographs. They were in color, at least, but there was so much brown and so much orange in the coloration. Patsy loved old things, and her interest in these photos intensified.

"Anyway," Laney said. "Some are of my class and whatnot, but then there's several of your family, Patsy. I thought you might like them."

"Are you going to throw them away?"

"I can't imagine what I'd need them for," Laney said. "So yes, I'm going to throw them away." She settled one hand on her stomach while the other picked up a photograph. "I've just been trying to go through a cupboard or a closet every now and then to clean things out. Anything I don't need, I'm getting rid of." She turned the photo toward Patsy. "But look. That's me."

Patsy took the photo, and she could see the youthful version of Laney standing on the edge of the orchard, squinting into the sun. A sense of happiness, of easier times, flowed from the picture, and Patsy wanted all of them.

"I see that," she said, smiling. She hadn't seen any of her mother and father though, and she went back to the array of pictures on the table. "What year were you in ninth grade?" she asked.

"Oh, let's see," Laney said with a sigh. She sat down at the table, and she looked tired. Bailey had said Ronnie was sick, and Patsy determined not to leave without asking Laney if she needed dinner. A break. Something. She certainly looked like she could use both. "I turned sixteen in tenth grade. I'm forty-six now."

"Nineteen-ninety," Cy said without hardly missing a beat. Both women looked at him, but he just reached for a photo.

"I was born in eighty-nine," Patsy said. "I would be a year old in these." She started looking for herself as a baby, and only three pictures later, she found one. Her mother held her in her arms, a bright smile on her face as she held out an apple to Joe, who was probably seven in the picture.

Patsy marveled at the emotion on her mother's face. She looked so *happy*, something she claimed she hadn't been in Coral Canyon. She'd said the orchard wore on her, and she just couldn't live surrounded by apple trees for the rest of her life. Patsy didn't understand her, because all she wanted to do was live under the shade of the apple trees.

"Your mom and dad," Cy murmured, sliding another picture on top of the one Patsy couldn't look away from.

She blinked and took in her parents sitting on the bench they'd kept in the garden for years. They had more than one family picture on that bench, and Patsy pulled in a tight breath. They were holding hands and looking at each other while they laughed.

Joy filled her next breath, and she knew it came from the picture. So something had definitely happened in the following years, because her mother had certainly been in love with her father at this point.

"Aren't they great?" Laney asked. "Anyway, I thought you might want them." She sighed as she stood, using both hands against the tabletop to do it.

Patsy stacked the pictures. "I do want them," she said. "I'll take all of them if that's okay."

"Totally okay."

Patsy did like seeing the trees from thirty years ago, because these ones closest to the house were so much bigger now. The house had gotten bigger over the years too, and Patsy wanted to take the pictures to the orchard and compare them to what was there now.

"You can stack them all in that shoebox," Laney said. "Take the whole thing."

She and Cy packed up the pictures, and while Cy put the lid on, Patsy turned to Laney. "Are you okay, Laney? Want me to bring down some lunch? Dinner?" She glanced toward the mouth of the hall, where she assumed bedrooms were. "How's Ronnie?"

"He's very sick," Laney said with a weary smile. "Graham went to get some things in town for him."

"Will he be okay?" Patsy asked.

"We took him to the emergency care center this morning," Laney said. "He has the flu. Liam told Graham what to get, and yes, he'll be okay."

Patsy sensed there was more, and she wondered if this was one of those feelings Cy had talked about. "Are you feeling okay?" she asked, wondering how much to press Laney.

"Just tired," she said, turning away.

"We'll bring you dinner, then," Cy said, his voice rumbling through Patsy's soul. "What's your favorite thing?"

Patsy expected Laney to protest and say they were fine. Instead, she looked up and said, "If you'd bring us a pan of scalloped potatoes from Mama Marie's, I would love you forever."

Cy chuckled, and even Patsy smiled at Laney. "I'll call them right now," Patsy said, and she pulled her phone out to get the job done. She wandered down the hall while she talked to the girl about doing a take-out order. Her own stomach growled, and she saw no reason not to get food for her and Cy too. Perhaps they could go back to his house and eat and enjoy the rest of the day together.

She couldn't believe she was going to take the rest of the day off, but as she turned back toward Cy, her decision solidified. "I got us food too," she said. "Drive me down the canyon to get it?"

"Of course."

"We'll be back in a little bit," Patsy promised Laney, and she waved to them.

Out in Cy's truck, Patsy buckled her seatbelt and said, "I thought we could take her the potatoes and then you could take me on a tour of your shop and your house."

"Oh, there's nothing to see at either of those," he said with a light laugh.

Patsy debated about how to respond. *Maybe I just want to get you alone again.* Too bold.

Maybe she could say, *I took the whole day off to spend with you.* That gave away too much.

Thankfully, Cy said, "But we can do that, if you want. I've been working on this new mailbox for Gray and Elise, and it's pretty cool."

"I'd love to see it." Instead of saying the bold things inside her mind, Patsy reached over and took Cy's hand in hers.

He glanced at her and squeezed her hand, and Patsy suddenly felt like the radio was playing a chorus of angels. He didn't say anything, and Patsy's mind wandered around her to-do list at the lodge, the pictures in the shoe box between her and Cy, and what was really wrong with Laney Whittaker.

CHAPTER 11

Cy blended the greenish-gray paint with the beige paint, making it look like the gradient coloring on a cutthroat trout. Gray and Hunter loved fishing with their whole souls, and they'd fed him more than one trout dinner this past summer and fall when Cy had first looked at relocating to Wyoming.

He wanted to do something to fill his time while he waited for his building to be finished, and Gray didn't have a mailbox at his new house. Cy had a certification in welding, and he'd been using the back shed here at the house he rented, which had a workshop and plenty of heat.

He'd made a great fish-shaped tube, and the paint was really bringing it all together. The front of the mailbox, which Gray or Hunter would open to get their mail, would be the fish's mouth, and Cy couldn't wait to show it to them.

The radio played, and the heater pumped, and Cy worked. He never paid attention to a clock anymore; he much preferred choosing a time to be done working and setting an alarm. That way, he didn't have to constantly wonder if he'd be late. This strategy had alleviated some of his anxiety in general, and it allowed him to relax and enjoy whatever he was doing.

When his alarm went off some time later, Cy quickly finished dabbing on a few more dark spots for the trout's skin, and reached over to tap off the chiming noises. His shoulders ached a little, and he rolled them out as he surveyed his work for the day.

He started cleaning up, and when he had the brushes soaking in paint thinner and all the newspapers in the recycling bin, he reached for the radio and turned it off. He had to trek through the frozen wilderness to the house, but it was only about thirty yards. In the house, he wished he had a dog to keep him company, and Patsy had told him about a great dog rescue operation in Dog Valley.

They'd made plans to go after the New Year, and Cy had been telling himself to be patient for several days now.

Tonight was New Year's Eve, and that meant it would be "after the New Year" in literally two days. Gray and Elise would be back from their honeymoon on the second, and Cy wanted the mailbox done by then. So he could wait to get a dog to take care of.

He showered, scrubbing extra hard to get all the paint flecks off his skin and hopefully all of the fumes out of his hair. He shaved and brushed his teeth, styled his hair—

which he *really* liked—and dressed in what he hoped would be a fashion statement but not embarrass Patsy.

They were going to the New Year's Eve ball at the community center, and Cy's nervousness increased in relation to his excitement. When he was with Patsy, he didn't experience nearly as much anxiety and worry. When he wasn't, he could feel himself spiraling.

His parents had gone back to Ivory Peaks with Ames a couple of days ago, but Cy could still hear his brother's counsel from breakfast a few days ago. *You need to go see someone, Cy. There are medications for this kind of thing.*

He knew there were. He'd taken them before. He didn't like them. They made everything in his mind soft. They put a wall between him and his feelings, and he didn't like it. He *liked* feeling all the things he felt—at least he liked feeling over not feeling.

He'd rather flip a rubber band on his wrist to calm himself than exist behind a medicated cloud.

He looked at himself in the mirror, thinking the jeans were normal. He wore a cream shirt with a greenish-brown tie—very much like the skin of the trout he'd been painting that day—and he shrugged into a suit coat jacket he'd found at the secondhand shop here in town. It was at least thirty years old, with wide lapels and boxy shoulders and a ton of charm.

He loved the jacket, and he'd been pleasantly surprised that it fit as well as it did. He'd paid seventeen dollars for it, and he made sure everything lay right in place before reaching for his cowboy hat.

"Only one more thing," he muttered to himself, picking

up the shades he'd also found at the secondhand shop. His brothers didn't understand why he went there; they sat and reminded him of how much money he had. But to Cy, it wasn't about the money at all. It was about finding something rare. Something used and forgotten and breathing new life into it.

With the shades on—he could still see his eyes through the brown lenses—he completed his New Year's Eve look. He wouldn't wear the glasses inside, and he probably wouldn't wear them at all except for the few moments where he stood on Patsy's porch to pick her up for the ball.

They completed the outfit, that was for sure, and he hoped he'd have an opportunity to use them in the future.

As it was, he was ten minutes late leaving to pick up Patsy. As he grabbed his keys and wallet from the kitchen, he paused. Right there in the bowl where he kept his pocket items sat the rubber band.

He wanted to take it, if only to help him focus on the drive up the canyon. In the end, he walked out without it, still cycling through his thoughts about medication and homeopathic remedies for his anxiety and nervousness.

Thirty minutes later, he stood on Patsy's porch, smoothing down his jacket after he'd knocked. The door opened, and Sophia stood there, wearing a pair of black leggings and an oversized sweater. Jonas, the little black and white dog that had taken to Cy, rushed right out onto the porch.

"Oh, my goodness," she said, scanning him from boot to hat. A smile spread across her face, and she shook her head. "You are something else, Cy."

Cy took that as a compliment, and he grinned back at her as he scooped Jonas into his arms. "I'm assuming Patsy's here." He chuckled as the dog licked his face, and he leaned away saying, "No, buddy. No licking."

"She's finishing her makeup," Sophia said. "Come on in. I'll go warn her."

"Warn her?" He laughed, though he supposed she should be warned. Although, if she didn't know he was going to show up in something a little off the beaten path, then she didn't know him at all.

He'd like to think she did know him—at least a little bit. They'd gone out a few times since Christmas, and he talked to her every day, either on the phone or through texting.

He waited in the living room with Jonas while Sophia left, and because the cabin was so small, he could hear their female voices in the bathroom. He glanced at the fireplace where he and Patsy had made s'mores, and then into the kitchen where he'd flirted with her shamelessly as they'd made pizzas.

He sure did like her, and so far, there were no red flags or obvious sirens telling him not to fall for her.

When she came around the corner in a devastatingly beautiful bright blue dress, Cy dang near leapt off the cliff. He'd go anywhere and to any length to have this woman on his arm. She smiled at him, her lips painted a bright red.

"Oh, wow," he said, wanting to laugh but suddenly not knowing how. Her dress had a high collar, short sleeves, and fit her like a glove to the waist, where it flared.

"Not quite a ballgown," she said. "But a party dress." She spun on the toe of a bright yellow pair of pumps, and Cy was floating toward heaven now.

"You're gorgeous," he said, and Patsy glowed. He took a step toward her, and in this small space, he only needed to take two more to reach her. "That dress is *amazing*. Brings out the color of your eyes like crazy."

"What about the earrings?" she asked, her voice full of fun.

And if there was one thing Cy really liked, it was having fun. He could barely tear his gaze from her mouth to look at her earlobes. When he did, he found a dangling pair of yellow rubber chickens, and he burst out laughing.

He took those two steps and swept her into his arms. "I should've gotten a memo about the color scheme," he said, still chuckling. "I could've worn a blue tie, at least."

"Oh, no," she said, grinning up at him, her hands securely on the back of his elbows. "It would have to be mustard yellow to go with this jacket."

"You like this jacket, don't you?" he asked, clearly teasing her.

"You know what? I do."

"It's from nineteen-seventy-four," he said. "I wasn't even alive then."

Patsy tipped her head back and giggled, and Cy basked in the happiness the two of them could produce together. "So we'll take a bit of the past with us into the future," she said.

"That's right." He backed up slightly and cocked his

elbow, a zing moving up and down his legs and into his spine. "Shall we?"

"We shall," she said with a slight British accent. Cy forgot all of his manners and didn't say good-bye to Jonas or Sophia. He didn't even close the door behind him. He wasn't sure how he'd gotten from the cabin to the truck, but he had.

"Seat heaters," he said, finally breaking out of the trance he'd fallen into. Patsy smelled like something petally and soft, and he wanted to hold her close and dance the night away with her.

Luckily, that was exactly what they'd signed up for, and when they entered the dimly lit gymnasium in the community center, it had been transformed into a fairytale ball.

"Wow," Cy said, trying to take everything in at the same time. Purple and green fabric had been stretched from the walls to the ceiling, and white tea lights were the only source of light. Vines snaked up the walls, and a perfectly round carriage sat in the corner nearest to him. People stood by it, clutching their significant other while a photographer snapped pictures.

"I thought this might feel a little like high school prom," he said. "But it's great."

"It's wonderful," Patsy said, glancing around. "I don't even know where to look."

In the middle of the room stood a statue, and it looked like a goblin or a troll to Cy. He supposed that made sense, since they had literally just entered the enchanted forest.

"The buffet is on the far side," a man said, and Cy brought

his attention back to his near proximity. The man there wore a navy velvet suit and a top hat, and Cy thought Ames would simply love this ball. "There are drinks on the other side of the carriage. Pictures on this side. Plenty of space to dance in the woods." He beamed at them like this was going to be the best night of their lives, and Cy actually thought it would be.

"Do you want to eat first?" he asked. "It's not too crowded yet." They'd gotten there a little after eight, and dinner had started at seven-thirty. It went until ten, so they had plenty of time.

"Sure," Patsy said. He kept his hand on the small of her back as they navigated the "woods" to the other side of the gym. Nothing had been overlooked, that was for sure. Little woodland creatures peered out from behind fake tree trunks. A pumpkin patch took up the front part of the gym, with a family of rabbits up on their hind legs, sniffing out danger. "It all looks so real," he said.

"Can you imagine doing this?" she asked. "I need to know who did this and recruit them to the lodge to be my activities director."

"Still looking for one of those?" he asked.

"Yeah," she said. "It's really hard to find people right now. There are so many job openings in Coral Canyon."

That was very good news for Cy, and though he'd heard it before, the fact that he wouldn't have a problem hiring people to work in the shop always made him happy. "Maybe I could do it," Cy said.

Patsy slowed and stopped, gaping at him. "You?"

"Yeah," he said. "Me. I ran a motorcycle shop, Patsy. I

can put on a few events at a luxury lodge." He took her hand and tugged her gently to get her moving again. "I'm not doing anything right now. The shop won't be done until at least March. Why not me?"

"Well." She opened her mouth to say more, but nothing came out. "I don't—I don't know. What experience do you have putting together events?"

"Uh, none," he said. "But I know how to build a custom bike. I know how to get people on the same page. I can schedule a snowshoeing…thing, and get the boys in the stables to feed the horses on time." He knew what the event coordinator at the lodge did. And if he didn't, he could literally call his sister-in-law and ask her. Bree would help him, and he said that next.

Patsy picked up a fancy paper plate, the kind that almost looked like real china. "You know what? This isn't a bad idea."

"I'm full of good ideas," Cy joked.

"I'm serious, Cy." She went down the food line, putting things on her plate she liked. Cy followed along behind her, wondering what he'd just gotten himself into.

A job, he thought. *One where you'll get to see Patsy every morning, and maybe every afternoon, and maybe kiss her good-bye before you go back to your house.*

That certainly made him smile. She took her food to a nearby table, and Cy joined her. "Let me think about this for a day," she said. "Talk to a few people." She pointed her fork at him, suddenly serious. "And you can't be a beast at the lodge."

"A beast?" Cy burst out laughing again. "Come on, Patsy. When have I ever been a beast?"

"Oh, you can be," she said. "I've seen it. Things don't go your way, and you're snapping those jaws all over the place." She gave him a raised-eyebrow, pointed look that said, *So there. And don't do it on my watch.*

Cy conceded the point, though he didn't find himself that beastly. Maybe he'd snapped at her in the orchard all those months ago—but she'd nearly hit him with a one-ton vehicle. Maybe he'd disappeared after publicly asking her out over the PA—but he'd been mortified and embarrassed. Maybe he'd argued with her on Christmas Day at her father's—but she'd just told him she wouldn't go out with him after first agreeing to go.

"I won't be a beast," he promised. "If you'll promise to kiss me tonight." He lifted his own eyebrows and grinned at her, scooping up a bite of mashed potatoes.

Patsy froze, her fork filled with ham and gravy halfway to her mouth. "Tonight?"

"It's New Year's Eve, Patsy. Everyone kisses at the stroke of midnight." Cy really didn't want to leave that community center without a taste of Patsy's bright red lips. Oh, he wanted to kiss her so badly he almost lunged toward her and did it right then.

But that would be a *beastly* thing to do, so he just smiled at her and waited for her to say whether or not she'd kiss him in less than four hours.

CHAPTER 12

Patsy wasn't sure why Cy was smiling at her like that. "What?" She finally put her ham and gravy in her mouth. "Wow, this is actually good," she said around the food, and that made Cy chuckle.

"I'm waiting for a yes or no on the kiss," he said.

A flush flared inside Patsy, and she took another bite, this time with a swoop of mashed potatoes with her meat and gravy. She chewed as she looked straight at him, her heart pounding like a jackhammer. "I suppose it's a yes," she said.

"Oh, you sound like it's going to be terrible," Cy said, that handsome smile still stuck in place.

"Well, it might be," she said airily. "When's the last time you kissed a woman?"

Cy flinched. "Dagger to the heart."

"It's been a while for me," she said, glancing down at

her plate to give herself a moment to collect her thoughts. "About ten months since I've been out with anyone."

"My last girlfriend broke up with me eighteen months ago," he said. "But I think I know how to kiss a woman. It's not something a man forgets."

Patsy saw him reach for his wrist though, and his fingers danced away quickly when he realized he hadn't put on his rubber band. For some reason, the fact that she made him nervous tickled Patsy. He was so *big*—everything about him. Big, broad shoulders. Big personality. Big cowboy hat. Big smile. Big charisma.

She liked him in a big way too, and she couldn't admit out loud to him that she'd been hoping he'd kiss her that night. In fact, if he hadn't made a move later, she would've done it. She could kiss him just as easily as the other way around.

"All right," she said, her voice filled with doubt. "If you're sure."

"I'm sure."

Patsy smiled at him and reached for her cup of ginger ale. "And do you know how to dance?"

"I'm definitely a better kisser than a dancer," he said.

Patsy giggled, because she thought he'd do just fine at both. Cy Hammond was good at everything, and Patsy hurried through the rest of her dinner just so she could get herself back into his arms.

He cleaned up their plates, and she tossed their cups into the trashcan. They both faced the dance floor at the same time, and Cy slipped his hand into hers. "I think dancing is going to be my thing."

"Your thing?" she asked, looking at him. Her yellow heels brought her closer to his height, though he still had plenty of inches on her.

"Yeah," he said, still gazing out at the magical place someone had transformed this gym into. "Remember how you asked me what I'd like to learn to do? I think it's going to be dancing." He looked at her then, some measure of trepidation on his face. "This might've been a terrible idea."

"No," she said, shaking her head. "When's the last time you went dancing?"

"Uh, high school?"

"You sound like you're guessing."

"I am guessing," he said. "I didn't know adults did this." He reached up with his free hand and pushed his cowboy hat further forward. "Maybe we should just go to a movie. We can hang out until midnight, and then I can get that kiss, and—"

"Oh, you're going to *earn* that kiss, Mister," Patsy said, stepping in front of him and taking both of his hands in hers. "Dancing is not that hard. If I can do it in these heels, you can follow me."

Cy looked doubtful, but his dark eyes glinted like fool's gold from underneath the brim of his cowboy hat.

A smile curved his mouth, and Patsy's eyes dropped to his lips. Desire shot through her, and a giggle escaped from her mouth, taking a bit of her nerves with it. She dropped his hands and backed up a couple of steps, thrilled when he stalked after her.

"Okay, so where would you put your hands?" she

asked, and Cy took her easily into his arms, putting both hands on her waist.

"Yeah, you fit here," he whispered.

Patsy sure did like this embrace, and she put her hands on his chest and pressed her cheek to his heartbeat. She did fit here, and she wondered what that meant. She'd never fit with a man the way she did Cy.

She wasn't sure this was real, but the warmth from his hands seeped through the fabric of her dress, and it sure did feel real.

"Patsy," he whispered. "I have to tell you something."

Her heartbeat sank into her stomach, and she opened her eyes and leaned away from him so she could see him. The wide brim of his hat seemed to create a pocket of privacy where just the two of them existed.

He swallowed, his fingers along her waist tightening.

"Just spit it out, Cy." She didn't like it when he radiated so much tension. She was used to the serious side of Cy, though, as they had had plenty of opportunities for him to show her what was important to him. She'd toured his building, and he'd taken her back to his house after they'd delivered food to Laney last week.

He mostly came up to the lodge to see her, and sometimes he just sat in the chair in her office and they talked while she paid bills, sent emails, and combed through resumes. He helped her with her chores, and he took her to dinner.

He was a hard worker, and he had a mind that thought through way too much. He liked history and roast beef sandwiches with Swiss cheese, and Patsy had started introducing him to the many ways one could eat and enjoy an apple.

He claimed not to like warm apples—he called them too mushy—and that severely limited her recipes, but she hadn't given up.

"You're supposed to be the fun one, remember?"

He blinked and finally seemed to remember where he was. "The last relationship I had was eighteen months ago." He drew in a breath and cleared his throat. "I was in love with her. I was getting ready to ask her to marry me."

Patsy suddenly didn't like this conversation. She wasn't sure where he was going with it. Maybe the talk of when he'd last kissed a woman had reminded him how much he'd loved this other person. Maybe the current Patsy felt every time Cy looked her way was only in her blood.

How could she have missed it?

"She obviously didn't feel the same," Cy said. "But that's not the real—that's not what I wanted to tell you. She would've been my second wife." He looked away then, and Patsy saw his pulse bumping in his neck. "If we —you know, you and me—get married, it would be my second time."

"You've been married before," Patsy said.

"Yes."

"How long ago?"

"Years," he said. "Eight or nine. It only lasted six months. We weren't a good fit, and it was about that time that I started paying more attention to my feelings and all the red flags I'd seen but ignored."

Patsy nodded as the song changed from the slow ballad to a more upbeat tune. Cy slowed and stopped. "I don't know what to do with this."

"How old are you?" Patsy asked, tucking her arm through his and leading him out of the forest.

"Thirty-eight," he said. "You're thirty-one."

"Mm."

"So you got married when you were thirty. It lasted six months. Any kids?"

"No."

"And you've been in love since then, it didn't work out, and you think you want to kiss me tonight."

"That sums it all up," he said. "What would your love life sum be?"

Patsy pushed her hand through her hair and tapped her toe to the music. Couples danced out on the floor, some doing a two-person swing or just a rocking back and forth to a faster rhythm.

"Uh, it's less impressive than that."

"Have you been married?"

"No," she said. "Never married." She thought of the chat she'd had with Celia. "Honestly, everyone I've been out with in the past has been a loser. That's what I do. I seem to pick the losers for some reason." She looked at him, realizing what she'd just said. "Until now. Until now, Cy. I didn't mean to say you were a loser."

"Maybe I am," Cy said.

"No," Patsy said. "You're not."

"How do you know?"

Patsy needed to fix this. She needed to make this

moment lighter, and she needed to salvage this night. "Let's see, I dated this guy once who was unemployed. He literally did nothing, and he'd get upset with me when I couldn't do things with him because I had to work. I spent eight months feeling guilty because I had a job. A job, Cy."

He watched her with something streaming through his gaze she couldn't identify.

"Then I dated this other guy who'd been out with Betty when we were younger. He was her age, and she's quite a bit older than me. Turned out, he really only wanted to get close to me so he could find out if she was happy in her marriage."

"You're kidding."

"Oh, it gets better." Now that she'd started the stories, she wouldn't be able to stop. "The last guy I dated didn't notice when I cut ten inches off my hair. Ten inches, Cy. He didn't say a word about it. When I asked him if he liked my new haircut, he admitted he hadn't even noticed."

Cy shook his head, but he wasn't smiling.

"The man before that borrowed so much money from me, you'd think I was a bank. Oh, and this is the best one. I once had a boyfriend who cheated on me with my best friend. So that was a real fun time, with a real winner."

She exhaled, the storm that had gathered in her chest starting to blow itself out. "Sorry, I sounded so bitter just then."

"You're fine," he murmured.

"So you have a job. More than a job—you own a successful business. You've never been out with my sister. You haven't cheated on me. You've never asked for a dime.

In fact, you've been nothing but kind, and funny, and I love it when you come to the lodge and sit with me while I work, and I appreciate it when you buy me dinner so I don't have to cook after a busy day."

She took a big breath, mostly to get herself to stop talking. She looked away, but her eyes couldn't find any one thing to settle on, and they quickly migrated back to Cy's. He seemed to have a magnetic pull on her, and she knew that was part of his big charm.

"And I'm going to offer you the job at the lodge if you're serious about taking it," she said.

"Oh, I'm serious about everything when it comes to you, Patsy."

"So you're not just having fun?" she asked.

"Are you worried that I'm just playing with you?"

"No." Patsy had never considered that. Cy was fun—he was quick to laugh, and he could adapt to any situation with ease. But he was serious too, and Patsy liked both sides of him equally.

"Because I'm not," he said. "I like to buy old clothes and pair them with new stuff. I like to tease and joke with my brothers. But I would never take your heart and hurt you."

She nodded, because when he spoke in such a low, husky voice, she absolutely believed him.

They seemed to move at the same time, and Cy eased her into his arms at the same time she tipped her head back. She closed her eyes, and she breathed in through her nose, waiting.

Finally, Cy's mouth touched hers, and fireworks

exploded through Patsy's mouth, throat, and chest. She held onto him then, sliding her hands up his shoulders and around to the back of his neck to keep him right where she wanted him.

And he was one-hundred percent right—he had not forgotten how to kiss a woman.

CHAPTER 13

Cy fitted the fish mailbox over the wooden pole in front of Gray's house and screwed the square base into the wood. He wore heavy leather gloves, but his breath still steamed in front of him.

Colton had called five minutes ago to say Gray, Elise, and Hunter had left his house and were on the way to theirs. Cy had been taking care of it for his brother, and he'd shoveled the driveway and sidewalks every time it snowed, sprinkled salt on them, and made sure the furnace was working so the pipes wouldn't freeze.

Gray had bought a beautiful home in the woods, set back from the road that ran in front of the lake he and Hunter loved to fish in the summer. He and Elise would only live here part-time, because Hunter wanted to attend school in Colorado with his friends.

As far as Cy knew, Gray still owned the house in the

suburbs of Denver too, as well as the farm where they'd all grown up.

Cy owned twenty acres of an apple orchard, and he fought against the sense of inadequacy that came when he compared himself to Gray. His mother had told him over and over he didn't need to be Gray. Or Colton. Or Ames. She'd always been really good at keeping the two of them separate, and while they looked a lot alike, they were definitely their own person. Ames didn't seem to have a confidence problem, and on the surface, no one would ever guess Cy did either.

He'd come right out and told Patsy he wanted to kiss her at midnight on New Year's Eve. Then he'd gotten that kiss a couple of hours early—and more later that night.

He focused on the mailbox and finished with the last screw. He checked the sturdiness of it, and he felt confident this fish wasn't going anywhere. He opened the mouth to see inside, and he really loved this creation of his. He'd painted the fish twice, and then sealed it with a clear, weather-resistant varnish. The trout practically gleamed in the sunshine, and Cy strode to his truck that sat down the driveway and put the cordless drill in the back of it.

He returned to the mailbox and stood by it, wanting to welcome Gray and Elise home personally. Thankfully, Gray's dark brown truck came trundling down the road only a minute later, and Cy put a big smile on his face and started waving.

He watched their faces light up, and he pointed to the trout mailbox. Gray pulled into the driveway, but didn't go all the way down it. They all spilled out of the truck, and it was Hunter who reached him first.

"Uncle Cy, that is sick," he said.

"It sure is," Cy said, because he knew "sick" meant "amazing" or "cool." He beamed at Hunter and hugged him. "You and your dad like fishing so much, and I wanted to make something for you."

"Cy." Gray took him into a tight, brotherly hug, and Cy closed his eyes as he pounded his brother on the back. "You're amazing," Gray said, and in that moment, Cy belonged to Gray. They'd had a special bond the past several years, due to both of them having been married and then divorced.

That carried a special kind of pain, even if the divorce was actually a good thing.

Gray stepped back and reached to open the mailbox. "This is so cool. I love it."

"Happy wedding," Cy said, reaching to hug Elise too. "How was the beach? Amazing, right?"

"Amazing," she said. "I just get my energy from the mountains."

"They have a special charm too." Cy stepped back and looked at his trout mailbox. "All right, we don't have to stand out here in the cold. You'll have plenty of time to admire the mailbox when it's not twenty below zero."

Everyone herded back to the truck, and Gray drove down the long lane to his garage. Cy got behind the wheel of his truck too, but he wasn't going to stay. Gray and Elise would be leaving for Ivory Peaks tomorrow, and everyone was gathering at Wes's for dinner later that night. They had things to do—and so did Cy.

He'd reached the end of the road and had his right blinker on when Gray called. "Yep," Cy said.

"You left?"

"Yeah, you guys have stuff to do, and I have to get up to the lodge."

"Oh, I see."

"It's not a big deal," Cy said. "I'm actually taking Bree's job for a few months, until my shop is ready."

"You're taking Bree's job?" Elise asked, and Cy realized he was on speaker with both of them.

"Yeah, well, Patsy needs the help."

"I'm sure she does," Gray said.

"I'm hanging up," Cy said. He hadn't spent much time with his brothers since Christmas, for exactly this reason. He hadn't made fun of Gray or questioned his long-distance relationship with Elise. He'd welcomed Wes to California with open arms when he'd broken up with Bree and fled the state of Wyoming. He hadn't done anything but support Colton when he met Annie, fell in love, and got engaged, all within the space of six weeks.

He could date Patsy without their sly comments and side glances.

"Cy," Gray said. "Don't hang up."

"Take me off speaker," Cy said.

"You're off," Gray said. "I'm sorry. I just thought you were coming in. Elise and I have gifts for you, and we really appreciate you taking care of our house. It snowed a lot while we were gone."

"Yeah," Cy said, because he had taken good care of Gray's house. "And you didn't need to get me any gifts."

"We know you love the beach, and we're grateful for your help." Gray cleared his throat. "Hunter said you took him to the arcade a couple of times, and we appreciate that too."

"Yeah, sure," Cy said. "Hunter's my favorite human on the whole earth."

Gray chuckled, and that broke the tension between them. "I'm sorry I said anything about Patsy," Gray said. "I think it's great you're pursuing her. You were…a little hung up on Mikaela for a while."

"Yeah," Cy said, looking out the window. When he'd moved here, he hadn't been over her. In fact, it wasn't until after Gray's wedding when he'd passed Grams to Patsy that he'd *seen* her. Really seen her. And he'd finally been able to look past Mikaela.

"Anyway, I'll bring your gifts to dinner tonight. You'll be there, right?"

"Of course," Cy said. "You're taking my favorite person away from me, so I have to be there to say good-bye."

Gray chuckled, and the call ended. Cy tapped the button on the screen again and said, "Call Patsy Foxhill."

A few moments later, the call connected, and Patsy picked up with, "Hey, Cy. Are you on your way up?"

"Yes, ma'am," he said. "And I was wondering how you felt about dinner tonight?"

"I'm always up to go to dinner."

"It's at my brother's house," he said. "With all my brothers that live here—and their wives. And us. And

Hunter." Cy pulled in a slow breath so she wouldn't hear it and held it.

"So your three married brothers, us, and Hunter."

"Yes."

"Boy, you don't pull punches."

"All three of the women there are your friends," he pointed out. "And you know, I don't think I mentioned this the other night, but I'm not in a rush to get married again."

"You're not?"

"Not particularly," he said, though he had to force a bit of casualness into his tone. "I want to make sure I do things right this time."

A couple of beats passed in silence. "Okay," Patsy said. "I'll go to dinner with you tonight."

———

"Here we go," Cy said, flipping the rubber band on his wrist over and over again and not feeling a thing. He'd taken the last spot in Wes's driveway, which meant they were the last to arrive.

"Cy." Patsy reached over and took his hand away from his wrist. "Stop it. You're going to hurt yourself."

He turned away from the squares of yellow light, and they stayed in his eyes as he blinked. He looked at Patsy, and she wore concern on her face. "What?"

"You didn't even know you were flipping that band," she said. "It sounded painful to me."

Cy looked at his left wrist, and it suddenly sent pain shooting up his arm. "Sorry."

"Hey, look at me," she said.

He did, and once again, so much came into focus for him. "Maybe this was a bad idea."

"You tell me," she said. "I'll do whatever, but I think it'll be fine once we get in there. You'll feed off the energy, and you'll transform into the fun version of yourself."

Frustration and embarrassment spiraled together, and Cy looked away from her again. "I'm sorry, Patsy."

"For what?"

"For having to wear a rubber band."

"Tell me about it," she said. "You haven't said much of it."

"You said your brother wore one."

"To focus during tests and stuff," Patsy said. "I think yours is for something else."

"It's sometimes a habit," he admitted. "Sometimes it's to help me release the anxiety building up inside me. Sometimes it helps me focus, like your brother."

"So tonight, it was for anxiety."

"I have a lot of anxiety," he admitted to the darkness beyond his window. "Especially in the winter. I hate being cooped up inside all the time, and I hate waking up in the dark, and I hate not being able to ride my motorcycle."

"That's why you lived in California."

"Things will definitely be harder here," he said. New doubts flew through his mind. What had he been thinking, buying twenty acres here and starting to build a new shop? He should've stuck to the coasts, where he could ride his motorcycle year-round and listen to the waves roll ashore every day if he needed to.

"Let's go in," he said. "Wes might not be a CEO anymore, but he likes to start things on time."

"You're sure?"

"Yes," Cy said, opening his door. He got out of the truck, and he slipped the rubber band off his wrist. He stretched it between two fingers and shot it out into the darkness. He did not need that in his life tonight.

He met Patsy at the front of the truck and swept his arm around her waist. "I'm sorry I'm a mess."

"You're not a mess," she said.

"Mm, I kind of am." He leaned down, and they breathed in together before Cy pressed his lips to hers. She kissed him back, and he kept the kiss sweet because he stood in his brother's driveway, and he honestly couldn't add any more emotion to what he already had streaming through him.

"A beautiful mess," Patsy whispered when he finally pulled away.

Cy smiled gently, feeling bled out now. They went up to the front door, and he knocked as he entered. Chatter came from the kitchen in the corner of the house, and since Wes had a huge, open-concept house, Cy could see everyone mingling as Bree and Annie worked in the kitchen.

Hunter held his cousin, and Colton was the first to glance toward Cy and Patsy. He nodded, and Wes turned. Cy kept Patsy's hand in his, because he wasn't afraid to show his brothers who he was dating.

"Hey, brother." Wes drew Cy away from Patsy and hugged him. "Patsy." He hugged her too, and Cy watched her eyes widen in surprise. He smiled at her, and hugged Colton.

"How are things now that the wedding is done?"

"Oh, my word," Colton said. "So much better." He smiled and nodded toward the kitchen. "There's soda over there."

"You're drinking soda?" he asked. "Doesn't that make running harder?"

"I'm not the one training for the Boston Marathon," Colton said, lifting his can to his lips. "You should see Gray." He lowered his voice as he glanced over to where Gray stood with Hunter and Elise. "He was inspecting every single thing in the kitchen."

"It was annoying," Wes added, his voice also low. "I mean, I get it. But come on. If what you eat is that big of a deal, bring your own dinner."

"If he did that," Cy said. "You'd be annoyed by that too."

Colton and Wes both looked at him, and Cy chuckled. "You know I'm right. You'd be all, 'we invite him to dinner, and he brings his own food? Come on.'" He looked back and forth between Wes and Colton. "Tell me I'm wrong."

Colton just took another drink of his soda, and Wes glared into the kitchen. "You're not wrong," he finally said. "I guess I shouldn't be annoyed."

"Boston's in four months," Cy said. "Let's try not to kill

him between now and then, and he'll ease up once he races."

"Hopefully," Colton said. "Otherwise...." He crunched his now-empty can in his fist, which caused Cy to burst out laughing.

He realized that Patsy had left him with his brothers and joined Elise and Gray. In fact, he watched as Hunter passed baby Michael to her, and he sure didn't miss the new light that filled her face as she gazed at the infant.

Cy fell a little bit more in love with her in that moment, because he'd always wanted kids, and by the look on her face, so did Patsy.

She lifted her eyes, and they came straight to his. They exchanged a smile that said so much without a single word, and he ducked his head.

"Oh, my heck," Colton said. "You're falling for her already."

"Maybe," Cy whispered. "Can you not do this right now?"

"Yeah, leave him alone," Wes said. "We're lucky he came in at all." He offered his fist for Cy to bump, which he did. "Glad you did, brother. We're not complete without you." He nodded and walked toward Gray and the others.

Cy stood next to Colton, who said, "I guess I can't talk. I got engaged only a couple of months after being stood up on my own wedding day."

"Yeah," Cy said. "You have no room to say anything." He looked away from Patsy and that baby, and met his brother's eyes. They both laughed, and finally, the rest of Cy's anxiety went with the sound.

He wondered, though, if he was being fair to Patsy. He knew he was a mess, and maybe he shouldn't saddle someone else with his mental illness and anxiety. That had been one of his biggest regrets with his first wife. He hadn't been honest with her about his health.

So go get help.

The words were right there inside his mind, and this time, they were in his own voice and not Ames's.

And be honest with Patsy.

CHAPTER 14

P atsy pulled up to the farmhouse where she'd spent her childhood, and instead of getting out of the car immediately, she reached for the shoebox on the passenger seat. She took out the top photo and studied it, a sense of nostalgia and love filling her.

She absolutely did love this orchard, and she did not want to lose it. She didn't want another thirty years to pass and have someone else living in this house and tending to these trees.

This was her legacy.

She looked up and held the photo out in front of her, matching the house from back then to what it was now. It had been autumn in the pictures, and it was winter now, so the leafy trees didn't match up. The house was more stark now, and Patsy could clearly see how certain things had fallen into disrepair.

The roof sagged on the left side, and that would need

to be addressed come spring, which was only weeks away now. Most of the snow had melted, though Mother Nature still liked to freeze everything overnight. Wyoming often saw isolated snow storms through May, so they weren't out of the woods yet, though March had been trucking along for a week or so now.

Patsy lowered the photo, because the steps also needed to be resealed, and the pillar on the corner of the porch had started to splinter. They needed a professional to come look at the house and determine which structural improvements needed to be made.

They had all the money from the sale of the twenty acres across the highway, and Patsy knew her father hadn't spent it all. She and her siblings had put it in a special account that they controlled, and they paid him a salary every month for living expenses. She just needed to talk to Joe and Betty about making the repairs around the house, the farm, and the orchard.

Betty should be the one doing that, as she technically ran the orchard, and a vein of bitterness spread through Patsy as she got out of the car and walked toward the steps and to the front door. "Dad," she called as she went inside. "It's time to go to the doctor."

She didn't mind making the trip down the canyon to take her father to his appointments, and she and Betty split the load about fifty-fifty. Betty's daughter had a dance concert at school that morning, so Patsy had made the trip. She'd be stopping by the grocery store and Cy's shop later too, and it sure was nice to get away from the lodge.

They'd made it through their extremely busy Valentine's Day season, and Patsy, Eli, Beau, and Wes had started orchestrating their Spring Fling—a brand new event that had sold out in fifteen minutes. All ten days of it.

Patsy was tired just thinking about it.

Cy had been doing an amazing job with the events, and he'd made metal charms for everyone who'd stayed at the lodge in February. Heart-shaped charms, and Patsy reached up to the one she wore around her neck.

"Dad?"

She walked into the kitchen and found the evidence of his breakfast in the sink. He didn't eat a whole lot while he was doing his treatments, and she wasn't surprised to see the half-eaten plate of eggs with the empty bottle of Ensure on the counter beside the sink. If he could get that down and keep it down, he did okay.

"Coming," he said, and Patsy turned to find him walking down the hall, one hand against the wall for extra support. She hurried to meet him, love filling her whole soul. "Hey, my beautiful daughter." He smiled at her, and how he had the strength to do that when he felt so poorly, Patsy didn't know.

She hoped she could be as faithful and fierce as him with whatever the Lord sent her way. "Hey, Dad." She hugged him and added, "Do you have your insurance card?"

"Yes, yes," he said. "Let's go."

Patsy helped him get outside and down the steps, then into the car. He heaved a sigh as he finally sank into the seat, and Patsy offered up a prayer as she went around the back of the sedan. "Help him to do well with this treatment. It's his last one, and if it be Thy will, we'd love to see significant shrinkage on his scans next week."

She paused at her door, a desperate pinch in her chest bringing tears to her eyes. Thy will.

She knew God was merciful. She knew He could perform miracles. She wanted one so badly for her father, but she'd been praying for such a thing for over a year now. What was she doing wrong?

She went to church. She served when opportunities came up. She prayed. She tried to be kind and loving to everyone around her.

She thought about the resentment and bitterness she still held for her siblings. Perhaps that was holding her prayers at the door to God's ears. Maybe He wouldn't grant her desires when she carried such negative things in her heart.

Patsy sighed too when she sat down behind the wheel. She didn't know how to get the infectious feelings out of her heart. Just when she thought she was over them, they came creeping back in, especially when she got things like the aged photos her father was now leafing through.

"Where did you get these?" he asked, his voice full of awe.

"Laney Whittaker," Patsy said. "She came here for a field trip in high school." She'd also learned that Laney and Graham were expecting another baby. That was the reason Laney had been so drawn and so tired over Christmas.

The Whittakers had asked anyone who could to pray

for Laney, as she'd had a rough pregnancy the first time around, and she was in the high-risk category because of that, as well as her age.

Patsy hadn't forgotten to pray for Laney and Graham, as well as their children, once. She loved them, and it was easy to pray for someone she loved.

"Look at your mother," he said, and Patsy heard the wonder and sadness as they intertwined.

"I saw them," Patsy said. She put the car in reverse and turned around. Her mind spun with all the things she wanted to ask her dad; she hardly knew where to start. "Dad, do you know why she left?" She flicked a glance at him and pulled onto the highway that led toward town.

He didn't answer as he shuffled through the photos. When he reached the end, he tucked them into the box and looked out the windshield. "She hadn't been happy for a few years," he said. "I told her we'd wait until you finished school, and then we'd look at selling the orchard and doing something else."

Pure surprise hit Patsy like a bucket of icy water. She hadn't known that. Her parents had never talked about it in front of her. "What would you do?"

"She wanted to travel," he said, his voice growing distant. "She wanted to live in a big city. She's from Miami, you know."

"No," Patsy said. "I did not know that."

Dad chuckled, but Patsy's chest hollowed out. She hadn't known where her mother was from? How was that possible?

"She lived there until she was ten," Dad said. "Then her family moved here."

"Do you think she's back in Florida?"

"I don't know," Dad said. "But she left when I finally told her I just couldn't do it. I couldn't sell the orchard or land that had been in my family for five generations." He looked out his window. "Sometimes I wonder if it was worth it."

"I would've bought it all," Patsy said, looking at her father. "Honestly, Dad, I would've done anything to buy it. It would have stayed in the family." She wanted it all, even now.

He reached over and patted her arm. "I know, dear."

"I want it now." Patsy's mouth turned sticky. "I hate that Betty's in charge of it. She doesn't even do what needs to be done."

Her father finally looked at her. "What do you mean?"

"What do I mean? Dad, come on." She shook her head. "You know what I mean."

"No, I don't."

"We sold the north twenty, because the apples were just falling to the ground," Patsy said. "Betty didn't hire the people to harvest. She doesn't put on the fertilizer four times a year. She doesn't prune. The farmhouse is a wreck, and the horses get out every other day, Dad. All of that would be fixed if I was running the orchard."

She drew in a breath, because she didn't want to talk badly about her sister. At the same time, the dangerous, dark feelings she harbored bled out of her when she spoke about it. If she could rid herself of those feelings, maybe God would hear and answer her prayers.

"I had no idea," Dad said. "She told me she was doing all of that."

"You're kidding," Patsy said, looking at him again. "Why do you think we sold the north twenty?"

"Because we needed the money."

Patsy shook her head, her nerves firing with anger now. She gripped the wheel until her knuckles hurt and she turned into the hospital parking lot. "If Betty had been managing the orchard properly, Dad," she said, her tone even and her delivery very deliberate. "We would have more than enough money. Beyond enough." She pulled into a space and put the car in park. She kept her gaze out the windshield as she said, "We lost fifty thousand dollars every fall when she didn't harvest the north twenty. Over the past four years, Dad, that's five times what we made by selling it."

And now Cy was building a motorcycle shop and a house for himself on her land. Her throat closed, and she got out of the car. Why hadn't she been stronger? Why hadn't she insisted Betty let her run the orchard? She could've saved them; she could've kept the land her father had worked, and his father before him, and his before him.

A keen sense of failure filled her as she went around to help her father stand. He met her eye once he did, and he said, "I didn't know, Patsy. I believed what she told me."

"Let me show you the books," she said, seizing the opportunity. "She doesn't even like working on the orchard. That's why it doesn't get done. I could do it, Dad. I *want* to do it."

He set his mouth in a thin line and nodded, which was farther than Patsy had ever gotten before. She wasn't sure why he believed her now when he hadn't before. "Let's look at the books soon," he said. "I should be feeling better in a couple of weeks, after this last round wears off."

"Okay." Patsy went with him inside, and she sat with him while they administered the poisonous drugs that would hopefully control the cancer raging in his body. She took him home and helped him into bed, where she sat watching him sleep.

For a few moments, her mind and body detached, and she wasn't sure how she'd come to this reality.

Then she heard her sister's voice call that she was there to sit with him, and Patsy gathered herself together and went down the hall to greet her. Familiar resentment filled her, though Patsy hugged Betty.

"How did it go?" Betty asked, her eyes flitting around without truly settling on Patsy.

"As good as can be expected," she said. "Betty, I have to talk to you for a second."

"All right." Betty set her designer purse on the counter along with her coffee cup. She finally looked at Patsy, who felt the weight of being the youngest sister like a vice tightening against her vocal cords.

"I want the orchard," she said. "I want to fix up the farmhouse and the barns and the stables. We've already lost forty percent of our legacy, and I'm not going to stand by and watch you drive the other sixty percent into the ground."

Betty's eyes widened, and Patsy waited for her quick refusal. Her sister opened her mouth, most likely to reprimand Patsy—something she was very good at—but Patsy said, "I'm laying everything out for Dad soon. All the books. How you didn't pay for the proper fertilization for the past two years. How our crop diminished because of it. How the fruit in the north twenty fell to the ground because you were too busy being PTA president."

Patsy turned and put on her coat. "You can't hide this from him anymore." She turned back as she pulled up the zipper. "I'm going to ask you and Joe to be there, and I'm going to ask for control of the orchard. I actually want it, and it seems a great disservice for you, me, Dad, granddad, and all Foxhill's back five generations to let you keep destroying it."

With that, she walked out, despite the stammering of her sister.

"You should've seen her face," Patsy said, releasing a pent-up breath. She paced in Cy's office while he perched on a stool and watched her. "I can't believe I just did that." She met his eye, but she was too keyed up to hold his gaze. "She's going to be livid."

"Maybe it's about time she was," Cy said. They'd been getting along so great, though Patsy had worried about that when Cy had come to work at the lodge. He was much more laid back that she was, and he'd been on his best behavior with the guests.

She'd mentioned her desire to take over the orchard, and he'd never once suggested she talk to her family about it. After all, she had in the past, and she didn't see anything changing.

Until now.

"I don't handle her very well." Patsy's fingers started worrying around each other. "She always treats me like I'm so stupid."

"Patsy." Cy stood up and intercepted her on her next pass in front of him. He put both hands on her shoulders. "You are not stupid. You are the *least* stupid person I've ever met, in fact."

She looked up into those dark eyes, and she liked the intensity burning there. While he was laid back about some things, he carried a certain passion for things too. And when that came out...watch out.

"She makes me feel that way."

"Then don't let her." Cy said it like such a thing was so easy. "I get how you feel. I do. You just have to stand up to her and make a new boundary for her. That's what I've done with my brothers."

Patsy nodded and tried to swallow the lump in her throat. It didn't quite go, and she drew in a deep breath. "Will you go over the books with me? Help me lay out my case?"

"Of course I will," he said. "Did you want to see the showroom? We painted the floor a couple of days ago."

"Yes," she said, further settling. "Show me all the new

stuff." She'd been coming to his shop every week for the past few months, and now that they were close to finishing, there was always so much to see.

He held her hand as he led her on the tour, showing her the beautiful showroom with two floors of windows that let in a ton of natural light. The floor had been painted a light gray and flecked with black and navy geometric shapes no bigger than a dime. He explained where their showpiece would be, and what furniture they'd bring in.

"Should be here tomorrow, actually," he said. "Carpet is going in upstairs, as you saw. And then I've got my people coming next weekend."

"I can't believe it's so close," she said, finally realizing what was happening. "You're quitting at the lodge."

"Yeah," he said. "But you've got Melinda now. She's going to be great."

Patsy had hired a woman named Melinda Corrinth to take over for Cy. They'd been working together for a week, and she'd moved into Bree and Elise's cabin just a couple of days ago. Patsy liked her, and it was nice to have more help around the lodge. Once spring truly hit, Patsy would need a gardener too, and she'd already put the job up online.

In fact, she had interviews tomorrow. A sudden urge to get back to the lodge hit her. She had so much to do there, including check her schedule to see when she could stage the takeover she wanted to do at the orchard.

"So you're sure you don't want to come work for me?" Cy asked at the end of the tour, gathering her close to his chest. "I still don't have a general manager."

"You said you were going to be the GM." Patsy wrapped her arms around him and swayed with him as he moved. To her knowledge, he hadn't started his dancing lessons. He'd taken her to a barn buster the week after Valentine's Day, because she'd worked so much on the actual day. He'd danced with her easily then, his confidence higher than it had been at the New Year's Eve ball.

"I don't want to be the GM," he said. "I want to be the carefree owner who pops in to go over the veteran bikes." He chuckled. "I'm going to have to accept you aren't going to come do it." He pulled away and looked at her, that passion burning in his eyes. "Aren't I?"

"If I get my way," she said. "I'll be quitting at the lodge to run the orchard." She wanted to make him happy, but she didn't see how. "I can't do that and run your shop."

"But it's on the orchard grounds," he said. "Maybe it could just be part of what you manage at the orchard."

"Cy, *you* own this land," she said, stepping out of his arms. "This isn't my family's orchard anymore."

"I've hardly taken out any trees," he said.

Patsy sensed he was saying more than what he'd actually said, and she cocked her head at him. "What's happening in your head?" she asked.

"Nothing," he said, turning away.

But Patsy reached out and grabbed his arm, which made him stop. "Whoa, there, cowboy. Look at me."

Cy did, but she could tell he didn't want to.

"You told me to ask you what you were thinking in times like these," she said gently. "You said you needed to be honest with me about what was in your head. So tell me."

Cy just shook his head, that longer hair on top flopping with the motion. "I need a minute."

"Cy," she said as he walked away from her, but she let him go. She had to give him a minute if he needed it. He'd asked for them only a couple of times in the past, and he'd told her about his depression and anxiety after one of his "minutes."

He'd admitted he should probably be in counseling and on medication, but he wasn't doing either.

Patsy sure did like him, and she'd even started to fall in love with him. She needed to go slow, and she'd told him that. He'd been fine with it, because he wanted to go slow too. So they'd spent time together, and worked together, and there'd been plenty of kissing at the end of the day.

This felt like a big step for her, though. Taking on her sister and asking Cy what was really in his head.

"Please let it be something easy to solve," she prayed under her breath, but she knew it wouldn't be. The things that stretched her the most and forced her to grow were never easy to solve.

CHAPTER 15

C y hadn't worn the rubber band around his wrist to the shop that day. He hadn't put it on for weeks. He found he didn't need it as much when the sun was shining, and Patsy was nearby, and his shop was coming along.

When life was good, Cy felt unstoppable.

But right now, a major hurdle had just manifested itself. He'd been putting off hiring a shop manager, because in the back of his mind, he'd convinced himself Patsy would come do it. He'd ask her again—beg her, really—and she'd say yes.

They'd work the shop together, and she'd help him with the design of his house, and they'd sail off into the sunset together, blissfully in love.

Cy could really be a romantic fool sometimes.

"Idiot," he muttered to himself as he left Patsy behind in the mechanic bay he'd just finished showing her. He headed for the front of the building, where the showroom spread out in all its glory. He couldn't wait to get the motorcycles out of storage, and he couldn't wait to be riding one.

That was what he wanted to do right now. Storm out of the building, hop on his best, biggest bike, and just leave. Leave everything troubling him in the rear-view mirror.

He paused in the middle of the showroom and took a long, deep breath. He needed to calm down for a second. Think about why he'd literally just run away from the best person in his life. Identify what he wanted to say.

What was in his mind?

That there was no way he could manage this place. Oh, he could intellectually. He knew the concept forward and backward. He knew all the parts of a motorcycle and where they went. He knew the public relations, and the social media aspect of the business. He knew about all of it. He'd done all of it.

He didn't like it. He didn't want to be the CEO. He wasn't Wes.

Cy couldn't handle the stress of the day-to-day operations at Rev for Vets. He wanted to meet with the veterans before they started the motorcycle, and when it was done. He liked getting updates in between. He liked coming to work later in the day, and he liked getting under a bike every now and then.

But mostly, he just wanted to do exactly what he'd said —he wanted to ride his motorcycle and pop in on the happenings at the shop when it was fun and convenient for him. He worked—he worked a lot. He knew what was happening in his building. But he didn't want to be there constantly, overseeing all of it.

He turned back to the back half of the building, where the maintenance would take place. All the meeting rooms were back here, as well as storage for their parts and equipment. Or all of that would be back here, once his team arrived from California, and the twenty-six people he'd hired here in Coral Canyon showed up next weekend.

Then, the first week of April, Ames would make the drive north, and Cy would have a grand reopening of Rev for Vets.

He'd already set up his first veteran for whom they'd custom design and build a motorcycle, and he'd announce it at the grand reopening.

There was so much to do between now and then, and Cy needed to keep his head on straight. He returned to the bay to find Patsy waiting for him. She looked up from her phone, concern in those pretty blue eyes.

He loathed that concern as much as he appreciated it. "Sorry," he said. "I didn't mean—I don't mean to make you worry."

"It's fine," she said. "We all need a minute sometimes."

"Yeah." He wished he'd worn his cowboy hat to the shop today, but he hadn't. He usually only wore it to work at the lodge, because the guests there expected an authentic western experience. Plus, he liked the cowboy hat, shocking as that was.

He'd shared a lot with Patsy over the past few months. Two months. However long ago Christmas was. In his head, it had been a while, but he knew it was still March.

"You can tell me, Cy."

"I haven't told you everything," he said, his anxiety starting to tap through his veins. A huge roar filled his ears, and everything seemed to be moving in super-speed. He forced another breath into his lungs. He was nowhere near a panic attack—he'd never had those. He just felt like someone had connected him to a live wire, and then forced him to drink a ton of coffee. Everything buzzed, and it was very hard to hear his own thoughts through the noise.

He deliberately moved slowly, tried to breathe slowly.

"I started dancing lessons at the beginning of February," he said. "I never told you that."

Her eyebrows went up, but Patsy said nothing.

"I'm getting pretty good," he said. "I'm in this private class with just me and a couple. He teaches me, and I dance with his wife. They have this whole studio in their basement."

"Wow," she said.

"Yeah." Cy ran his hand up the back of his head. "They want me to invite you, but I know how busy you are, and I'm about to be swamped." Heck, he was swamped now. "But what do you think? Would you come to the class with me?"

"Of course I would, Cy." The way she didn't hesitate, and the hint of exasperation in her voice, told Cy that he needn't have hidden this from her. He wasn't sure why he had. He'd just wanted it to be his little secret for a minute.

"Okay." He looked around the bay, but there was nothing to hold his attention. "I haven't started therapy."

"I know."

He nodded, because of course she knew that. "I can't run the shop," he blurted. "I mean, I can. But I can't. I don't want to. I just…can't do it."

Patsy held his gaze, refusing to release him. She took a step toward him, and then another, finally sliding her hands up his forearms to his biceps to his shoulders. "I really wish I could come work for you," she said. "Honestly, Cy, I do. But it doesn't feel right."

"Right," he said. "I know."

"Do you?"

"I've asked the Lord over and over for a solution to this," he said. "He hasn't given me one, and I've just let it go."

Something perked up in her expression. "Why do you think He does that?"

"Does what?"

"Doesn't answer our prayers."

"I think He has," Cy said. "It just isn't the answer I wanted." He flashed her a brief smile as he shouldered the load. "So I'm going to get on it. I'll call down to the employment office this afternoon while you're getting groceries. Get the job put up. Someone will want it." He had to believe that, because he really needed someone to manage the shop, the mechanics, the schedule, all of it.

"So you're saying if we've been praying for the same thing over and over, and nothing's happened, it's simply that the answer isn't what we want." Patsy looked thoughtful, as well as troubled.

"Usually," he said. "For me, at least." He watched her

retreat from him, dark clouds gathering over her eyes. "Hey, what's going on?"

She shook her head and turned her back on him. That was somewhat new behavior. Patsy faced everything head-on, usually with blazing blue eyes and a solution that would fix the problem.

He stepped up behind her and wrapped his arms around her. "You can tell me."

"I know I can," she whispered. "I'm just absorbing it for a minute."

"Mm." He pressed his lips to her neck and held her tightly.

A few seconds later she said, "I've been praying for my father to be healed for over a year." Her voice broke, and she turned quickly into his arms. "It's not going to happen, is it?"

Cy's heart started to beat faster and faster. "Oh, now, I don't know, Patsy. No one knows that."

"He's not getting better. He's done round after round of chemo, and the mass is the same size." She looked up at him, tears clinging to her beautiful lashes. Cy wanted to reassure her that everything would be fine. That the Lord would ensure that everything worked out.

But the truth was, people died. Accidents happened. People lost loved ones, and they lost buildings. They had to figure out how to move on, and physically move to a new location.

Cy had had to do both of those things.

"I'm so sorry," he whispered to Patsy. She closed her eyes and nodded, melting back into his embrace. Cy loved holding her like this, and he slipped a little further in love with her. He wanted to tell her how he felt, but now didn't seem like the right time.

So his imagination took off, and he envisioned the two of them living in his house, with the orchard right outside the front door. Patsy would manage those, and she'd help with the shop too. Cy would work on her father's house and help out with the horses, as well as do what he wanted to do in the shop.

It was a perfect life, the two of them, beneath the apple trees and the scent of grease not far away. He sighed and closed his eyes, wishing life could be so simple and so serene.

After several minutes, Patsy had composed herself. She pulled away from him and looked him straight in the eye. "You can run this shop, Cy," she said. "You're smart, and capable, and no one is more passionate about what they do than you."

He nodded, fierce appreciation filling him. "Thank you, Patsy. So…do you think I should hire someone or not?"

"Up to you," she said. "But you can do this."

Cy suddenly had a whole lot more to think about. He took Patsy's face in his hands and leaned in closer to her. "I sure do like you, Patsy Foxhill," he whispered. "The day I met you, my whole life changed." He kissed her then, because that was as forthcoming about his feelings as he was willing to be right now.

She kissed him back like she liked him too, and that the day she'd met him, her life had changed…for the better.

———

"No, no, no," Cy said, leaping from the barstool and toward the dog he'd brought home a couple of days ago. He clapped loudly, startling the downy soft pit bull mix. He scooped her up while she was still leaking all over the floor and took her to the back door.

"You ring the bell to go out," he said, nudging her nose against the bell there. "Potty. Potty." He slid open the door and dumped Blue Velvet onto the deck. "You go potty outside."

He slid the door closed and faced the puddles on the floor. "Shouldn't have gotten an untrained dog," he muttered to himself. "Why didn't You warn me?" He walked over to the sink and bent to get out the cleaning wipes. "I thought getting a dog was a good idea. You never led me to believe it wasn't." He continued to vent his frustrations to the Lord as he cleaned up.

"At least it wasn't on the carpet," he said. "So thank You for that." He returned to the back door and let Blue Velvet back in. "Sorry, girl." He picked her up and let her lick his face. "But you really have to go outside."

He looked back to his bowl of cereal, now soggy. "We're going up to the lodge, and you'll need these." He unlooped the bells from the handle on the door and tucked them in his pocket. "I'll bring them with us, okay?"

He gathered up a bag of beef treats, a leash, and a little sweater for the pup. "Patsy wants to see you in the sweater she bought you. She loves sweaters, Blue, so no complaining." The dog didn't complain at all. She was more like a sack of potatoes and he had to manhandle her to get her front legs into the sweater.

After tugging it down over her back and chest, he stood and looked at her. "It's cute," he told her. "It's got a big purple heart on it. Patsy's going to love you in it." He clipped the leash to Blue's collar, and she didn't like that. But she had to learn to walk on the leash, and no one but Cy was going to teach her.

By the time he'd gone around the block twice, he was sweating under the hat, gloves, and coat. Wyoming was still plenty cold, but he could see the piles of snow on the sides of the road getting a little smaller day by day.

"Come on," he said to the dog. "We're going to the lodge. Get in the truck."

She did, her tongue hanging out of her mouth. The cold didn't seem to touch her, but his sweat was cooling now, and the chill infected Cy and went right down deep into his bone marrow. He shivered as he got behind the wheel, and he got the heater blowing and his seat heater warming.

He'd met with Bree several times when he'd first started at the lodge, and he'd learned that she usually did a bunch of stuff in the morning. But Cy had worked out a different system. He didn't go up to the lodge until breakfast was in full swing, and he made a live presentation of that day's events. He got everything organized and ready the night before, and he sent the morning reminder texts on a scheduler so he could enjoy a later start to the day.

Patsy said she didn't care what he did, as long as the

job got done and the guests were happy. No one had complained yet, so Cy's system was working for him.

His stomach flipped as he turned to go up the canyon, because while he'd been at the lodge for a couple of months now, he still wasn't sure what the day would bring. He hadn't worked a real job in...well, Cy didn't think he ever had. He'd grown up working on the farm, and while his father was a taskmaster, he didn't have to report to work in a uniform, wear a silly hat, or beg for time off.

He hadn't gone to college after high school, but he'd taken a few mechanic classes and earned a welding certificate. He'd traveled to a high-end motorcycle shop on the East Coast and studied what they did. He'd shadowed the owner and asked him questions. When he'd met his first veteran, Cy knew exactly what he was supposed to do with his life.

And he'd been trying to do it ever since.

His phone rang as he pulled into the parking lot at Whiskey Mountain Lodge, and he really didn't have time for a call. But it was McCall, and Cy really did need to talk to him.

"Hey," he said to the other man after connecting the call. "What's up?"

"What's up?" McCall asked. "Dude, you said it would be warmer by the time we had to come to Wyoming."

"It is warmer," Cy said with a smile. He reached for the leash and tried clipping it to Blue Velvet's collar, but she dodged him.

"I don't know about this," McCall said. "It's freezing here. What am I supposed to tell Julie?"

"She didn't come with you?"

"They're not making the move until April," McCall said. "I just showed up to meet the realtor, and Cy, it's *freezing* here."

Cy chuckled, but he couldn't argue. "Let's meet for dinner. I can show you the building, and we'll get everything in line for this weekend." He looked at the lodge as he spoke. He couldn't believe he'd only be here for a few more days.

"Oh, you're definitely buying me dinner," McCall said. "Maybe for a year."

Cy laughed fully then, glad when McCall did too. But the man was a born and bred Californian, and he probably was seriously doubting his decision to move to Wyoming to run Cy's mechanic shop.

"Come on," he said to Blue Velvet, and he slid from the truck, turning back to get her leashed. Before he could, she jumped out behind him and took off for the lodge. "You have got to be kidding me," he grumbled under his breath.

He left the bells behind and barely thought to close his door before he went after the pit bull. She was a sweet thing, but she had absolutely no manners whatsoever. He'd brought her to the lodge before though, and she knew better than to jump out of the truck uninvited.

"Blue," he called, his chest collapsing when the double-wide front doors opened. A couple came out, and Blue Velvet put her front paws up on the gentleman.

Cy watched in horror as the man shoved Blue away,

and then tried to shield his wife from the thirty-pound dog as if Blue was a monster. "Hey," he called. "Come on, Blue."

The pit bull didn't come, and Cy's frustration morphed into anger when the man looked up, disdain on his face. "You should have a leash on your dog."

"I'm aware," Cy said, holding it up and still crossing the parking lot. "She just got away from me."

The woman screamed as Blue sniffed her feet, and the man kicked at her.

"Hey," Cy said, finally arriving. "That's not necessary. She was literally just sniffing." He grabbed Blue by the collar and clipped the leash to her, his stomach bubbling.

He straightened and faced the couple, fire licking through his chest. Something awakened in him, and he actually felt superhuman. "You didn't need to kick her."

"I'll do whatever I have to," the man said.

Cy advanced on him, and the man and his wife pressed into the closed door. "I was right here. She wasn't going to hurt you. She's a rescue dog, and she just needs to be trained up a little. The last thing I need is someone like you making her life worse." He glowered down at them, his head so hot.

"Someone like me?" Though the gentleman looked afraid, he wasn't going to back down.

Cy rolled his eyes and kept Blue Velvet right as his side. "It looked like y'all were leaving. Have a good day." He stepped to the side and gestured for them to go.

They both glared at him as they passed, and he sighed

as he turned back to the door. It opened before he could reach for the handle, and Patsy stood there.

She wore a frown and a glare, and she said, "My office, Cy. Right now." She glanced down at Blue Velvet, who was wearing the sweater she'd bought for her. She loved the dog, and Cy had enjoyed going with her to pick her out a week or so ago.

"You can come too, Blue," she said, turning on her heel and marching back into the lodge.

CHAPTER 16

Patsy shook her head, and Cy stopped talking. "I don't care what he did or said, Cy. You can't treat guests like that." He was quitting in four days anyway.

He nodded, his lips pressed together. "I'm sorry. I let the beast come out."

Patsy smoothed down her own sweater and looked at Blue Velvet. "You didn't help either, little miss," she said to the dog, who took a couple of slow steps toward her, her head down. Patsy had chewed Cy out for the way he'd treated Mr. and Mrs. Jameson, some of their best customers.

She reached down to pat Blue. "What an adorable sweater you have on." She grinned at the dog, and then looked up at Cy. He still wore an echo of the beast she'd seen on the security cameras on his face, and Patsy hated that she'd had to discipline him.

Tension rode in the air between them, and she wished

she could wave a magic wand and make it all disappear. "Are you on schedule for this weekend?" she finally asked.

"Yes," he said, his voice tight and clipped.

Patsy nodded, because she was used to having everything tight and clipped in her life. "Good." She sat down at her desk, enjoying the way Blue Velvet curled in a circle and then finally lay against her feet. A smile ran through her soul, but when she looked down at her desk, she realized what she'd been in the middle of.

Going through her father's books. She and her siblings were meeting next weekend, the one after all of Cy's employees started filling his shop with helmets, parts, potted plants, and family pictures.

"I'm sorry," Cy said again. "Can I go?"

"Yes," Patsy said. She hadn't realized he was waiting for her to release him. "Sorry, I thought it was clear we were done."

Cy sighed and sat in the chair across from her. "Are you sure you don't want to come work at the shop?"

"Not getting any good applicants?"

"I've had three," he said. "One was a woman named Bunny."

Patsy smiled, but she wouldn't laugh. "Hey, she didn't name herself," Patsy said, quirking her eyebrow. "Right? I mean, look at me."

"Good point," Cy said with another very big sigh. "I guess I'll call her. I just know I'm going to be a beast at the shop without you there." He gave her a hopeful look, but Patsy just shook her head.

"Nice try, buddy."

Cy finally smiled, the last of his beastly persona slipping away. "I'm going to miss it up here."

"We'll miss you too," she said, flipping a page in the ledger. "I know McCall is supposed to be here today, and if he makes it—"

"He made it," Cy said. "I just talked to him."

"Oh, okay, great," Patsy said, her voice pitching up. "Maybe we could go over these tomorrow?"

"Let's do it next week," he said. "Right before your meeting. You can deliver it to me the way you would them, and I'll give you feedback."

"Okay," she said, looking back at the ledger. "I just… don't feel confident."

"Hey, remember what you said to me last week?"

She looked up, trying to remember.

"You said I was smart, and no one had the passion for my shop that I do. Anyone could—and would—say the same about you and that orchard." He leaned forward and put one palm against the book. "You don't even need the ledger, Pats. You don't."

She nodded, though she felt like her whole life had been anchored to the ledger and what it showed. "Thank you, Cy."

He grinned at her, and the softness that lent to his features made her pulse behave erratically. He really was an amazing person, and Patsy felt lucky to know him.

His phone rang, and he looked at it. "Oh, holy cow." He fumbled it, and the device fell to the floor. "No, no," he moaned.

"Who is it?" Patsy asked, rising to her feet. Cy picked up his phone and stood too. "It's Wyatt Walker."

"No." Patsy sucked in a breath and pressed it to her heartbeat. "Answer it, Cy."

"Right." He flipped the phone over and swiped. "Hey," he said, his voice smooth and casual. "Wyatt Walker, the rodeo king." He chuckled, his face full of pure joy now.

It was torture to listen to only half the conversation, mostly because all Cy said was, "Yes, that's right…it's on April second."

Then, "Yes, it's a weekend. It's beautiful up here. I'm sure we can find a place for you to stay."

And "We'd love to have your wife and family join us." He paced in the office, his eyes on the pictures and then her as he went back and forth. "Yeah, of course I can pay for it…oh, you don't need to do that."

He thrust his free hand into the air, his fist raised in triumph. "Sorry, Wyatt, I only make motorcycles for veterans…yes, that includes rodeo kings." He laughed then, and the conversation finished up quickly.

"Ho-ly cow." Cy sighed and sank into the chair he'd been sitting in when Wyatt had called. "He's coming, Patsy. He's coming to the grand reopening, and he's bringing his family."

"That's amazing." Patsy squealed and rounded the desk to give Cy a hug. "It's going to be *huge*, Cy." She sat in his lap and hugged her arms around his neck.

"I need to start praying for good weather," Cy said, a panicked look in his eyes as he settled his hands on her waist. "Will you pray for me?"

"Of course," she said, her eyes drifting closed as she leaned down to kiss him. She didn't let him kiss her for too long, and when she pulled back, she rested her forehead against his. "I'm so proud of you."

"Don't be going there," he whispered back. "I have to get everyone here, and get the entire shop loaded in less than three weeks."

"You can do it," she said. "I can come help with anything, Cy. Really."

He nodded, and Patsy slid off his lap to return to her desk. She sat, her heartbeat still elevated. She wasn't even sure what she'd been working on before she'd gone to get Cy from the front porch as he'd towered over the Jamesons.

He stood up and said, "Well, I'm late for my announce-ments. Can I use the PA?"

"Sure," she said. "You know how it works."

"Me and you and lunch at your cabin?" he asked from the doorway, and Patsy looked up at him again. So hand-some, and so eager to spend time with her. Cy Hammond was practically perfect in every way, and she smiled and nodded

He left, and she sagged against her chair. No, Cy was not perfect, and she knew it. He let his temper run away with him sometimes, and he claimed to have some mental issues. She'd seen him be moody and depressed, but it didn't seem to affect him the way she'd seen it affect others. He still got up every day. He still came to work. He did have some anxiety, especially surrounding his shop, but she supposed that was normal for someone doing what he'd done. He'd moved his shop halfway across the country, to a new state where he knew no one.

He'd hired dozens of people to work for him, and he'd taken his concept for a motorcycle shop and showroom from his head and delivered it to someone who could build it. He'd booked Wyatt Walker to come to his grand reopening —and every cowboy in the state of Wyoming knew who Wyatt Walker was. Heck, even Patsy knew who the famous rodeo star was. One evening when she sat with her father, she'd bought one of his signature hats from a shopping channel for one of her boyfriends a couple of years ago.

Even if Cy did have some depression and anxiety, he was still about a thousand times more of a man than anyone else she'd dated.

She liked that he had a nickname for her, and she liked that he was protective of his rescue dog. She liked that he saw his brothers often, and that he also carved time out for the two of them. There was so much to like about Cy Hammond, in fact, that Patsy knew she was well on her way to being more in love with him than just liking him.

She pushed the thoughts out of her mind and looked at the ledger again. With a slap, she closed it, because she was at work, and this had nothing to do with Whiskey Mountain Lodge. She could deal with her family later.

She also needed to figure out how to deal with her feelings for Cy, too.

Later, she told herself sternly. Right now, she needed to put in another order for hay for the horses. Summer couldn't come fast enough.

—————

PATSY TOOK THE STEPS TO THE CABIN'S FRONT DOOR TWO AT A time and burst through the door. "Sophia," she called. "We're going to be late."

And they couldn't be late. Patsy should've been down at the grand reopening already, but there had been an emergency with one of the guests. A literal emergency, where the paramedics had been called and everything.

"I'm right here," Sophia said, rising from the couch. "Let's go."

Patsy practically jogged to her car, glad Sophia understood the urgency of the situation.

"You called him, right?" Sophia asked.

"Yes," Patsy said. "But he can't hold it, and I *really* don't want to miss it."

"We're not going to miss it," Sophia assured her. "It's not for another hour, and it only takes forty minutes to get there."

Patsy took a deep breath and buckled her seatbelt. Sure enough, they pulled down the newly paved lane that led through the orchard to the big building in the back corner. She'd been down the road many times, but it felt different this time.

The parking lot was full, but Patsy drove around to the back of the building and right into one of the bays. Cy stood there, talking to none other than Wyatt Walker, and Patsy dang near pressed harder on the accelerator instead of the brake pedal.

"Oh, my goodness," Sophia said. "That really is the rodeo king."

"Cy says he hates that," Patsy said. "Just so you know."

"He's married besides," Sophia said. "I'm not going to flirt with him."

"Hm," Patsy said as Cy came toward her. Sophia flirted with everyone, and Wyatt wouldn't be immune just because he was married. He held a boy on his hip and his pretty, blonde wife watched another child who ran around nearby.

She got out of the car and stepped right into Cy's arms. "Sorry. I'm so sorry."

"You're fine," he said. "You didn't miss it." He looked at her, his eyes sparkling like dark stars. "Come meet Wyatt." He took her hand and turned toward the couple and their children. They all looked perfectly at-ease and like they belonged to each other.

"Wyatt," Cy said. "This is my girlfriend, Patsy Foxhill. She owns the orchard here."

"You don't say." Wyatt grinned and reached up to touch his cowboy hat. "Pleased to meet you, ma'am."

"It's great to meet you too," she said, extending her hand to shake his. They did, and he introduced her to Marcy, his wife, and his two boys, Warren and Cole. "And Cy's not been entirely truthful with you." She glanced at him as Wyatt's eyebrows went up.

"Oh?"

Ames, Cy's twin, edged closer, his gaze suddenly sharp.

"He owns this twenty acres of the orchard," Patsy said. "My family owns the other side of the highway."

"They used to own it," Cy said. "I kept as many trees as I could. In fact, I only took out some four-year-olds that weren't producing fruit yet."

Ames glanced at Cy, and Patsy wished she could understand their silent twin language. She met Wyatt's eyes, and he started chuckling. "Oh, I have twin brothers, and I know that look well."

"You have twin brothers?" Cy asked.

"Oh, yeah." Wyatt grinned like he was thrilled to be there, in their tiny town, at a motorcycle shop reopening. "Liam and Tripp. They have whole conversations without saying a word." He looked at Cy and Ames. "It's highly annoying."

Cy blinked, and then he burst out laughing. Ames did too, but Patsy noticed his was much shorter than Cy's. Wasn't as loud either. He kept glancing around like he expected a problem to arise, and he was going to solve it singlehandedly.

"All right," Cy said. "It's getting close to time. We should get out there." He stepped back to Wyatt's side. "Thanks again for doing this. We've got a great lunch planned at my brother's afterward. It's up in the woods, and you'll love it."

"I love this place," Wyatt said, handing his smallest boy to his wife. "We're in Three Rivers now, and it's small like this. It's nice to be part of a community."

"That's what I'm hoping to do," Cy said as they walked away, and Patsy marveled at the two of them side-by-side.

Wyatt was a little taller, but not by much. They both had those broad shoulders, and cowboy hats, and jeans. Cy had bypassed his eccentric fashion choices, and today he wore a polo with his logo on the front, jeans, the cowboy hat and boots.

He was perfection to her, and she sighed as he and Wyatt went through the doors that led to the showroom.

"You can come with me," Patsy said to Marcy and her boys. "Come on, Sophia." Patsy turned just as an earsplitting clatter filled the air. She caught sight of Sophia going down, pure alarm on her face as she tried to find something to grab onto.

There was nothing.

CHAPTER 17

S ophia Cooke had never experienced such humiliation in her life. Her tailbone hurt, and tears sprang to her eyes. She couldn't cry, because she'd spent far too long on her makeup to look amazing for this grand reopening.

She had no special role in it, but she was going to Gray Hammond's afterward for lunch, and Ames would be there.

To add further shame to her humiliation, it was Ames himself who appeared in her sight first. "Hey, you okay?" He reached for her, and Sophia put her hand in his. He was big and strong, and he helped her to her feet easily.

Her heart rebelled against the idea of starting a relationship with him. Number one, she'd already witnessed all of her friends falling in love with these Hammond brothers. She felt like a tagalong. Number two, Ames was far too broody for her.

Handsome, sure.

The perfect blend of cowboy and cop, of course.

But he scared her, and Sophia didn't like feeling like the weak one in a relationship.

"What happened?" Patsy asked, also appearing on the scene.

"Nothing," Sophia said quickly. "Just me being my clumsy self." It was that, true. But it was more, too. She'd been trying to lean against the toolbox in a sexy pose to try to catch Ames's attention. She hadn't realized it had wheels and would roll.

One of Marcy Walker's boys began to fuss, and Patsy turned her attention to her. "Come with me," she said, scooping the child right into her arms. Patsy was so good with kids, and Sophia wondered how she did that.

Sophia could get the little ones at the lodge to play with her now. It had taken a long time for them to warm up to her, but she didn't know why. She adored children—she'd even thought about becoming a nanny for a career—but they needed time to get to know her before they liked her.

"I need to clean this up," Sophia said, looking at the mess she'd made.

"If you do, you'll miss the ceremony," Ames said. "Leave it. We can come do it after that ribbon is cut."

"But Cy—"

"I can handle Cy," Ames promised her with a smile. It fled as quickly as it had appeared, and Sophia wished it would stay longer. She followed Patsy and Marcy out the door and across the showroom floor.

Ames touched her elbow and nodded toward a side door. "I don't want to be center stage."

Neither did she, and she wanted to be closer to Ames, so she followed him to a door that led outside on the edge of the crowd. And what a crowd. It felt like everyone in the town of Coral Canyon and Dog Valley had converged on this building in the corner of an orchard.

It couldn't be seen from the road, and up until the moment the building had emerged from the trees, Sophia had doubted they were in the right place. But they were, and she stayed close to Ames so she wouldn't have to stand through the ceremony by herself.

"Welcome, everyone," Cy said into a microphone. "What a great turnout. I know why you're all here, but I wanted to take a couple of minutes and explain what we do here at Rev for Vets." He explained that they were a full-service motorcycle shop, a sales floor, and their specialty was custom designed bikes.

"Our first veteran that will get a custom-designed motorcycle is Major Andy Archer." He gestured to a man standing down at one end of the long, wide red ribbon that separated Cy and the microphone from the crowd. His brothers held the ends of the ribbon, and Sophia realized Ames had slipped away from her.

She looked around for Patsy while she clapped and the Major walked over to Cy. They shook hands, and embraced, and Cy said, "The Major here likes Captain America, so we're planning a patriotic bike. He'll be in the shop next week to go over initial designs, and then our mechanics start to build. We employ twenty-six people from right here in Coral Canyon, and I want you to meet them too."

The front row of the crowd surged forward, and several people began calling out their loved one's name. Sophia wondered what it would be like to have a cheering squad. Someone who cared at all that she was doing something good with her life. Heck, someone who cared would be enough for her.

Patsy cares, she thought. And Bree did, and Elise. Celia was forever asking Sophia how she was doing, that was for sure. It was almost like Celia knew Sophia didn't have anyone in the world concerned for her well-being, and she could admit she'd enjoyed spending time with Celia and also Amanda, the older women at the lodge.

She liked them more than women her age, but she couldn't explain why. And she got along great with Patsy. She finally spotted the blonde woman—her best friend— only a few paces away, in the front corner of the crowd.

Sophia edged through a few people to her friend's side. "Oh, Sophia," Patsy said, relief in her voice. "There you are." She reached over and squeezed her hand. "Are you okay?"

"Fine," Sophia said. Only her ego was bruised—and maybe her tailbone. She cut a glance at Ames, but he didn't look at her. Of course he wouldn't. A man like Ames likely had a dozen women in Colorado he could call for a date. He didn't need her, a mousy woman five hundred miles away.

"And now," Cy said. "The man you're all here to meet." He turned back to the glass door Sophia hadn't wanted to walk through. "Mister Wyatt Walker, the rodeo king himself."

The crowd went wild, and Wyatt Walker came through the door, a wide smile on his face and one hand already up in a wave. He went to Cy's side, and they looked at one another, practically identical smiles on their faces.

Then, as if they'd rehearsed it—which they probably had—they both reached up and removed their cowboy hats and started flapping them at the crowd.

A roar rose up and every hatted person in the crowd took off their hat and returned the gesture. In that moment, Sophia wished she wore a cowgirl hat, but she didn't. Patsy just used her hand, waving her wrist up and down while she giggled.

"He's full of charisma, isn't he?" she asked, not taking her eyes from the two men at the front of the crowd.

"Yes," Sophia said, but she had her gaze glued to Ames. Ridiculous, she knew. The man didn't even know her name. The public servant in him would've helped anyone who'd flopped to the ground with such a racket.

Wyatt took the microphone and said, "I'm thrilled to be here. I've been wanting to learn to ride a motorcycle. Now that my back is healed, my doctor says I can." He glanced at Cy. "Horses are out, but apparently, motorcycles are in, and I thought maybe they'd be somewhat similar."

Beside her, Patsy burst out laughing, and it was loud enough to draw the attention of several people, Cy included. He grinned for all he was worth, and he leaned toward the mic. "Not even close, Wyatt, but I'm sure we can outfit you with something that will be a smooth ride for your back."

"Great," Wyatt said. "I'll be in the shop next week, too,

folks. This is a great thing Cy has here, and you're lucky to have him as part of your community." He handed the microphone back to Cy while everyone clapped again, and Cy faced the crowd.

"All right, let's do this. Then the showroom will be open. Wyatt will be signing in the back corner. We have refreshments for everyone. Thank you so much for coming." He looked toward Patsy, and she darted forward with a giant pair of scissors Sophia hadn't even seen.

She handed them to him, and he put one hand on each of the handles. With one big chop, he cut right through the red ribbon. Cheers and whistles rent the air, with the Hammond brothers making some of the loudest of the noises.

Sophia could admit the Hammonds knew how to throw a party—who got Wyatt Walker to come to a motorcycle shop opening?—and she couldn't wait to go to Gray's. She'd been to Colton's wedding, but that was all. Elise had tried to get her to come to other events last year, but Sophia didn't fit. She didn't belong to the Hammonds the way she did the Whittakers.

Maybe if she started dating Ames….

She banished the thought, because when she looked to where he'd last been standing, he'd disappeared. Sophia wished she could disappear too, because that would be easier than constantly being overlooked.

CHAPTER 18

A mes Hammond couldn't stop grinning at his twin. Cy had a unique way of endearing everyone to him, and Ames had just watched him win over an entire town in a ten-minute ceremony.

The motorcycle shop crawled with people, and Ames stood a few feet from Wyatt Walker and his wife, both of whom sat at a table Ames had set up himself. He'd covered it with a white cloth, and he'd put several permanent markers out for the two of them. They were signing everything from T-shirts to cowboy hats, and they seemed to be the happiest people on the planet.

Ames had done a little reading on Wyatt once Cy had called to say he'd booked the celebrity rodeo star for the grand reopening. He'd endured several back surgeries in the recent past, so Ames knew his life wasn't as charmed as it looked from the outside. Ames knew that hardly anyone's life was what it looked like to other people.

He'd brought his mother with him to watch Cy's reopening, but their father had stayed in Ivory Peaks with Grams. Ames hadn't told anyone else yet that he had a feeling Grams wouldn't be alive very much longer. He'd been going out to the farmhouse every chance he got, and Grams was very nearly one hundred years old.

He couldn't even imagine living that long, and he certainly didn't want to do it alone. Now that Cy was dating Patsy, it was only Ames who didn't have a significant other. He'd been looking, but the last few dates he'd been on had been disasters. He'd been hit on by a woman in the back of his patrol car, and his desperation had become apparent when he'd actually considered saying yes.

He and Gray ran at the gym together a lot, but they'd moved outdoors in the past couple of weeks, and they'd talked a lot about how Ames could find a girlfriend. But Gray was worse than Ames when it came to dating, and he'd gotten very lucky when he'd found Elise.

He'd traveled to Coral Canyon to do it, and Ames kept looking around, thinking perhaps the woman of his dreams was right here in the crowd. His eyes kept going to Sophia, one of Elise's friends. He didn't know her last name, though he was sure he'd met her before. Maybe. He couldn't entirely remember.

But all of those women from Whiskey Mountain Lodge had come to Colton's wedding, and Ames had been there too. So surely he'd met her before.

He could ask Gray or Elise for Sophia's last name, but he didn't want to. He didn't want either of them to know that he was considering starting a long-distance relationship with any woman who'd be willing to talk to him on the phone.

Pathetic, he told himself, because he was.

He kept an eye on the Walkers at their table, his stance and his folded arms a warning to everyone that they should behave, or he'd escort them right back outside. Eventually, the line dwindled, and the crowd thinned.

When it was just family left, as well as Patsy and Sophia, Cy clapped his hands together and said, "Thank you, everyone." Silence followed, and Ames knew Cy was holding back his emotion.

Ames didn't feel a whole lot of emotions, as he'd learned to stuff everything away in the police academy. He showed nothing while on the job, and he reminded himself he wasn't on the job anymore.

"Lunch at my place," Gray said. "Everyone meet over there, and we'll plan to eat in about a half an hour."

Everyone started to head out, and Ames stuck close to Cy, Patsy, and Mom. Sophia stayed with Patsy too, and he remembered the two of them arriving together. He had nothing to say to a woman, so he just shuffled along with his mother, making sure she had a firm footing as they left the building.

"It's a beautiful shop, Cy," she said, and Ames faded further into the background. He was the older twin, but he felt like he was constantly jostling for a position in the family. He loved his brothers, and he didn't mind marching to the beat of his own drum. He just didn't know what that beat was anymore. He couldn't hear it. And he was terrified he'd spent thirty-eight years listening to the wrong rhythm.

He helped his mother up into his truck and waved to Cy as he got in his. Patsy and Sophia climbed in with him, which didn't make sense to Ames. Patsy's car was in the back; Cy would have to drive her all the way back here, when they'd be halfway back to the lodge by the time they reached Gray's house.

Ames shouldn't care. It wasn't him who had to make the drive. And yet, the wasted time gnawed at him to the point of frustration. He masked it well and made the drive to Gray's house in near-silence. Only the radio played music from his phone, as the two connected the moment Ames got behind the wheel.

"Coral Canyon is a beautiful place," his mother said, and Ames didn't know how to respond.

"Yes," he said, and that was all. He could admit this town had a specific charm. The views of the Grand Tetons were magnificent, and Ames had never met a pine tree he didn't like. He pulled in behind a few other trucks, and Colton opened their mother's door before Ames got out.

"Come on, Ma." He smiled at her, and then Ames, and Ames just nodded back. He'd worn a cowboy hat to the grand reopening, mostly because Wyatt had brought them for everyone in the family.

He could admit he didn't hate wearing a cowboy hat. He had grown up on a farm, after all, and he still rode a horse whenever possible. He watched Colton and Annie take Mom toward Gray's front steps, and he watched Wes and his family follow them.

Cy arrived with Patsy and Sophia, and they went in as well.

Gray pulled in next, with Wyatt Walker right behind them. A few minutes later, Ames was officially the only one who hadn't gone inside, and he wondered how long it would be before someone noticed.

"Who'll come out?" he wondered aloud, though he knew who. Cy. Cy would definitely come get him, and then Ames would have to explain things he'd rather not. If not Cy, then Gray, as Ames had grown close to him over the past several months. If not Gray, then Colton, who seemed to be the glue that kept the family together.

And honestly, Wes would come out too.

Ames couldn't fault his brothers for anything. They had unique personalities, sure. But they worked hard to get along, and though life had pulled them in different directions, they were still a unified family.

He got out of the truck and started for the house. No sense in making someone else come get him. And he certainly didn't want anyone talking about him. He opened the front door to plenty of noise, because no one in the Hammond family knew how to talk quietly when they got together.

In the kitchen, Annie worked with Elise, and Ames hung back near the foyer he'd passed through. Mom had baby Michael in her arms, and Wyatt's boys played with Colton's dog in the living room. Hutch, Elise's dog panted too, and Cy had just brought Blue Velvet in from the back yard as well. The boys giggled with three canines all trying to lick their faces.

Ames wanted a couple of boys too, and he knew that wasn't going to happen without a good first date. *Just one,* he prayed. Then he could make it a second date, and then maybe a third.

"Are you afraid they'll bite?"

He pulled himself from his thoughts and looked at the woman who'd spoken. Sophia. "A little," he admitted. He looked back out at all of them, trying to find the empty space where he'd fit. "You?"

"Oh, yeah," she said. "I'm used to crowds, but this one's different than the one at the lodge."

"Cy's been up at the lodge. Wes was too."

"Yeah." Sophia wrapped her arms around herself. "It's different though."

"How so?" He turned toward her fully now, thinking perhaps he'd found a space to be for right now.

"Different family," she said. "I don't know you Hammonds very well."

"But you're friends with all the women."

"True." She glanced at him, as if only realizing he'd looked at her fully. Her attention drifted away and came right back to him. "I'm Sophia Cooke."

"Cooke," he said, smiling. "I knew the Sophia part." He extended his hand toward her. "I'm Ames. The oldest twin."

"I know who you are." She smiled too and shook his hand anyway. Her eyes crinkled in a pretty way, and Ames tried to decide if he thought she was pretty because she was talking to him, or because she actually was.

"Have we met?"

"Not officially," she said. "I saw you at Colton's wedding though. You wore a top hat." She tried to cover her giggle with a cough, but she didn't do a great job.

Ames grinned even wider. "Yes, well, he said we needed to dress up. Hats were *not* optional, and he never specified that it should be a cowboy hat."

She simply shook her head. "And you're the cop."

"I'm actually a captain over the detectives in my department," he said. "But yes."

"Wow. A captain." Sophia definitely had a flirtatious tone with him now, and Ames did like that. He'd never had to work very hard to get a date, but everything felt hard right now.

Sophia gestured toward the kitchen. "I'm a culinary instructor on the weekends, and I cook at the lodge during the week."

"I can sometimes get water to boil," he said.

She burst out laughing then, and everything about her transformed for Ames. She had a great laugh, and beautiful eyes the color of the dark mountains in the distance. Ames's pulse hopped in his chest, but he didn't know what to say next. He couldn't ask her to dinner, as he'd only be in town for one more night.

So he just smiled, and it seemed Sophia didn't have anything more to add to the conversation either. Thankfully, Gray lifted both hands above his head a few minutes later and said, "Okay, quiet down. Lunch is ready."

He'd taken one step toward the fray when Sophia said, "Ames?"

He paused and turned back to her. "Yeah?"

"Could I…would you give me your number?"

He blinked, sure he'd heard her wrong. "My number?"

"Yeah," she said, her face turning a pretty shade of pink. "I have a feeling Patsy is going to, I don't know, fall madly in love with your brother, and I'm going to be the only one left at the lodge."

Ames frowned, because he wasn't sure why her having his number could do anything about that. "I—"

"It would be nice to have a friend to talk to," she said, shrugging.

"You don't have other friends here in Coral Canyon?"

"Ames," Cy said. "Sophia. Come on."

Ames looked to his brother, and everyone in the house was watching him and Sophia. "Yeah, coming," he said, glancing back at Sophia. "Let's pick this up later."

"Forget it," Sophia said, brushing by him. Ames watched her go, confused about what had just happened. He frowned and pushed his cowboy hat down even further, only to have to take it off a moment later for the prayer.

He stayed out of the way while the others loaded up their plates, and by the time he finished getting food, he turned to find just one seat left—right next to Wyatt Walker.

He thanked the Lord above and took the chair. "Thanks for coming to do this for my brother."

"We've been wanting to get up to the mountains," Wyatt said, looking at Marcy and then putting a piece of elbow macaroni in front of his two-year-old. "I like this area, and Gray said he only comes in the summer."

"Well, you wouldn't want to be here in the winter," Ames said. "It's freezing."

"See? That's what we need, Marce. A summer home in the mountains. Get out of the Texas heat."

"Yeah," she said in a deadpan from across the table. "We *need* a summer home in the mountains." She shook her head, though her blue eyes broadcasted love for her husband. "Wyatt, the bulk of my business is in the summer."

"You have other pilots now."

Ames had the feeling that Wyatt was used to getting what he wanted, and he grinned at Marcy as he picked up his brownie.

"I'll think about it," she said.

"Can't ask for more than that," Wyatt said, turning to Ames. "You're still in Colorado, right?"

"That's right." Ames felt like someone in the Hammond family should be, but he'd already started thinking about leaving too. Gray and Hunter had bought the family farm, and while they did come to Coral Canyon for the summer—or they would this summer for the first time as a family—they planned to live in Ivory Peaks on the farm for the bulk of the year. "I'm a captain in the Littleton Police Department."

"My oldest brother is a forensic veterinarian," Wyatt said. "Works with a lot of cops."

"Yeah, I bet," Ames said. "Down in Texas. Three Rivers, you said?"

"Yep."

"Do they need more men on the force?" Where the

question had come from, Ames had no idea. He only knew he needed a change. He wasn't sure what that looked like for him. Relocation? Simply a new girlfriend? A transfer to a bigger department?

A new job….

Ames was willing to consider anything at this point, and he glanced down the table to where Sophia had sat next to Patsy and Cy.

"No idea," Wyatt said. "But I can text Rhett real quick. He might know."

Ames just nodded, because so much of his attention was being taken by Sophia. He should've just smiled and ducked his head and given her his number. Why had he acted like a cop, questioning her and making her feel stupid?

Cy laughed, and it was too loud. Ames's concern spiked, because when Cy laughed like that, he was headed for a big fall. While Wyatt texted his brother, Ames quickly pulled out his phone and texted his oldest brother too.

Can Mom stay with you tonight? I want to stay at Cy's, and I know he doesn't have room for both of us in that rental.

Ames watched Wes, and he met his brother's eye once he'd read the text. Wes nodded, and Ames lifted his hand in acknowledgement.

"Rhett says they're always looking for more people on the force," Wyatt said. "Three Rivers is in a growth spurt right now."

"Like Coral Canyon," Gray said on the other side of Wyatt, and his eyes easily moved from the rodeo king's to Ames's. "You thinkin' about moving here, Ames?"

"Not really," Ames said, his phone buzzing beneath his palm. He glanced at it, and saw Wes had texted back.

Worried about Cy?

Of course Ames was worried about Cy. That could be a full-time job, and no one did it better than Ames. He could usually shoulder it just fine, because he wasn't worried about himself. But right now, Ames needed to hear Cy's reassurances just as much as his twin needed to hear his.

Maybe more.

CHAPTER 19

After Ames confirmed that yes, he was worried about Cy, Wes watched him, and it sure was good to see his youngest brother so happy. Not a moment went by where his smile slipped or the light dimmed in his eyes. Wes wondered what kind of crash that would produce for Cy, and then his heartbeat would flutter in his chest.

Because Wes knew what it took to hitch a smile in place, shake hands, nod, smile, and converse like he cared. He knew Cy did care about his motorcycle shop and his family—the two most important things to Cy. Still didn't mean the effort he had to put into social events like this didn't drain him completely.

He took a break from watching him with Patsy and Gray to look at his mother. She wouldn't let go of Michael for longer than it took to feed him, and now that Bree supplemented his feedings with a bottle, she hadn't even had to do that. A twinge of guilt pulled through him that he didn't live close enough for her to see her grandson every day.

A pitchy voice at the table reminded him that his mother had a grandson at the farm, and he smiled as Hunter said something about school that Wyatt Walker found funny. The man chuckled and shook his head, and he seemed so normal.

Wes should've known he would be. Even the most superhuman of humans were still human. Just because Wyatt had climbed onto the back of a bull and ridden it for eight seconds didn't make him any different than Wes. He wondered how the rodeo king would fare in a marathon meeting, with lawyers and sharks and falling company stocks. That was stress. That was worth a medal or a title or whatever Wyatt had earned on the backs of those bulls.

He was a very nice man, and Wes liked the energy he put off. Marcy was as equally impressive, especially with how she handled her rambunctious children who didn't want to sit at a long table while grown-ups chatted.

Wes barely wanted to, and he got up and picked up his plate along with Bree's. He took them into the kitchen and rinsed them in the sink before turning to say, "All right, who wants to come with me down to the lake? I'm taking the dogs." He looked at Hunter. "Hunt?"

"I'm in," he said, standing up.

Wes looked at Marcy, who faced the house. "I'll take your boys, Marcy," he said. "If you don't mind."

"It's okay, we—" she started.

"She'd *love* for you to take the boys," Wyatt said. "I'll get them ready." He stood up and left his plate where it was and turned to his kids. "Come on, kiddos. You need coats and boots. You're goin' down to the lake with Wes."

He set about getting them ready, and Colton got up to help Wes get all the dogs leashed. "You okay?" he asked.

"Yeah," Wes said. "I'm just…restless."

"It's getting warmer."

"Yeah," Wes said. "I can't wait until we can get out on the hiking trails. I bought a new backpack for Michael."

"I'm sure you did." Colton gave him a tight smile, and Wes saw something flash in his eyes.

"Are *you* okay?"

"I think so." Colton bent and clipped a leash to Hutch's collar while the silver doodle smiled.

"You *think* so? That's not reassuring."

Colton turned his back on Wes, and there was definitely something wrong. What it could be, Wes didn't know. Annie wasn't planning any more weddings—both of her daughters were married now. Colt worked in the lab at Springside a couple days a week, and he'd found he liked building furniture and running in his spare time.

"You want to come on the walk?" Wes looked down at Hutch, already straining against his leash. "I've got three dogs and three kids and could use some help."

"Sure," Colton said. He still didn't look at Wes as he continued with getting his coat and gloves.

"Want me to come?" Wyatt asked, but he looked like he couldn't stand for much longer.

"No, we're fine," Wes said. He looked at the biggest of the small boys. "Warren, right, son? You're with me. We'll make Cole go with Colton. Your name starts with a W and so does mine. Colton with Cole." He grinned at Warren, who hugged his father's leg though he smiled.

"You say, 'yes, sir,' Warren," Wyatt prompted.

"Yes, sir," the child said.

Wyatt crouched down, a groan accompanying the wince on his face. "You listen to Wes real good now, y'hear?" Wyatt reached out and adjusted his son's collar. "Love you, bud, and Mama just needs a break, okay?"

"Okay," Warren said, and Wes wondered why Marcy needed a break. "Can I ride Bucky when we get home to grandpa's?"

Wyatt shook his head and chuckled. "Only if you're absolute perfection on the walk. I'm gonna ask Wes." He put his hand on the back of the couch and used it to stand up. He looked at Wes. "Pure perfection."

"Oh, I'll keep my eye on him," Wes said, marveling at the love Wyatt had for his son. At the same time, Wes knew exactly what that felt like.

"Colt, you've got Cole."

"Got 'im." Colton opened the front door and retook the little boy's hand. He handled Sparky in the other, and Wes had Blue Velvet and Hutch.

"All right," Wes said. "Let's go."

"I'll get the door," Wyatt said. Once there, he leaned in closer to Wes and added in a low voice, "Thanks, Wes. Marcy just found out she's having another baby, and she's exhausted."

"Gray has bedrooms upstairs," Wes said. "Have her go lie down."

"I'll talk to her." Wyatt grinned them out of the house

and closed the door behind them. The sun was high overhead, and it shone down merrily on everything.

Wes caught up to Colton, who wasn't moving that fast due to having two-year-old legs walking beside him. "So spill," he said, glancing at Hunter, who walked on Colton's other side. The boy had started spending more time with the adults in the past six months, and Wes didn't mind. He adored Hunter, and he was really mature for his age. Having Gray for a father would do that, Wes supposed.

"I don't want to upset you." Colton kept his gaze on Cole while he spoke.

"Why would I be upset?"

Colton sighed and looked away from the small person at his side. Warren kicked rocks a couple of feet to Wes's left, and that was just fine with him. Wes waited, because he knew Colton extraordinarily well, and sometimes his brother just needed time to get his words together.

"Mom won't hardly talk to me and Annie when she comes here," he said. "She never stays with us, and...I guess I'm jealous."

Wes opened his mouth to respond, because as the oldest, he always knew how to respond. All that came out was, "Oh."

"It's not your fault," Colton said miserably. "I guess I thought I was okay not having kids, and I am. Ninety-nine-point-nine percent of the time, I'm okay." He still wouldn't look at Wes, and he imagined that point-one percent could feel really big sometimes. Really deep, and really heavy, and really dark.

"I'm sorry," Wes said. "Ames needs somewhere for

Mom to stay tonight, because he wants to stay with Cy. She should stay with you."

"It's okay."

"She doesn't even know she was going to come home with me," Wes said. "I'm sure he asked me because I'm the oldest. That's all."

"You don't care?"

"Not at all."

"Mom will." Colton gazed down the road as the lake started to peek around the corner. "You watch. She'll say something."

"Just tell her, Uncle Colton," Hunter said. "Dad did that last week. He sat her down and said, 'Look, we're going to Coral Canyon, and you don't get to say anything about the baby.' And she hasn't."

Wes sucked in a breath, and he and Colton both looked at Hunter. He smiled back at them. "She'll listen to you. You say, 'Mom, it makes me feel bad that you won't even talk to me because I don't have kids.' She'll get it."

"Hunter," Wes said slowly. "Take Hutch, would you?" He passed the dog to his nephew. "And tell me…is Elise pregnant?"

"Yeah," Hunter said. Wes couldn't tell if he was happy about it or not. He was still smiling, so that was something.

Wes exchanged a glance with Colton. "Were you supposed to tell us?" Wes asked.

"Yeah, Dad said I could," Hunter said. "He's telling everyone at the house too."

Wes suddenly wanted to get back and be there for that announcement. At the same time, he was glad he wasn't, because his family could be a bit overwhelming, especially when they were all together.

"That's amazing," Colton said, and he sounded pretty normal. "I can't wait to tell them congratulations."

"Yeah," Wes said. "Are you excited, Hunter?"

"I don't know," the boy said truthfully. "Dad and Elise are super excited, so I feel like I should be too." He kicked at something in the road too.

"But?" Colton prompted.

"But I don't know," Hunter said. "Like, I love your baby, Uncle Wes. I just don't know what to do with him."

"Believe me, Hunt," Wes said dryly. "Neither do I."

Colton burst out laughing, and Wes joined in with a chuckle. Even Hunter did.

"You'll love that baby so much when it comes," Colton said. "And you'll know exactly what to do with him."

"Maybe," Hunter said, and another red flag shot up in Wes's mind.

"Keep talking, Hunt," he said.

He took a few steps before even making a noise. "I don't know, it's just…Dad says I'm not broken. He says it's okay not to have any feelings about the baby. I just wonder…." He exhaled. "It's fine. I'm going to talk to Lucy about it next week."

Colton looked at Wes again, and Wes nodded. His turn to keep Hunter talking. "Who's Lucy?" Colton asked. "New girlfriend?"

Hunter scoffed and shook his head. "She's my therapist."

"Oh." Colton tugged on Cole's hand to keep him moving. "How long have you been seeing her?"

"Couple of months," Hunter said. "I, uh, kissed Molly, and I told my dad it was kind of weird. I didn't know if I liked it or not, and that's when I told him I might not have the same kinds of feelings as other people. You know, because of my mom."

"What about your mom?" Colton asked, and Wes was glad he hadn't had to.

"Lucy thinks I might have boxed up how I really feel about her leaving me and Dad, and because of that, I don't feel much of anything." He looked at Colton and Wes with wide open eyes. He was so innocent and so vulnerable, and Wes wanted to find Gray's ex-wife and ask her if she knew what she'd done to her beautiful boy.

"Get over here, son," Wes said, his voice a little gruff. Hunter stepped between Colton and Wes, and they both put their arms around him. "You're a perfectly fine human being, Hunter. I love you no matter what."

"I do too," Colton said.

"I just want to feel things like other people," Hunter said.

"I can see why," Colton said. "I would've never told my dad I'd kissed a girl."

Wes couldn't smother his chuckle fast enough, and thankfully, Hunter laughed too. "You're sure you didn't like it?" Wes asked, grinning at his nephew.

"I liked it better the other times," Hunter said, still smiling.

"You be careful with the girls," Colton said, turning

serious in a flash. "You're way too cute to be leading them on."

"You sound like Elise," Hunter said, rolling his eyes. "I've heard it all before."

"Yeah, well, you have the killer Hammond genes," Colton said. "Trust me, Hunt. They're lethal to girls."

"Oh, boy," Wes said, rolling his eyes too. "Don't listen to him, Hunt. You kiss as many girls as you can."

Hunter looked at him, his eyes widening. "Really, Uncle Wes?"

"Don't tell your dad I said that," Wes said, smiling. "And just kiss the ones you like—while you're not dating someone else. No cheating, Hunter."

"No cheating," the thirteen-year-old repeated. "I can handle that."

"And I don't think you're broken either," Wes said. "Either of you. I've seen you get really emotional, Hunter."

"Yeah, remember when your dad broke up with Elise?" Colton asked. "You were super upset then."

"Yeah," Hunter said. "It just feels like it's all or nothing. I'm not sure that's normal."

"No one's normal," Wes said, and he called to Warren to wait at the corner. The conversation moved on to something else, something lighter, but Wes didn't forget that his brother was struggling, or that his nephew was in therapy and Gray hadn't said anything.

He sent his mother home with Colton and Annie, and he hugged Gray and Elise and told them congratulations, and then he went back to his house with his wife and baby.

When he knelt down to pray, he spent a long time on

his knees, begging God to watch over and help his family. For the wounds he knew about, to the ones he didn't.

For Cy, and Ames, who Wes loved dearly. For Gray, who would be running in the Boston Marathon in just three weeks. For a clear mind for himself, and for the love they all needed to feel in their lives. For Grams and her health. For his father, who was alone in Ivory Peaks.

He hadn't realized he'd started to weep until Bree's hand landed on his shoulder and her kind voice said, "Wes, honey, are you okay? You've been down there a long time."

"I'm okay," he whispered and climbed into bed with her. He gathered her close and stroked her hair, whispering, "I love you so much, Bree."

"I love you, too, Wes," she said against his chest. Extreme gratitude overcame him, and Wes pressed his eyes closed and left the care of his loved ones in God's hands.

CHAPTER 20

P atsy drew in a deep breath and got out of the car. Betty's car also sat in front of the farmhouse, and Patsy felt like she was walking into a battle. A major battle, and if she didn't win it, she'd be out on the streets. Betty probably wouldn't talk to her for a while, and Patsy didn't want to be cut off from her nieces.

She tucked the folder under her arm and climbed the steps, ready for this fight. "You want this," she murmured to herself. "She doesn't, even if she fights you on it. Please, Dear Lord. Soften her heart."

She knocked on the door and opened it a moment later. "Dad? Betty?"

"In the kitchen," her sister called, her voice almost a sing-song. Patsy worked hard not to roll her eyes. Her fingers tightened on the folder as she walked back into the kitchen, where she found Betty sitting with Dad at the kitchen table. They both had coffee cups in front of them, and a bowl of sugar on the table between them.

"Morning," Patsy said as cheerfully as she could. She kept the folder with her as she turned toward the coffee pot. It was empty, and it felt deliberate. Patsy turned back to her family, her breath lodging in her lungs. "Do you need anything, Dad?"

"He's good," Betty answered for him, and when Dad didn't say anything, Patsy got an idea of how this meeting would go.

She lifted her chin and sat down at the table. "All right. Maybe we should just get started then."

"Joe's not here," Dad said.

"He's not coming," Patsy said gently. "Remember I told you that earlier this week? He said he doesn't want to be involved with the orchard anymore. He also said he thinks I should start to manage it." She cut a glance at Betty, who pursed her lips. "I don't want to accuse anyone of anything." She laid the folder on the table and nudged it closer to her father.

"Dad, I want the orchard. I want to run it full-time, and make sure we're bringing in the profit we should be, and which will allow us to preserve the land we have into the future."

"I can—"

"I'm going to respectfully ask that you don't interrupt me," Patsy said, giving her sister a hard look. "I have things to talk about and show Dad, and then you can say anything you want. Is that fair?"

Betty's blue eyes blazed with fire, and she practically

burned Patsy with her glare. At this point, Patsy always backed down. But not this time. She stared steadily back, and finally, Betty nodded.

"Thank you," Patsy said politely, thanking the heavens above for her courage. Working with the Whittaker brothers had given her a voice, and she'd never been more grateful.

"Now, let's start with the maintenance this orchard requires." She opened the folder. "Dad, you used to do a rigorous schedule of spring fertilization and clean-up in the orchard. I know, because I did the four-step program starting in April with you for several years. According to these records, the trees have only been fertilized once in the past three years, and the debris on the orchard floor has not been raked out once."

She flipped a page. "For the past four years, the north twenty has been neglected. This is a balance sheet on what that section of the orchard made from the previous four years." She pointed to the six-figure number in the first column. "We made plenty of money when we had people harvesting those apples. You were selling them all over the west, right, Dad?"

"Yes," he said. "Hammerstein bought almost all the apples in the north twenty for years. They're the leading applesauce producer in Idaho."

"Hmm, yes," Patsy said, flipping the page. "And yet, we didn't sell to them the next year. Or the next. Or the next. Or last year." She could still see the apples on the ground from last fall. "I'm not sure what happened or why it didn't get done. But it didn't."

"It was too expensive to hire the people," Betty said.

"You're wrong, Betty," Patsy said. "To hire the people we need to harvest the north twenty, it costs us fifteen thousand dollars. We make fifty-four from the apples in that section." She had proof of that too, but no one asked to see it.

Patsy continued to lay out what had gone wrong and how she would fix it. Ten minutes later, she stopped talking. "That's it. I want to take care of the orchard. Betty is busy with her family, as she should be. But Dad, the Foxhill Farm has been in our family for generations. We can't lose it because Betty's pride will be hurt."

She nodded at her sister, who had steam pouring from every hole in her head.

"This has nothing to do with my pride," she snapped. "I'm the oldest, and this has already been decided." She looked at Dad. "Dad, tell her."

"Betty," Dad said. "Is what Patsy saying true?"

Patsy kept her eyes on the folder, which she'd closed. If Betty lied, well, she'd have to live with that.

"Some of it," Betty said. "But Dad, I'm doing the best I can."

"It's not good enough," Patsy said quietly. "Please, Betty." She'd told Cy she wasn't above begging, and she'd just proven it.

"It's not fair," Betty said. "No one taught me how to do this."

"No one taught me either," Patsy said. "I worked with Dad around the orchard, and I know what needs to be done. You have a family, Betty. Don't you just want to take care of them?"

"I used to enjoy managing the orchard," Betty said. "It's not as fun as you think it is."

"I understand that, but—"

Betty got to her feet and leaned into the table, her expression furious. "You've always thought you were better than the rest of us. Perfect Patsy, and her perfect organization."

"That is not true," Patsy said. "I've lived in your shadow for my entire life." She drew in a deep breath, because she had not come here to trade jabs with her sister. She didn't want to say things she'd regret later. It wouldn't accomplish anything.

She exhaled and stayed in her seat. "Dad."

"Sit down, Betty."

"No, I'm done here." Betty stomped away, pausing in the hallway and turning back. "I need some time to think about this," she said over her shoulder.

Patsy stood up and met her sister's eye. "Do I have your permission to start the spring fertilization in the meantime?"

"I'll do it," Betty clipped out, and that said, she left the house.

Patsy sat back down and let her pent-up energy leak out in the form of a sigh.

Dad reached over and patted her hand. "For the record, Patsy," he said. "I believe everything you said."

"Really?"

"Yes." He gave her a sad smile. "I'll talk to Betty."

Patsy nodded, her chest cinching tight with emotion. "Thank you, Dad."

———

A couple of weeks later, Patsy rocked back and forth in the recliner in Bree's bedroom while her friend packed. "I wish you were coming," she said.

"There's no way I could," Patsy said. "I'm going to try to watch on TV. Elise said they show the marathon from beginning to end."

"Only the lead runners, though," Bree said. "Gray won't be in the lead."

"Probably not." Patsy looked down at the sleeping baby angel in her arms. She did want babies of her own. A lot of them, and she'd started to imagine them with dark hair and eyes like Cy's. She was blonde and blue-eyed, and she had no idea what a child with the mix of their genes would look like. Both Bree and Wes were dark, so Michael was too.

"He's such a good baby," Patsy said. "You're so blessed, Bree."

"I know," she said. "Makes me terrified to have another one."

Patsy looked up. "He's five months old."

Bree placed a pair of shoes in her suitcase. "Oh, I know. We're not trying yet. But Wes definitely wants more kids, and he's almost fifty years old. So he's not keen to wait."

Patsy looked back at the sleeping baby, a vein of joy moving through her. "Well, he's perfect."

"How are you and Cy?"

"Good," Patsy said, and that was the truth. "He's not shy about what he thinks or feels, and I like that."

Bree smiled at her. "He seems to really like you."

"He says he does."

"And you like him?"

"Definitely." Patsy grinned back at Bree and stood up. "Okay, I'm not elaborating." She laid Michael in his swing, and the baby grunted and squirmed while she tucked his blanket around him. "I wish I was going to Boston with everyone, but I'm not, so I need to go say good-bye to my boyfriend."

"You do that," Bree said. "Thanks for bringing that medicine. Wes refuses to stay home."

Patsy understood. It wasn't every year that one's brother got to run in the Boston Marathon. She drove quickly to the house on the north edge of town and parked behind Cy's truck. Now that spring was more evident, this house had a beautiful yard with a square of emerald green grass. Two big trees stood in the front yard, and Cy had cleared out the flowerbeds and put in some petunias.

His house in the orchard would be finished in a few weeks, and Patsy wanted to rent his house if she got to manage the orchard. Betty still hadn't decided, and Patsy's patience was growing thin.

Betty had not done any of the fertilizing, and Patsy had made a bold decision to do it herself. So she had. Most days after a long day at the lodge, with plenty of stress and an endless to-do list, she drove down the canyon and worked around the farm. She'd never seen

Betty in the small office in the barn, and she'd arranged to have the orchard raked out, so the leaves from last year wouldn't prevent the fertilizer from getting to the roots.

She'd hired the crew to do that, and she'd ensured the irrigation system was working in every row. She'd hired a crop duster to spray for pests the first week of June, and Patsy felt sure they'd have an amazing crop this year. A crop she could sell for a profit.

She knocked on Cy's door, and he called, "Come in," from inside. Patsy entered the house to a living room with comfortable furniture. She'd sat on it plenty of times with Cy while they talked about their lives, watched movies, and expressed their dreams.

He came into the room from down the hall. "Hey." He grinned at her and took her into his arms. "You sure you can't come to Boston with me?"

"Beyond sure." She tipped her head back and looked up at him. "Betty hasn't decided yet, but if she does let me take over the orchard, can I take over your lease here after you move into your house?"

"Mm, I see what's happening here." He grinned down at her, his hands warm on her waist. "You're using me for my house."

"Oh, yeah," she teased. "This tiny two-bedroom rental on a street all by itself. That's what you're good for."

They laughed together, and Patsy tipped up onto her toes and kissed him. "Is that a yes?" she asked.

"Sure," he said. She expected him to release her or kiss her again. He had to leave to make his flight in just a few minutes. Instead, he gazed down at her, a sober look in his eye. "Patsy, have you thought about a future with us?"

"A future with us?"

"Yeah," he said. "What if we get married? Just go with me, and don't freak out."

"I'm not freaking out." Yet. Sure, she'd thought about a future with Cy. It was hard not to, because he did speak directly.

"I own twenty acres of the orchard. If we get married, you could definitely manage that, no matter what Betty says."

Hope fired through Patsy's soul. "Yes."

"And you wouldn't need this tiny rental, because you'd live with me." He pressed his cheek to hers, and Patsy let her eyes drift closed as she imagined the future he spoke of. She could see it with perfect clarity, and she wasn't sure if that was a good thing or not. If it didn't come true, it would hurt so much. And if it did…she couldn't hope for such joy. It almost felt selfish.

"It's a nice future," he whispered. "In my head."

"Mine too," Patsy said.

An alarm sounded on his phone, and Cy touched his lips to her jaw. "I have to go."

"I know." Neither one of them moved, and Patsy turned and dipped her head so she could kiss Cy one last time before he went to Boston.

A few minutes later, she had Blue Velvet's leash, her food and water bowls, and her dental treats. Cy told the dog to get in the back of Patsy's sedan, and she obeyed. He kissed Patsy again, and they both got in their vehicles.

Patsy went back up to the lodge, her fantasies about the future continuing on a loop. Had she finally found the man who would stick by her side through thick and thin? Who'd notice when she cut and colored her hair? Who cared about the things she was passionate about?

It sure seemed like it, and Patsy didn't understand the fear running through her.

CHAPTER 21

Nervous energy ran from one side of Gray Hammond's mind to the other. He'd worked for months and months—over a year—to be here in Boston.

His legs felt good. He'd done a gentle, easy run with Elise yesterday. She was having a good day, and she'd gone two miles with him, and then let him do two more on his own.

She could run four miles with him now, and there was nothing Gray loved more than running with his wife. Maybe fishing with his son. Or living with both of them in the farmhouse on the land where he'd grown up.

Yes, he definitely liked that the best.

He hopped up on his toes, keeping his calves warm.

A sea of people filled his vision, and his familiar anxiety roared back to life. He reminded himself he was ready for this. He wasn't competing against all of these people. Only those in his age group. He wouldn't be at the front of the pack, no matter what he did.

He hoped he would be on television at some point, because he knew his parents would be watching with Grams. Elise had been ill for the past couple of months as she dealt with morning sickness, and they'd both spent plenty of time on their knees, begging God to allow her to feel well enough to come to Boston.

Gray hadn't run a marathon without her in the crowd for a while now, and he didn't want to be there by himself.

Of course, he wasn't here by himself. Hunter had come and had always been planning on coming. Colton and Annie had both come. Wes had brought his wife and baby. Ames and Cy were there, though Cy hadn't brought Patsy. Apparently, she had a lot going on with the family orchard and trying to get it transferred to her name. Not only that, but Whiskey Mountain Lodge was entering the summer season, and Patsy had a lot of work to do.

Gray didn't mind, because it wasn't like Cy and Patsy were married. Even if they had been, Gray understood that it wasn't all that fun to stand around for hours watching people run by.

He bent and stretched his back, an alarm on his watch going off as he felt the age in his spine.

But he felt good today. Very good. He was going to give this his best effort, because he wasn't sure he'd ever do anything like this again.

He silenced the alarm and put his sunglasses in position, tucked beneath the elastic band of his visor.

This was just another run. He'd done a marathon in St.

George, Utah in the fall, and he'd done two more in the past six months, once on a treadmill, and once just a few weeks ago as the weather started to warm around Denver.

He'd beaten his Colfax marathon time in St. George, but his time a few weeks ago was slower.

Gray wasn't going to let it bother him. Not today. Nine people had flown here to see him run, and he had many more watching for a glimpse of him.

He was going to give them what they'd come for. He was going to start strong like he usually did, and put in a good, fast five miles. Then he'd pull back and conserve some energy. He'd push through miles seventeen to twenty, his worst stretch.

And he'd finish strong.

A man came over the loudspeaker, and Gray perked up. He stretched his arms again and rolled his ankles.

He was ready.

This needed to start.

"The traditional gun will go off. Please don't surge forward. Wait until the crowd in front of you starts, and then begin. Your time won't start until you pass the sensor at the starting line, and it concludes at the finish line."

Gray knew all of this, and while he normally didn't run with his cell phone, today, he'd kept his device with him. He pulled it out and took a quick selfie as the announcer finished his directions.

Gray had mere seconds to get the picture sent, and he quickly tapped and added it to the group text. He wished he had time to tell Elise how much he loved her, and Hunter that he was so glad the boy was his son.

Instead, they got a picture of him at the starting line of the Boston Marathon.

The gun went off, and Gray's pulse bounced into the back of his throat. He was ready to go.

He was in the first third of the crowd, and he could wait until the sea thinned if he wanted. But he didn't want to. He took a moment to tuck the phone in the waistband of his running shorts and zipped it in securely against his back.

Up ahead, he saw people start to move, and Gray bounced one last time on his toes, and then he started moving.

He didn't go very fast, because he wasn't to the starting line yet. He could use this couple hundred yards or so to find his breath and stretch his muscles one final time.

He never came exploding out of the gate anyway. This wasn't a sprint.

He caught sight of the starting line up ahead, and he increased his speed. By the time he crossed it, he was moving at his top speed for the first five miles.

Hunter had said they'd get a spot along the lines near the beginning, so they'd know he was there. Elise had done that in Denver, and Gray had really appreciated it. Her presence early in the race had impacted him more than he'd known, and he'd asked his family to do the same here.

The cheering on the sidelines nearly deafened him in the beginning, as did the rush of his own adrenaline.

Then the first mile ended, and the second was easier,

faster, and quieter. Gray sometimes ran with headphones in, and plenty of other people were.

Today, Gray wanted to experience everything around him. The city. The route. The smells.

Mile two ended, and Gray checked his watch. He was moving fast, and it felt so good. So easy. So natural.

He didn't think about his feet, or his legs, or the fact that by the end of the year, he'd be a father for the second time.

He just existed in this moment, and then the next, everything he'd been training inside his body working together seamlessly.

"Dad!"

Gray heard Hunter's voice, because it was ingrained in his soul. He thought he'd probably be able to hear it across great distances if Hunter cried out to him.

He looked right and down the line a bit, and he saw Hunter jumping up and down with the sign he'd made. And then the noise of his brothers hit his eardrums, and Gray grinned at them, moving from the center of the route toward the side.

Cy whistled between his teeth, a shrill noise that made Gray's heart take flight. Wes whooped and clapped, and Colton's voice seemed to be made of thunder. Ames yelled his name over and over, and Gray started laughing.

He held out his hand, and several strangers slapped five with him as he went by. He just wanted to touch his wife.

Elise stood at the far end of the row, her face alight with joy as she cheered for him too. He couldn't hear her voice above his brothers, because they were *so loud*. But it didn't matter. Elise's support existed way down deep in his soul.

His family leaned over the barrier to give him five, and Gray took strength from each of them as he raced by.

He wouldn't slow down for them, because he had an amazing stride going right now, and he was *running in the Boston Marathon*.

A zing shot down his arm as Elise's fingers touched his for a fraction of a second, and then Gray was past them.

That high kept him running faster than normal until mile six, and then Gray forced himself to slow down. He couldn't run a half-marathon at a pace of six-fifteen per mile and expect to be able to finish at all. He'd been running long enough to know what worked for him over twenty-six miles.

He ran, and ran, and ran, not really noticing anyone else around him. He passed a lot of people, including a mother pushing three children in a triple stroller.

He appreciated the atmosphere and camaraderie of the people on the course with him, and their effort spurred him to keep going through ten miles, and then twelve.

A van came up beside him, and Gray ignored it. The media vans had been all over the course, and they mostly stayed out of the way. This one moved in front of him and seemed to match his pace.

The back doors opened, and a cameraman knelt there, recording him. Gray wondered if they had isolated him because he was fairly alone on the course right now.

"Wave to your mother," another guy in the van yelled, and Gray did, a huge smile on his face. He wouldn't put it past his father to know someone he could call to make sure Gray got filmed during the marathon.

He kept his pace in a medium range, and he caught up to the van as it slowed. Another camera recorded him through the side door, and a woman clung to a handle and pressed into the back of the passenger seat.

"Here we have Gray Hammond, who's forty-three years old. He took third in the Colfax Marathon last year in Denver to qualify for Boston, and he's our current forty-to-forty-five age range leader."

Gray really wanted to turn toward the reporter and ask her if she was kidding. That couldn't be right. She just meant he was the leader right now, because the other forty-to-forty-five year olds had started behind him. They'd surely end with a faster time.

It didn't matter. He was on TV, and surely his mother would get to see him.

Eventually, the van slowed, and Gray let it fall behind. He made it through the hardest miles of the race, and he let himself go as fast as his body wanted to and could go.

The finish line was almost near when the noise level increased, and Gray couldn't believe he'd done this.

This was one of his major bucket list items, and *he'd done it*.

"You did it, Gray!"

"Good job, Dad!"

"Run fast, Gray!"

He loved that one the best, because that was Elise's voice, and she'd said that in Colfax.

He ran hard across the finish line, and only then did he

start to slow and allow his body to tell him he needed to stop now.

He did, sucking at the air and reaching for his phone in that back pocket. He unzipped it, but it didn't matter. His family knew how to find him, and several minutes later, after he'd downed several gulps of Gatorade and found his normal breathing, he heard Colton call his name.

He turned toward the sound, and the group of them engulfed him. They ended up all laughing, and Gray found the one person who always reminded him who he was and who he wanted to be.

Elise.

"You did it, baby," she said, grinning up at him.

"Thanks for coming," he said to her, bending down to give her a quick kiss.

"You were on the big screen," Hunter said, turning his phone toward Gray. "I got it on video. Look, it has your name at the bottom and everything."

Gray took the phone and watched the clip, in complete disbelief. "This is awesome."

"Mom's called three times," Wes said. "You better call her as soon as you feel like you can."

"All right," Gray said. "But I have to eat."

"We've got a reservation at Steakson's," Ames said. "In thirty minutes."

"Let's get going then," Gray said. "I'll call Mom later." He handed Hunter's phone back to him.

"Do you think you'll be the leader in your age group?" Cy asked.

"No way," Gray said. "I just happened to start in the first third of the race."

"I think you'll be wrong about that," Wes said. "And I really like it when you're wrong."

"Well, I turned in my sensy-thing, so I can find out once it's all recorded."

"Doesn't that drive you nuts?" Colton asked. "Not knowing."

"Not really," Gray said, shrugging. "I ran fast today. It felt great. I know I did well. Where I place doesn't matter after that."

"Oh, boy," Cy said, rolling his eyes. "Thanks, *Dad*."

"Yeah, can you keep the lectures to a minimum while we're on vacation?" Wes teased.

"Vacation?" Gray practically roared. "I just ran twenty-six miles. Someone else is buying my dinner."

"By choice," Ames said, joining into the ribbing. "You ran that far *by choice*. We're just not as crazy as you are."

"Okay," Gray said. "Okay." He laughed again, because while running was a solitary event, he sure did like having his loved ones here with him once he finished.

He met Cy's eye, and something passed between them. Cy put on a good front, and Gray recognized it because he'd spent a lot of time doing the same thing. Something was going on there, and Gray determined he'd ask his brother when they were alone, or when he could text him singly.

Then he'd get the real story about what was going on in Coral Canyon, with Cy's new shop, his new house, and his new girlfriend.

CHAPTER 22

"Okay, close your eyes and turn around." Patsy grinned at him when Cy looked up from the computer screen. He drank in the womanly shape of her, the curve of her hips in those sexy jeans, the extra height she gained from her heeled sandals, and that short-sleeved sweater with rainbow stripes.

"Look at you," he said, standing. He wanted to look and touch.

"I mean it, Cy," she said in a stern voice. "It's your birthday, and you can't see what I have planned."

"You sure?" He swept her into his arms, and she giggled as he growled. "I want my birthday kiss."

She tipped her head back and kissed him, and Cy didn't care what the rest of the day brought. With Patsy, he was complete.

"Okay," she said. "But seriously, Cy. I didn't get up at the crack of dawn to kiss you."

"No? Too bad." He touched his mouth to hers again. "How'd you know I'd be here?"

"Because the house is almost done," she said, giggling and dancing away from him. "Now, come on. I have a blindfold, and I'm not taking no for an answer."

Cy's blood ran hot, but he didn't say what was on his mind, as it probably wasn't appropriate. "You should've been this assertive with your sister," he said.

"I was," Patsy said. "That's why the orchard is passing to me in ten days."

Cy was just about to close his eyes, but he stalled. "Patsy," he said slowly. "What are you saying?"

"She gave in." Patsy squealed, and Cy swept her right off her feet as laughter pulled through his lungs and chest.

"You're kidding," he said among the chuckles. "That's so great, sweetheart."

Patsy had been trying to get the ownership of the orchard given to her, and it had been a long month since she'd sat down with her father to show him her sister's mishandling. She hadn't wanted to hurt Betty, but she didn't want to lose what her ancestors had invested their entire lives in.

Patsy exuded pure joy, and Cy simply basked in it. He set her on her feet and gazed at her. "You're amazing, you know that?"

"You should reserve judgment on that until this day ends." She grinned up at him. "Now, close your eyes and turn around so I can put this thing on."

"Yes, ma'am." Cy did what she asked, and while he didn't normally come over to the shop this early, Patsy had been right. He'd come early because the painters had shown up at the house where he'd been squatting. His house, but he wasn't supposed to be living in it quite yet.

He still had the rental, and he could've slept there. He simply wanted to be in his house, and Cy sort of did what he wanted, when he wanted to do it.

"Okay," Patsy said, tying a tight knot in the blindfold at the back of his head. "Let's go. You hold onto my hand, and I'll get you where you need to go."

"Okay," he said, taking one tentative step. He trusted Patsy, but it was still hard to walk when he couldn't see. Painstaking step by painstaking step, she led him to her car, and then she drove him somewhere. It didn't take very long, so they had to be somewhere nearby, and when she let him out of the car, it still smelled like pine trees.

Up six steps, and through a door, and the scent of maple syrup met his nose. He started to chuckle at the same time his mind started telling him he did not deserve this woman.

"Surprise," she said, sweeping the blindfold off. "You said if your last meal was going to be breakfast, you'd want Belgian waffles with sausage."

A plate of sausage sat on the counter, and she quickly rounded it. "I'll have waffles ready in five minutes. You sit."

"Patsy," he said, still in wonder at the kindness of her heart.

"Sit," she said, smiling. "It's your birthday, Cy. You get whatever you want today."

He didn't sit but went to stand beside her. "Whatever I want?" He leaned down and pressed a kiss to her neck.

"Behave yourself," she whispered, but there was absolutely no power behind her words.

He chuckled and simply kissed her again. "I got you something for my birthday," he whispered.

"Cy," she said. "That's not how birthdays work."

"It is when you're me," he said.

She shook her head, and he couldn't tell if she was really upset or just trying to focus on the waffle batter.

Cy decided to do what she said and behave himself and sit at the bar. A minute later, she served him a toasty, brown Belgian waffle, and he smothered it in butter and syrup. "There's just a couple of things I want," he said.

"I know," Patsy said. "I've got all the meals planned for today, so don't ruin them for me." She grinned at him and cut into her own waffle. "And you're going to get your dance tonight."

He grinned at her. "Thank you, Patsy."

"I have another gift for you too," she said. "At your house. You'll get it when you go home tonight."

He nodded and stuck another bite of everything in his mouth. The waffle, the syrup, the sausage…it was a bite of heaven on a fork. After he chewed and swallowed, he asked, "When can I give you my gift?"

"Where is it?"

"The shop."

"Dinner is at the shop," she said.

"Dinner is at the shop?" He lifted his eyebrows. "I didn't see that on my schedule."

"Marissa knows," Patsy said with a smile. "I arranged the whole day with her. She won't call you unless the building catches on fire or someone dies."

Cy burst out laughing again, and he realized what that meant. He got to spend the whole day with Patsy, the woman he was falling in love with. Or maybe he was already in love with her. He wasn't sure.

They'd talked about going slow in their relationship, which was just fine for Cy. He was still working out some of his mental issues, and he hadn't yet gone to see anyone or get any medication.

At the beginning of April, after the grand reopening, Ames had stayed with Cy for a night, and he'd expressed his concerns. Again. Cy appreciated them, he did. He loved his twin, he did.

But no one knew how he was feeling. No one but him, and he thought he was handling things okay. The shop had experienced a few bumps in the past couple of months, but they'd worked out the kinks. Cy hadn't even been a beast —at least he didn't think he had.

"Okay," Patsy said once they'd finished eating. "Grab your wallet and your hat, cowboy, because we're going horseback riding and then to a movie.'

"A movie?"

"In the middle of the day," Patsy said, her voice filled with glee.

Cy swept one arm around her, the golden glow of happiness filling him. He loved this feeling, and he hoped he could hold onto it for a very long time. "Which movie?"

"Like that matters," she said, repeating a conversation

they'd once had. "I seem to remember you telling me it didn't matter what movie it was. It was a movie *in the middle of the day*." She giggled, and Cy drank in the sound of it.

"Plus," she added. "Your second meal of the day? A burger and fries from Down Under. They're delivering to the theater for me. You're welcome." She seemed proud of herself, and she should be.

"You're amazing, Patsy," he said, staying serious.

"Thank you, Cy," she said. "I know how to organize stuff."

He picked up his wallet and reached for his cowboy hat. Once that was settled on his head, he said, "All right, little lady. Lead me to the horses."

"We're going to the orchard to ride," she said. "And I'll tell you all about how things went down with Betty and Joe."

"Can't wait," Cy said, and he honestly couldn't. Whatever was important to Patsy was important to him. In that moment, as he followed her out of the rental house, he knew he'd fallen in love with her.

Gray had asked him about his relationship with Patsy, and Cy had been honest. It had been going well, and he and Gray had texted quite a lot about getting married for a second time.

Cy needed to ask him how he'd known he was ready for that next I-do. How had Gray handled it? Maybe if he had a plan, Cy wouldn't be so nervous about telling Patsy how he really felt. And when should he do that?

Not today, he told himself. If he told her today, and

things ultimately didn't work out with her, his birthday would forever be tainted. And he'd rather not be reminded of that every time he blew out birthday candles.

———

HE GOT HIS BURGER AND FRIES, AND PATSY HAD RENTED AN entire theater just for them. They got the top row, reclining seats, with their food, and one of Cy's favorite movies—*The Three Amigos.*

He couldn't believe she'd arranged all of that. He couldn't believe she could remember all of the little details he'd told her about himself over the past handful of months. He couldn't believe he'd somehow hoodwinked her into thinking he deserved her.

His thoughts spiraled on the way to the shop, and he tried to calm them. Keep them in order. Slow them down. He was definitely quieter on the way out of town, but Patsy didn't press him to talk.

She hummed along with the radio, both hands on the wheel, and Cy closed his eyes and had a silent argument with himself and the Lord. *Is this the right thing to do? She doesn't deserve to be with someone like me.*

Why not you?

Because of this exact thing.

He should be happy on his birthday. He shouldn't be so high one moment and so low the next. He hated the self-doubt, and with that came the self-loathing.

Tell me if it's not right, he prayed. *Just tell me. I can handle it. I don't want to hurt her.*

"Cy?"

He opened his eyes and looked at her. The golden rays of sunshine slanting through the window haloed her from behind, and he didn't want to give her up. It would be very, very hard to do, and Cy wasn't sure he had the guts to do it, even if God told him to.

"Hmm?"

"We're here. Do you want to go in?"

He looked at the shop, instant love for it filling him. The architect had done a great job on this building, and his grand reopening had been published online all over the country as Wyatt Walker had quite the reach. He apparently hadn't done any events since his line of western wear had come out. He'd done one initial tour and retired to Three Rivers, where he lived with his wife and children.

The grand reopening had been his first public appearance in over four years, and Cy was so, so grateful the man had come to Wyoming to talk to him in front of a crowd for ten minutes. He had vets applying from all over the country, and he'd booked out through October for custom builds within a week after the opening.

Things had started off with a bang, and the well of gratitude inside Cy kept getting deeper and deeper.

"Yeah," he said with a sigh. He met Patsy at the front of her car and took her hand in his. He lifted it to his lips, and said, "I'm grateful for you, Patsy. You know that, right?"

"Yeah," she said. "I know that." She smiled at him and added, "You know I did all of this for your birthday because I really like you, right?"

"Yeah," he said, though he was still struggling to

believe her. "I know that." He stepped up to the showroom door and opened it, his excitement growing. The showroom was open until seven, so the salesmen and receptionists there still had a few hours to work. "Come on to the back," he said. "And I'll show you what I got for you."

"I'm still not happy you got me something," she said.

Cy didn't respond, because what was he supposed to say? He had an astronomical amount of money. He'd paid for the building and his house with cash, after paying for the land with cash too. He could afford to get her whatever she wanted—and whatever he wanted.

He didn't take her too far into the back of the shop, where the motorcycles were built and repaired. He turned right down the first hall and went to the first private meeting room. A back hall went along the other side of these rooms, and that way, the motorcycles they built for people could be wheeled in and shown to their paying customers.

The only difference here was that Patsy wasn't paying. Cy was gifting.

He opened the door and flipped on the lights, and her motorcycle sat there, the chrome glinting and the leather seat calling to him to touch it. "Ta-da," he said in a falsely happy voice.

She stalled right inside the door and gasped. "Cy." She covered her mouth with both hands and gaped with wide eyes at the motorcycle. It was perfect for someone her size —a ladies model with a wider base and a wider seat for easier handling. He'd painted it yellow, because that was her favorite color, and he'd put the classic stitched leather seat cover on it. Classic handlebars, and a low-profile tire for a tricked-out look. That was the only thing he'd done to amp up her bike.

"It's the perfect size for you," he said. "I used your height to get it just right. It's yellow and black, and I even ordered you a helmet custom-made." He took a step toward the motorcycle. "It's warm enough now, Pats. You can learn to ride right here in the parking lot at the shop. I'll teach you."

He beamed at her, because this was what she wanted. He continued toward the machine, admiring it, and picked up the helmet which McCall had laid on the seat. "It matches. And look, it's got the texture of a sweater, because you love sweaters so much."

He held it out to her as if she couldn't see the helmet, but she made no move to take it. His pulse crashed inside his chest, sending out so many beats, they reverberated against each other.

"I can't, she said, lowering her hands.

"It's a gift."

"No," she practically barked. "I'm not taking it." And with that, she spun on her heel and marched out of the room and down the hall, leaving Cy alone in the private showroom, holding her helmet and wondering what in the world he'd done wrong.

CHAPTER 23

Patsy actually picked up her step every second or third one and jogged, spring truly present in Coral Canyon. The orchard smelled like flowers, and they had a real apple scent. She loved the orchard year-round, and signing the paperwork that put her name on it had been literally the highlight of her life.

She'd had everything in that moment. The orchard she loved. A man she was falling for more and more with every text he sent, every call of Cy's she took, every date he took her on.

"But not this," she told herself.

"Patsy." His voice filled the sky around her, but she didn't stop. She'd arranged for dinner at the shop, and if she could check her phone, she guessed it would be close to time for it to be delivered.

She wasn't sure where she was going. Her car was parked over by Cy's house, because he'd wanted to show it to her. He'd said it was almost finished, and she hadn't seen it with all the finishes—the paint, the appliances, or furniture.

The road through the apple trees loomed in front of her, and Cy's footsteps were running behind her. Patsy took a deep breath, her heart and mind racing. She couldn't outrun him. All of those Hammond men were so dang athletic.

Gray had literally won his age group in the most prestigious marathon on the planet, and the man was forty-three-years-old.

"Patsy," Cy said coming up beside her. He didn't touch her, and Patsy's skin itched. She glanced over at him, and he wore anxiety in his eyes, shoulders, and the set of his mouth. That got her to slow down, and a slip of rational thought filled her mind.

She took another couple of steps, forcing herself to slow down further. Cy adjusted his stride with her, and Patsy paused in the shade of a large apple tree. Cy said nothing, and Patsy knew she needed to explain. She didn't know how.

She faced Cy, and he only looked at her for a moment before dropping his chin. "You don't like the motorcycle."

"I do," she said, and that only confused her more. She didn't just like the motorcycle. She *loved* the motorcycle— but not for what it physically was. But what it represented.

Cy knew her favorite colors. He knew her favorite things. He'd made her a custom bike that would fit her height, and make it easy for her to handle, and she couldn't even imagine riding the motorcycle around town.

She'd feel like a complete Rockstar, and she wondered if Cy felt like that when he rode.

"I do like the motorcycle," she said. "But I can't accept it."

"Why not?"

"It's *your* birthday." She hoped that would be a strong enough answer, but Cy wasn't stupid just because he dealt with a little bit of anxiety. Sure enough, a sharp edge entered his beautiful eyes, and Patsy wanted to reach up and cradle his face, tell him how much she really, *really* liked him, and that if he could just give her a pass on this one, she'd make everything okay between them again.

"Patsy," he said, his voice almost a whisper. He was begging her to just tell him, and Patsy reached down deep into herself, imagining her strength to come from the roots of the trees that surrounded them.

"I had a boyfriend once," she said. "His name was Cody, and he was a real loser."

"I think we've established that all of your boyfriends have been losers."

"All of them?"

"Well, until now," he said with a smile. "Though I'm not perfect, Patsy. I'm—"

"I know who you are," Patsy interrupted. He'd worried so much about his weaknesses that she wondered if he even saw his strengths. "Cody didn't have a job, and yet he was always buying me gifts. Then he'd ask me for money, or when the check came for dinner, he wouldn't reach for it. Once, we sat there for another forty-five minutes while I waited to see if he'd pay. He didn't."

Cy just watched her, his hands tucked into the pockets of his jeans.

Patsy's feet hurt, and she shifted her weight. "For my birthday, he bought me a horse. A very expensive horse. A ten-thousand dollar horse."

"Wow," Cy said.

"And I know you've said like, a thousand times, that horses and motorcycles aren't the same, but in there, it felt the same." She gestured back toward the shop, surprised at how far she'd managed to get from the front doors. "I don't want expensive gifts. They make me feel…stupid." She nodded, done talking now.

Cy's eyes sparkled, but at least he took a few seconds to absorb what she'd said. "I get our names start with the same letter," he said. "But I'm nothing like Cody. I have a job. I own a business. I have so much money, I could literally buy you anything you wanted—every day, all day— for years and still have money left over."

"I know." Patsy heaved a big breath and blew it out slowly. "I know that, Cy. It's not about the money."

"You don't want your boyfriend to buy you gifts?"

Patsy heard how unreasonable that was. She did. And yet, the feeling still ran through her veins with the speed and strength of sound. "It just…it's too much."

"I've paid for dinner lots of times."

She nodded, and that gave Cy momentum. "I've paid for entertainment. Movie tickets and tours and all of that."

"I know," she said. "But there's a big difference between a plate of pasta and a custom-made motorcycle."

"But that's the thing, Patsy. Not to me."

"I don't even know what to do with that." Patsy turned and looked down the road, and then faced the shop again. She reached for his hand, glad when he let her slip her fingers through his. "The horse from Cody created a ton of tension between us. He had certain expectations after that. If I didn't want to do something, he'd be like, 'good thing I bought a horse for a woman who never rides it,' or 'too bad I got you that horse and you won't let me ride it.'"

Patsy's memories filled and overflowed. "He bought it for me, but he wanted to ride it all the time. He used it almost like this thing he held over my head." Patsy swallowed, her mouth sticky. "He pressured me, and I don't know." Her tongue felt so dry. "I don't want big, elaborate gifts."

They started strolling back toward the shop, and Cy's hand in hers stayed firm. "I don't want to check with you about gifts," he said carefully. "One of the ways I show how I feel is buying and giving presents. It's important to me." He squeezed her hand and tugged on it to get her to stop. "Will you consider accepting them? I don't know what that looks like for you, but I can assure you I didn't design and build that bike for you to make you feel stupid. I was actually hoping it would make you feel—" He stopped talking, his eyes rounding.

"Feel what?" Patsy asked.

The grumble of an engine came toward them, and they both turned to see the white delivery van that contained their dinner coming toward them.

"You ordered from Woodfired?"

"That's right."

"Tell me you didn't get the Calabrese and sausage pizza."

"I can't tell you that." Patsy smiled at him, glad at the joy pouring from him. She knew what his favorites were, and she'd gotten the huge gorgonzola salad too. She didn't understand why anyone would pepper bacon and call it good, but Cy loved it. He loved the halved grapes in the salad, as well as the homemade garlic croutons that were made in the high-heat oven at Woodfired. Patsy disliked moldy cheese, but this wasn't her birthday. Cy loved all of those things, and this meal was just for him

"What about the one with honey?" he asked.

"Who do you think you're dealing with?" She stepped away from him to take the food from the driver, and she took a moment to sign a receipt and thank him, before she turned back to Cy with two boxes of pizza, a smaller one with Woodfired's famous burrata, and the big bowl of salad.

"Are you hungry?" She smiled at him, wishing she could erase the last thirty minutes of her life. Maybe Cy would just forget that she'd run out on him.

"A little," he said. "But I can literally always eat pizza from Woodfired." He took the bowl from the top of the stack. "You got the gorgonzola salad." He looked up at her. "You don't even like this stuff."

"But you do, and it's your birthday meal."

"Should we go eat at the house?"

"Sure," she said. It was quite the hike from the shop to his house, and Cy had bought a golf cart to make the journey. He drove them across the parking lot and onto another road that led to his house, which was bordered by apple trees on three sides. He didn't want to live in a parking lot, and only the back yard butted up against the woods without apple trees. He'd left a strip of them between the house and the shop, and the front yard and west side of the house also highlighted the trees.

"Cy, this is amazing," Patsy said as he led her into the house through the back door. She couldn't even take everything in, and she let her eyes wander around at all the high-end finishes. He had quartz countertops and dark wood cabinets in the kitchen. The floor sported wood as well, to which Cy said, "It's a wood-like tile. That way, I don't have to worry about it getting wet."

He set the salad bowl on the island and turned to take the boxes from her. "I have a couple of stools we can sit on. The dining room table is coming, and I have rugs and curtains and all of that still to do." He swept his hand toward the living area. "So I haven't unwrapped and set up the furniture."

"A stool is fine," Patsy said. "We don't even need plates either." She flipped open one of the boxes, and it was the three-cheese pizza with a sprinkling of red pepper flakes and a drizzle of honey. Her mouth watered, and she slid the top box off the bottom one. "That one's yours."

He smiled, but it didn't stay long. Patsy had broken the mood of this day, and a strong pull of guilt hit her in the stomach. She still moved, taking a piece of pizza from the box and lifting it to her mouth as if nothing was wrong.

She loved this pizza, with its sweet sauce, spicy red pepper, creamy cheese, and the char on that crust. She couldn't even enjoy it tonight, and she ended up only taking two bites before she put her piece back in the box.

"I'm sorry," she said. "I ruined everything."

"No, you didn't," he said, reaching for his second slice of pizza. He loved the homemade pepperoni, sausage, and marinara pizza, and he'd taken the lid off his salad too.

"I did," she said. "I just…don't know how to accept large gifts."

Cy nodded, but Patsy knew he wasn't happy. "I'd love it if you'd try," he said quietly. "I promise I won't ask you to then pay for my dinner."

Patsy smiled, because Cy was trying to lighten the mood, and she appreciated that. "I'll try," she said.

"I can't ask for more than that." He lifted his pizza to his lips and took another bite. After chewing and swallowing, he added, "Thank you for an amazing birthday, Patsy."

A new ray of light entered the kitchen with them. "You liked it?"

"I'd like anything where we get to spend the whole day together." He finished his pizza and stood up, offering her his hand. "Dance with me?" He was still trying to make his birthday about her, and as she smiled and sighed and stood, she realized she was wrong.

He wasn't trying to make his birthday about her; he was trying to *include* her in his birthday.

So she tucked herself into his arms and against his chest and danced with him. She'd gone to several lessons with him by now, and the man was seriously light on his feet.

In the silence, Patsy tried to find a way to go back in time and just thank him for the motorcycle. Of course he wasn't Cody. Not even close.

Cy Hammond was unlike any other man she'd ever dated, and she felt like a fool for comparing him to anyone else.

CHAPTER 24

"You're fully moved in?" Ames asked his twin, glancing over his shoulder as he spooned sugar into his coffee. Cy had arrived in Ivory Peaks late last night, and they'd barely had any time to talk.

"Yeah," Cy said, rubbing his hand down his face. "A couple of weeks ago."

"And Patsy took your cabin?"

"She's going to," he said. "She's moving this weekend. It's been very hard for her to leave the lodge."

"I'll bet." Ames poured his brother a cup of coffee and turned to set it in front of him. He retrieved the sugar bowl, moved it to the island, and proceeded to get the cream out of the fridge. Cy started fixing his coffee the way he liked it, and Ames wondered if he'd have to push his brother to start talking.

"She told me to tell you thanks for coming to help her move."

"Of course," he said. "Her family sounds kind of whack."

"They're okay," Cy said. "Her sister is just busy, and her brother is still dealing with his divorce."

"Everyone has something, don't they?" Ames asked, lifting his mug to his lips.

"Yeah," Cy said, still stirring, stirring, stirring.

"What's going on with you and Patsy?"

"We're good," Cy said, but Ames thought his voice was a bit forced.

"Did she ever take the motorcycle?"

"It's still in the shop," Cy said. "I don't know what to do with it."

"Put it in the garage at your rental," Ames suggested. "She's moving there; she'll have it then."

"I want to teach her how to ride," Cy said. "Like how Elise and Gray run together now. She did that, because she wanted to spend time with him. Patsy said she wanted to learn to ride, and I thought if she had the perfect bike, and I taught her, we could spend the summer riding all the roads in Wyoming." He sighed, and Ames wished he could fix things for his brother.

"But it's almost July now," Cy said, frustration heavy in his voice. "And I'm just riding by myself."

Ames didn't react at all, which usually allowed Cy to keep talking. Today, though, he clammed right back up again.

"Cy," Ames said.

"No," Cy said. "Don't ask me, okay? If I'd done what you want me to do, I'd have told you."

"It's not what *I* want you to do."

"Yes, it is," Cy said. "I'm managing it."

"Okay," Ames said, keeping the doubt out of his tone. "So why'd you come down here? I know the way to Coral Canyon."

"I just needed a break," Cy said. "The shop is super busy right now, and with all the stress of Patsy quitting and packing and moving…I just needed a break." He looked at Ames. "So you're going to show me a good time for the next couple of days. You're not going to hound me about going to see a counselor or if Patsy and I are serious, and we'll have a nice drive back to Wyoming together." He smiled at Ames, who chuckled.

"You got it, bro."

"Thank you," Cy said. "Your turn. Five minutes on what you've been doing on the dating scene."

Ames scoffed, the sound loud and a little sharp in his throat. He took a sip of coffee to try to soothe it. "There is no dating scene."

"None?"

"One, I'm a cop." He held up one finger. "I actually had a woman tell me that was, and I quote, a 'turn-off.'"

"Why's that?"

"She thinks all cops are corrupt." Ames shrugged one shoulder. Some were, he knew that. And it seemed like the bad ones got the biggest headlines.

"What's number two?"

"My last name is Hammond," Ames said. "You realize Dad just donated two hundred million dollars to the research hospital? They're naming an entire wing after us.

Our name is everywhere, and it's been on the news for four solid weeks."

"I'd think that would be good for the dating scene."

"No, what it does is bring out all the women who're looking to get me to the altar without a prenup." Ames rolled his eyes, wishing he could get rid of the memories of the past month. The morning after the news had first broken, Ames had left his house to go to work to find at least thirty women on the sidewalk in front of his house.

The German shepherd he had right now, Daisy, had whined and given one bark, and that had clued Ames in to the crowds. The dog looked over at him right now, as if she knew he was thinking about her.

"Is there a number three?" Cy asked.

"No," Ames said. "Being a cop and a Hammond are bad enough."

"Well, it seems like being a cop—which you say women don't like—would cancel out being a Hammond—which they do."

"I suppose there are women who can live with me being a corrupt, criminal cop if I have a lot of money." He finished his coffee and stood up. "I don't want to talk about this anymore."

"I'm sorry," Cy said. "But I get it. So no talk about me going to counseling or Patsy, and I'm not going to ask you about dating again."

"You've got yourself a deal." Ames stepped over to the drawer beside the refrigerator. "Let's go get breakfast."

"And you've got yourself a deal." Cy stood up, a happy smile on his face. Ames knew his twin could paint that smile over almost anything, any feeling. Ames hated that he didn't just believe Cy's happiness, but he knew the man almost as well as he knew himself.

Ames knew he wasn't happy, and while Cy seemed to be doing well with his shop and hanging in there with his relationship with Patsy, he knew he didn't feel the joy that would counter his misery.

"Is it okay to talk about your job?" Cy asked once they were in Ames's truck. "I heard you were talking to Wyatt Walker about going to Three Rivers. Colton said he told you to come be on the force in Coral Canyon."

Ames didn't answer right away, because he had no idea how to do that. He'd give up seniority in Littleton, and he didn't want to relocate. He felt a strong responsibility to be a Hammond in the Denver area, though his mother and father had both told him to follow his heart.

The problem was, Ames felt like he didn't have one.

"I'm considering a lot of things right now," Ames finally said.

"Why don't you come work for me?" Cy offered. "You don't need to be a police officer. Come run my office, and meet a beautiful woman, and fall madly in love like the rest of us."

Ames opened his mouth to respond, but his mind stalled for a moment. Usually, he balked at the idea of giving up his career in law enforcement. They'd just agreed not to talk about his dating scene.

And….

"Like the rest of us?" Ames asked. "What does that mean? You're in love with Patsy?"

Cy looked out his window, and Ames had seen this tactic before. He also didn't need his brother to answer. He already had.

"How are you—?"

"You agreed not to ask me about her," Cy said coldly.

Ames released the wheel and regripped it. He couldn't just let this go. Cy had been in love before—twice that Ames knew of. Both of those relationships had ended and devastated his brother. Ames had been worried that Cy was headed for a huge fall before, but this only made things worse.

If things didn't end well with Patsy, Ames felt certain the Cy he knew would cease to exist.

He didn't say anything else on the way to breakfast, because he had agreed not to say anything else about Patsy that weekend. He'd do what he'd said he would—show Cy a good time, keep his mouth shut about Patsy, and drive them back to Coral Canyon to help the woman move.

―――――

MONDAY MORNING, AMES WOKE EARLY AS HE USUALLY DID, and he stretched, leashed Daisy, and said, "Let's go see what these trails are that Uncle Wes has been bragging about." He'd take off the leash once they got up in the mountains a little bit, and he'd expect her to stay immediately beside him.

He let his mind wander through the pines and aspens as his feet took him up and up, his breathing growing more labored, and Daisy doing exactly what he wanted her to do. He did love working with the police dogs, and if he quit the force in Littleton, he'd give that up. Neither Three Rivers nor Coral Canyon had K-9 dogs—and yes, Ames had done some research.

Maybe he could buy a piece of land somewhere and get it all landscaped. Build a nice house like Cy had done. Put in a dozen dog runs and start training the pups himself. He could sell them to police departments all over the country once they were ready for service. He knew how to do it. He'd trained at least a dozen dogs in the early stages of their careers, and he had a way with the canines.

He knew them, and they knew him.

"What do you think, Daze?" he asked her, and she looked up at him. He smiled and looked back up the trail. Something buzzed in the air, and Ames slowed his step. Daisy did too, and she hunched down, not quite laying down or sitting, but perching on her haunches, tight, ready to explode if Ames gave the right word.

She whined, and he didn't like that. He held out his palm to keep the dog back, and he stepped in front of her. "Stay, Daisy." He looked up the path again, definitely hearing something cutting through the panting of the shepherd and the sprinting of his pulse in his own ears.

Someone was crying.

"Hello?" he called, but no one answered. "Come on," he said to Daisy. "Slow. Behind." He went up the path first, the dog's hot breath on his heels as they crested the hill.

A woman sat on the bench there, her shoulders slumped as she gazed out over the valley. She lifted both hands to her face and sobbed into them again. Her voice filled the air, but it was too high-pitched, and she was too far away, for Ames to understand what she'd said.

"Ma'am?"

She spun toward him, and Ames froze at the beautiful sight of a familiar face. "Sophia?" he asked, the name thawing him enough to get him moving. He crossed the distance to the bench quickly, taking in her ankles and legs, elbows and arms. She didn't appear to be hurt.

"Are you okay?" He crouched in front of her, still trying to find an injury. In that moment, he realized her wounds weren't on the outside, and a connection formed between them as she looked at him with tears clinging to her eyelashes.

CHAPTER 25

Sophia could not believe who had appeared at the top of this hill. Of course, it had to be Ames Hammond. Hadn't she embarrassed herself enough in front of this man? Why couldn't the Lord just give her a break?

One little break, she thought. *Would that be so hard to do?*

She'd been praying for comfort for the past couple of months. When Patsy had first told her that she was going to try to get control of her family's orchard, Sophia's first reaction had been to pray that she wouldn't be able to.

She never had been able to bring herself to do it, though. She loved Patsy, and she wanted her to be happy. Since her sister had finally agreed to sign over the orchard, Sophia had known Patsy would leave the lodge.

It had taken longer than either of them had thought, and Sophia should've been ready. She should've been prepared to put on a brave face, help her best friend pack, and then help her carry the boxes into her new place.

Instead, Sophia had gotten up before Patsy, dressed quickly, and left Whiskey Mountain Lodge so she didn't have to face the fact that she'd be sleeping in the cabin alone that night.

Patsy had called, and Sophia had told her she'd be back in a little bit. That she'd just wanted to get in a hike that morning. Then she'd completely broken down right here on this bench, where Ames had found her.

"Sophia?" He'd asked her something, but Sophia couldn't remember what.

"What are you doing here?" she asked, reaching up to wipe her eyes. She hadn't put on makeup that morning, and she wasn't sure if she was happy about that now or not. Scratch that—she was glad she hadn't. She wasn't going to be the next sucker to fall for a Hammond cowboy.

In fact, this Hammond brother didn't even wear a cowboy hat. He was a cop, and her pulse jumped. Cops weren't regular humans, she knew that. They saw things other people didn't. Heard little inflections in someone's voice.

"I'm here to help Patsy move," he said. "Oh."

He knew already. Humiliation ran through Sophia like fast-moving water, and she needed to get away from this man. Now.

"I have to go." She exploded to her feet, causing Ames to fall backward. She didn't care, because everything was moving so fast now. She walked away while he said something to his dog, who went to his side though the German shepherd looked like she wanted to go with Sophia.

She started down the trail and back to the lodge, because she couldn't spend the day crying in the hills.

She could put on a brave face and a bright smile for her best friend. She could, and she would. She would not make this day harder for Patsy, though she had literally labeled all of her boxes already. Patsy didn't do anything without lists, labels, binders, and plans. It would probably be the easiest move in the history of moving, all thanks to Patsy's extreme organizational skills.

Graham Whittaker had hired a new manager for the lodge, and she'd moved in with the new event coordinator. Julianne and Melinda lived in the cabin where Elise and Bree had once lodged, and Sophia really would be living alone for the foreseeable future.

Instead of hiring a full-time groundskeeper, Eli had contracted with a company to come up and take care of the lawn in the summer and the snow removal in the winter. Sophia felt like her family was being disbanded one member at a time, and she didn't know how to stop it.

"Sophia," Ames said behind her, but Sophia couldn't get herself to slow down or stop. And turning around was out of the question.

"Daisy, stay," he said, and the dog whined. She could hear him walking and breathing behind her, and she wished he'd go away. But it was a public trail, and she couldn't demand he leave her alone. He wasn't doing anything wrong by hiking on the same hill as her.

She hated that she'd thought more about this man than she cared to admit. She never had gotten his phone number after the grand reopening of Cy's shop, because she'd slipped out of Gray Hammond's house before the meal had ended.

It had been a long three months of imagining what Ames might be doing in Colorado, and wondering why she thought about him so much. She'd already made the decision not to fall for the last Hammond standing. So why did her heart wail at her to slow down and let him come to her side? Why did the idea of asking for his number stick in her mind?

She wouldn't do it. Not again.

"I didn't know we were so close to the lodge," Ames said as the building came into view.

Sophia paused for a moment, because it was a beautiful sight. She often went up into the hills south of Whiskey Mountain Lodge, because all of the tourists went west, closer to the Tetons. Their guides had routes for everything from horseback riding to the family hike, and those all went into the forests and woods to the west.

The southern woods had become a sanctuary for Sophia—at least until now.

"You probably parked at the Pine Valley trailhead," she said as Ames came to her side.

"That's right," he said. "Is it far from here?"

"Yeah, you went over the rise. It's probably two miles to the summit. Half a mile down here."

"Two miles?"

"At least," she said. "You didn't realize you'd been hiking for two miles?"

Ames frowned at the lodge, parking lot, and grounds below. "I have a lot on my mind."

"Join the club," Sophia muttered.

Ames looked at her, but she refused to meet his eyes. They were deep and dark, she knew. She knew the shape of his jaw without looking, and she knew what she wanted to have come out of his mouth just before he kissed her.

She shook her head slightly. She'd definitely gone insane by even *allowing* herself to think about kissing this man.

Ames's phone rang, and he grumbled under his breath something about Cy. "Yeah," he said. "I know, I just didn't realize what time it was." Pause. Breath. "No, I have my truck. I'll be there. Fifteen minutes…yes…okay." He hung up without saying goodbye, and Sophia's skin tingled.

"I don't suppose you could give me a ride over to the Pine Valley trailhead? I may or may not have just told Cy I'd meet him here at the lodge in fifteen minutes."

Sophia looked at Ames then, and this man was so dangerous to her health. He wore a half-hooded glare and a half-hopeful glint in those eyes she had so well memorized.

"Even if we ran down to my car, you won't get there and back in fifteen minutes."

"Faster than if I try to hike two and a half miles back and then drive over."

"True." She looked back down to the parking lot, picking out her white SUV. She already knew she was going to say yes. So why couldn't she say it?

"I'll go ask someone at the lodge," he said, stepping past her. "Come on, Daisy."

Sophia watched them take a few steps away, and panic struck her in the chest. "Wait," she blurted.

Ames spun and came right back toward her, his expression definitely angry now. "I'm sorry I didn't give you my number a few months ago." He stopped in front of her. "Okay? I was going to, and then you left before I could, and I felt stupid telling Cy about it, and having him give it to Patsy to give to you." He sucked in a breath. "Okay?"

"Okay," she said, because that was what one said when asked such an aggressive question.

"Okay." He held her gaze for another moment, and then he turned back to the lodge. "I'm already going to be late."

Sophia wasn't sure if he was talking to her or not. She took a step forward, because if Cy would be at the lodge in fifteen minutes, that meant the move was about to happen. She'd be late by driving Ames too, and she really didn't want to disappoint Patsy.

Ames turned around again, something fierce on his face. He met her eye and said, "We're already going to be a little late."

"Yes," she said, though he hadn't phrased it as a question.

Without another word, he lifted his hand and slid it along the side of her neck to the back of her head. Sparks turned into fireworks in the space of two seconds, and as Ames pressed right into her personal space, Sophia's muscles burned as her pulse misfired.

He held her captive, and he probably didn't even know it.

He leaned down, and the next thing Sophia knew, Ames was kissing her.

Oh, wow.

She relaxed—melted, really—into his arms and kissed him back.

He pulled away after only a few seconds—not nearly long enough in Sophia's opinion, and asked, "Would you go to dinner with me tonight?"

"Mm," was the only thing Sophia could come up with, and Ames chuckled as he slid his hand away from her.

"I'm going to take that as a yes," he said, his voice throaty and deep. "And we really better go, because my twin is grumpy when people are late."

She followed him down the rest of the path at a near jog, and she didn't even mind, though she hated running. His kiss had filled her with energy, and she definitely needed something to burn it off.

CHAPTER 26

P atsy oversaw the removal of her things, as cowboy after cowboy came into the cabin, picked up a box or a belonging, and took it out to one of the remaining trucks. Moving was always such an ordeal. A great big mess.

Patsy hated messes, though she felt like her life had become one in the past month or so. Since Cy's birthday, things between them hadn't been the same. He'd disappeared into his shop and his house, and Patsy had realized how easy it was for him to do that. She'd been so busy working at the lodge, trying to train the new manager, as well as taking over the orchard simultaneously. She'd let Cy slip away, because she was so busy.

He'd gone to Colorado for a few days to visit his family, and he'd brought his twin to help her move.

Every time she looked at Ames, she had a flash of regret. She'd wanted to go back to Cy's shop and get the motorcycle he'd built for her. She did. She just didn't know how to bring it up. She'd honestly expected Cy to, as he'd never really held back with how he felt. He was brave and courageous and just said what was on his mind.

She'd given him the job of making sure everything coming out of the cabin would fit on one of the trucks. The last thing either of them wanted was to make more than one trip down the canyon. Everything had to go in one load, which was why Patsy had arranged for four pickup trucks—including Cy's and Ames's.

"How's it looking out there?" she asked Beau as he came inside.

"Good," he said. "You don't have that much stuff, Patsy." He flashed her a smile and picked up the last of the boxed kitchenware she was taking with her. Since her father still lived in the home surrounded by the orchard, Patsy was taking over Cy's rental. It was conveniently located only a ten-minute drive from her father's house, as well as the shop and Cy's new home.

She'd helped him move everything of his from the rental to his house once it had been finished and passed inspection. He'd had some trouble with the roof that had delayed him a week or two, but he'd been in the house for two weeks now. He'd promised her the rental was clean and ready for her, and she didn't doubt him.

With the last of the boxes gone, Patsy started instructing everyone who came through the door to take something else. "That recliner," she told Eli and Graham. "And Todd, I have a nightstand and a lamp in the bedroom."

"You got it," he said, moving that way.

Patsy tried not to look at Sophia, who stood out of the way in the kitchen. A lot of the stuff here belonged to the Whittaker brothers, as they'd provided the cabin for those working at the lodge. Even if Sophia moved out, she wouldn't take the dining room table, or either of the couches in the living room. But Patsy had brought a few things for herself.

She didn't own a bed, but the rental had one, and Cy said it was fairly comfortable. Nerves ran through Patsy, because she'd be in a new place that evening. By herself. She wasn't scared to live alone; she just didn't like it.

"What else?" Ames asked as he came in and she didn't see him.

"Oh, uh, I have a folding table in the hallway there," she said. "And the stand mixer in the kitchen."

"I'll take that," Sophia said, turning to lift the light blue appliance. She tracked Ames as he took the few steps to the table in the hallway, and the two of them left together.

Todd came out of the bedroom with the only furniture she'd take from there, and Patsy quickly swiped on her phone to check her list. "Oh, the rocking chair."

She couldn't believe they were to the outdoor items already, but she supposed having eight strong men to do the work made it go fast. She stepped out onto the front porch, deliberately not allowing herself to turn back to the interior of the cabin.

She'd lived here for four years, and she'd enjoyed it. She could come visit Sophia any time she wanted. Even as she rationalized her feelings—something she'd been doing for a month now—Patsy knew she wouldn't.

She'd throw herself into the orchard management, because that was what Patsy did. She seized onto something and *did it*, no matter the cost. The orchard needed a lot of work, and it was the height of the summer—the perfect time to get them up to speed and producing the best and biggest crop possible. She could improve next year, as she'd missed some key spring months while Betty fought with her over everything.

In the end, her sister had relented. Joe had practically disappeared, and Patsy wondered if her father had intervened with Betty. Someone had. Perhaps her husband.

"The rocking chair," she told Eli as he came up the steps. "And I have a bicycle, and that's it."

"That's it?" Graham asked from the bottom of the steps. He removed his cowboy hat and wiped the sweat along his forehead. "This is easy, Patsy."

"I told you it would be fast."

"Are you sure you have to go?" Graham looked up at her, and he was dead serious.

She smiled as she went down the steps to the sidewalk. "I'm sure."

"Yeah, I know." Graham sighed as he looked back toward the lodge. "Thank you for everything you've done for this place. For our family." He embraced her, and Patsy felt like she was hugging her son, though Graham was far older than her.

"Thanks for taking a chance on me," she said.

"No chance," Graham said. "I knew the moment I met you that you'd be great here."

"Well, thank you." She stepped back and brushed her

hair out of her eyes, suddenly unable to look at the man who *had* taken a chance on her—a twenty-seven-year-old with no experience in the hospitality industry. With hardly any management experience at all.

"Come up any time," Graham said. "Definitely for the holidays, and Sunday lunches, and all of it."

"I'll definitely take you up on that." Patsy faced the walk to the parking lot, several more people coming back their way. "We got it all, guys," she said, because she could wheel her bicycle out to a truck. She went around the side of the cabin to get it, and she did walk beside it as she headed toward the pickups that had backed up to the curb.

"Thanks," she told everyone as she passed them.

"We'll miss you, Patsy," Beau said.

"Don't be a stranger," Eli said.

"Thank you, Patsy," Andrew said.

She smiled and nodded as she acknowledged what they'd said. She'd miss them too, and while it had taken her a while to settle into the Whittaker family, she'd definitely felt a part of them in a way she hadn't in her own family.

"Just that?" Cy asked when he turned from the back of the truck where Ames was trying to situate the rocking chair.

"This is it," she said brightly. "Not too bad, right?" She surveyed the other trucks, and all four of them had something in them. Two were fairly full of boxes, while the other two held her few pieces of furniture.

"This is nothing," Cy said. "I rented a twenty-foot truck

to empty the storage unit where my stuff was." He smiled at her, but Patsy felt a keen sense of missing.

She missed him fiercely. He wasn't himself—at least not with her. He was hiding something, holding something back, and pretending.

Patsy couldn't blame him. She'd told him she'd try to accept the gifts he wanted to give her, but she'd never said another word about the motorcycle. Maybe now was the right time.

"Let's go," Ames said, jumping down from the tailgate. "Get this unloaded, and we can go grab lunch." He clapped Cy on the shoulder and headed for the driver's seat of his truck.

"Oh, you're going to go to lunch with him?" Patsy asked, her lungs pinching together.

Cy swung his gaze toward her, finally looking at her. They'd been revolving around one another for far too long. Texting and calling, sure. But when they were together physically, it was tense. Barely any eye contact. Stilted conversations about nothing.

Patsy hated all of it.

"No, I said I'd go get you lunch," he said. "So we'll get everything unloaded, and you can start unpacking while Ames and I go to town. We'll bring the food back to your house."

"Perfect," Patsy said. "Thank you, Cy." She hated that she sounded like his boss. So professional. So sterile. "Okay, well, we all know the way?"

"Yep," Graham said, jangling his keys.

"I'll follow him," Beau said. Cy was the other driver,

and he obviously knew the way to the house he'd once lived in.

Patsy nodded and turned to get to her own car. Her heartbeat thrashed in her chest, because she was leaving Whiskey Mountain Lodge. She'd loved this place, and she cast another look at the rustic, yet beautiful building. It was made of logs and perfect for a mountain getaway. She could see it in the winter, when the yellow squares of light welcomed everyone who dared traverse up the canyon. She could hear the laughter and smell something delicious that Celia had made for their Sabbath celebration.

So many memories streamed through her head, and Patsy wanted to hold onto each one individually and keep it with her always.

As she rounded the front of Ames's truck, she found Sophia lingering near the back bumper of her sedan. "Sophia." Her voice almost cracked, and Patsy held onto it with everything she had.

She hurried into her best friend's arms, and the two of them clutched one another. After several seconds where Patsy lost the battle with her emotions, Sophia said, "I'm going to miss you so much."

"I know," she whispered. "I'll miss you too."

Sophia stepped back her eyes filled with unshed tears. "I'm going to have to call you every night to talk to you about stuff here," she said. "I love this job, but things are crazy sometimes."

"Oh, I know." Patsy smiled at her and brushed at her own eyes. "Trust me, I'm going to be texting you daily vents about my sister and whatever new disaster I find around the orchard that day."

"I can't wait." Sophia half-laughed, but to Patsy's ears, it was mostly a sob. She hugged her again and made another promise to call her later. Then she got behind the wheel of her car and drove out of the parking lot, her shoulders square and her head held high.

She wasn't the first to arrive at the house, and the rocking chair sat on the front porch when she pulled up to the house. The three trucks already there had backed into the driveway, and there wasn't room for her.

She got out and hurried across the lawn to unlock the front door, and since she'd labeled every box with what room it went in, all she had to do from then on was point and say, "My bedroom," or "the bathroom," or "that one goes in the kitchen."

Another thirty minutes later, and everyone left again—even Cy and Ames.

A sense of being wrung out moved through Patsy, and she sighed as she closed the door and faced the house. The living room took up the front half of where she stood, and lots of natural light poured in from the two walls of windows. A hallway veered off to her left, and there were two bedrooms and a bathroom down that way. It was a much bigger place than the cabin, and she had to take several steps to even cross the living room.

The kitchen took up the back of the house, and her eyes landed on the light blue stand mixer. She barely used it, but it had been a gift from Sophia, and Patsy couldn't leave it behind. She wondered why she could accept the mixer from Sophia—which wasn't cheap—and not the motorcycle from Cy.

She wasn't sure, though she suspected it had something to do with the level of expectations associated with the gift. Cody had held that horse over Patsy's head at every turn, and she'd resented him for it. She'd ended up disliking the horse too, and she'd eventually broken up with Cody and sold the horse he'd bought for her.

She could still remember sneaking up to his front door and leaving an envelope of cash from the sale. No note. No nothing. He'd never responded to let her know he'd gotten it or appreciated it.

Patsy blinked her way back to the present and went to move her car into the garage. Cy had used it as a workshop for his welding, but Patsy wanted to park in it. That way, when it rained and snowed, she wouldn't have to deal with the mess.

The garage wasn't attached to the house, and it sat back about fifteen feet. It did have an automatic door, and Cy had given her the remote for it. So as she eased down the driveway, and the door lifted, she saw something blocking her from parking in the single-car garage.

That yellow motorcycle.

She pressed hard on the brake, her car jerking to a stop. "Oh." The word just came out in a whoosh of breath, and Patsy couldn't look away from the shiny chrome on the bike, that immaculately stitched seat, and the helmet Cy had perched on the handlebars.

Everything inside Patsy itched to go inspect the motorcycle, so she got out of her car and went to do just that. She picked up the helmet and tried it on, expecting it to be perfect—and it was.

Cy wouldn't have done anything wrong with this motorcycle, and she knew it. Warmth filled her at the same time a flood of tears gathered in her eyes. "You're so stupid," she whispered to herself.

It was the second week of July, and she knew Cy had been out on the winding roads around Coral Canyon, on the way to Jackson, and up into Dog Valley on his motorcycle for the past couple of months.

She could've been riding with him for most of that—if she hadn't been so prideful and so resistant to taking this gift.

"How do I fix this?" she wondered aloud as she swung her leg over the seat and sat on the motorcycle. Cy had made it to fit someone her height, and that was obvious. Everything about it was pure perfection, and Patsy let her tears fall.

She wasn't sure how long she sat on the motorcycle in the garage, but she knew she didn't want Cy to find her there, weeping and wondering what to do. Or maybe she did. Maybe then they could have a real conversation about it—about them—about their relationship—and maybe the awkwardness that had been blooming between them for months would finally wither and die.

She'd closed the garage and left her car where it was before Cy and Ames returned. When they did, they had plates of barbecue with them, and with the addition of Ames, the conversation wasn't so strained.

"All right," Cy finally said with a sigh as he stood from

the dining room table.. "I have to get to the shop." He leaned down and pressed a quick kiss to Patsy's forehead. "I'll call you later, okay?"

"Okay," she said, and she stayed in her seat as the twins walked out. She hadn't unpacked anything quite yet, and she wondered if she could get by until tomorrow without opening a single box.

In the end, that just wasn't how Patsy Foxhill functioned, and she started unpacking within five minutes of being in the house by herself.

CHAPTER 27

"What would you do?" Cy asked, after explaining the situation to Ames.

His twin exhaled slowly, his process for thinking through something before answering. Cy had put together a proposal over the course of the last month, and he'd laid it all out for Ames. He'd emailed him the map. Shown him where the shop was, and where his house was, and which part of the orchard he didn't need and would never use.

He wanted to give it all back to Patsy, and he'd put together a pretty powerful argument for why she should have it back. He just wasn't sure if it was good enough.

He'd left the motorcycle in her garage when she'd moved into the rental house just down the road and around the corner from the shop. She hadn't said one word about it, though surely she knew it was there.

Every day, his heart grew a little heavier. And a little darker, if he were being honest with himself. He tried really hard to be absolutely honest with himself, because he still hadn't gone to a counselor, and it was the only way he could see truth and reason in his life.

His thoughts had been twisting more and more recently, whispering things like, *You didn't even see the break-up coming from Mikaela, but you can feel something is off with Patsy.*

And he could.

They weren't the same, even now that she wasn't running herself ragged at the lodge and trying to manage the orchard. But, the orchard really was in a state of disrepair, and Patsy did work from sun-up to sun-down to get the land, the trees, and the little farm back to where it could operate properly. On top of that, she had to re-establish contacts and trust with those who used to buy Foxhill apples, and assure them that their crop this year would be worth coming to see.

"I think you should present it to her," Ames finally said. "Get it all out in the open, Cy. This bottling-up isn't good for you."

"You think it's clear enough?"

"It's crystal clear," Ames said. "And don't think I didn't notice how you just ignored what I'd said about bottling up your emotions."

Cy sighed, but he didn't argue. He stood in his kitchen, his eyes out the window above the sink on the woods that bordered his back yard. Blue Velvet sniffed around back there, but Cy didn't worry about her. The dog could come and go as she pleased, and she normally went to work with him, stayed by his side, and slept in the bed with him too. She did like a bit of outdoor time in the afternoon, and Cy watched as she barked and trotted over to a tree, looking up into the leaves of it.

He turned around and leaned against the counter. "I'm fine, Ames."

"You keep telling yourself that," his brother said.

"We both will," Cy shot back.

Ames didn't have an immediate comeback, and Cy was about to say goodbye and get on with obsessing over how to approach Patsy with the idea of returning fifteen acres of the twenty he'd bought from her last year.

He didn't need the front fifteen acres. If she'd let him keep the road leading back to his house and shop, she could have all those apple trees back. It was her family's generational land, and Cy knew it meant a great deal to her.

"I, uh, have to tell you something," Ames said, clearing his throat.

Cy's curiosity pricked, and he smiled as he said, "Is that right? What? You found a woman who doesn't care that you're a cop and doesn't know your last name yet?"

"Sort of," Ames said. "Actually, no. She knows both of those things. She just doesn't seem to…care."

"You should propose right now," Cy teased.

"Okay," Ames said with plenty of sarcasm. "This is why I didn't tell you."

"How long has this been going on?" Cy asked, because he'd detected no noticeable changes in his twin. Usually, he had some sort of twin sensor that would go off, but he'd literally felt nothing.

"A month or so," Ames said evasively. "About the time Patsy moved out of the lodge."

"So you must've met her right after that," Cy said. "Who is she?"

At that moment, he heard Ames's doorbell ring. And if he hadn't, he would've definitely heard his dog start to throw a tantrum. Ames growled at Thunder Ridge to be quiet, that police dogs didn't bark every time the blasted doorbell rang.

Cy chuckled as the dog kept right on barking, and he said, "I'll let you go. You need to train that dog."

"No kidding. Talk to you later." Ames had to shout the words to be heard over the barking, and Cy ended the call with his brother rebuking the Malinois.

He looked down at the folder of information, which included a color copy of the map Cy had rendered from the satellite images of the orchard, as well as the lot parcels from the county. He'd put a lot of effort and thought into this proposal, and though his pulse sped and tightened, he swept the folder into his hands and headed for the door.

Patsy would say yes or no, and it didn't matter if that happened today or tomorrow or next week.

The weather had already started to cool in Wyoming, and Cy wasn't looking forward to another winter. It felt like he'd just gotten his motorcycle out of the garage for that inaugural spring ride, though it had been four months now.

He took the golf cart through the parking lot and down the lane to the highway. Just a hop, skip, and a turn later, and he arrived at the orchard that Patsy owned. Her car sat in the spot it always did when she worked in the office, which was a prebuilt shed she'd bought almost the day she'd moved down the canyon.

She'd put a desk in there, and she used the Internet from her father's farmhouse. If she wasn't there, talking on the phone, arranging an order, or doing an interview, Patsy would be out on the land somewhere, doing whatever physical labor was required to improve the land, the harvest, or the functionality of the orchard.

Today, when he knocked, she called, "Come on in."

Relief streamed through him, because he just wanted this to be over with. As he reached for the door handle, time slowed down.

What, exactly, did he want to be over? This meeting where he tried to convince her to take back the unused part of the land he'd purchased? Or their relationship?

As he opened the door, time moved at a steady rate again, and Cy didn't know the answer to his questions.

"Hey," she said, plenty of pleasantness in her voice and the pretty smile on her face. Her hair had grown out from the extreme pixie cut of eight months ago, but she'd kept it on the short side. She now sported a cute A-line cut that left some pieces of her shockingly blonde hair to fall to her chin, while she had hardly any in the back. "What brings you here?"

"This." He practically threw the folder at her. It was actually pretty much a thrust, which felt aggressive to Cy. "It's the front fifteen acres," he said. "I don't use them, and I want you to have them back."

"What?" Patsy held his gaze for a moment and then flipped open the folder.

"I only need the back five acres," he said, because she'd figure it out soon enough. "If you'll let me keep the road going back there—which I'll maintain—you can have the fifteen acres of orchard back. All the trees. Everything."

She scanned the front paper in the folder, which detailed everything he'd just said in bullet points and complete sentences. She flipped the page, and Cy had put the map second. There wasn't much else to explain, but he'd put a contract as the third page. If she'd sign it today, so would he, and she'd be able to harvest all of the apples currently hanging in those fifteen acres of trees.

She frowned as she turned the page and didn't find another one. "There's no price."

"That's because I'm not charging you anything."

Her eyes shot to his, widening in shock. "Cy."

"It's a gift, Patsy," he said, his throat so raw. "Remember how you promised you'd try to find a way to accept my gifts?"

She shook her head, and that was all the answer Cy needed. A terrible, horrible, hot rush of anger moved through him, touching everything and setting little fires throughout his body.

"I can't just take the orchard back."

"Why not?" he challenged. "I'm done with all the construction on my five acres. It's just sitting there."

"Not without buying it." She closed the folder and extended it back to him.

A moment of clarity descended upon Cy. She hadn't

tried at all. She'd said she would, but she hadn't. That was why she hadn't said one word about the motorcycle, and why she couldn't just take these stupid fifteen acres.

Something's wrong, his mind screamed. *Don't let her play you like this.*

He would not be blindsided again, the way he had been with Mikaela. He would not be caught with a diamond ring in his glove box, only to learn the woman he was in love with was actually going to break-up with him.

He fell back a step, the whole world spinning now. Nothing made sense, and Cy's thoughts jumbled and tangled.

"I can't believe you," he said, his voice made of cruelty.

"What do you mean?" Patsy finally lowered her hand, because Cy would not be taking that folder back. He'd been stewing over it for weeks; he had the whole thing memorized.

"You're so selfish," he bit out. "You haven't tried at all to find a way to accept a gift from me. Sure, you'll take a plate of food, but nothing else. I don't get it."

"I can't just take fifteen acres," she said. "You paid a lot of money for that land."

"I'm *giving it to you,*" he shouted.

Patsy flinched and backed up, but Cy didn't care. He wasn't going to be the one left with his heart broken and bleeding. Not this time. If he broke up with Patsy, then he was in control. He wasn't left wondering what he'd done wrong.

She was the one who'd done something wrong. She

was the one who would have to pick up the pieces of her life.

Not that she would, because Cy could clearly see in that moment that Patsy would break-up with him in the future. Sooner or later, she would, and he'd be left gasping for breath and wondering how he'd let himself fall in love with another woman who didn't love him back.

"You're unbelievable," he said, plenty of disgust in his voice. "I'm done here." With that, he spun and marched out of the door he'd just come through. The world outside wasn't moving any slower, but Cy didn't care. He could see the golf cart, and he focused on that, everything else in his vision a bit blurred.

"Done?" Patsy said behind him. "What does that mean?"

"It means we're done," he called over his shoulder. "Over. Don't call me. Don't text me." He got behind the wheel of the golf cart, feeling a bit foolish. He wanted to speed out of her driveway, spitting gravel behind his big, manly truck tires. As it was, he'd just motor off in this wimpy golf cart.

He glared at her as she walked toward him. "I don't want to be with someone who won't even try."

"I'm trying," she said, plenty of anger in her expression too.

Cy laughed, the sound high and utterly cruel. "You keep telling yourself that, Patsy." With that, he pressed the gas pedal down in the golf cart, and sure enough, his exit wasn't nearly as dramatic as he'd like it to be.

She didn't call after him, though, and as Cy drove away

and back to his house, he left bits and pieces of his heart along the side of the road.

"You did the right thing," he told himself after he'd parked. He sat on a bench in the back yard and patted Blue Velvet, who seemed to know he was in deep turmoil. "You did the right thing."

He wasn't sure how many times he said it, but maybe if he just kept repeating those words, he'd start to believe them. Maybe they'd become true.

He spiraled, his emotions flying high and then taking a dive. A sob gathered in his chest, and Cy knew what came next.

The debilitating panic.

The thought to start throwing things.

The beastly mood that would follow him everywhere for weeks and months. He'd snap at his employees and miss meetings. He didn't want to be that person again.

A beast.

With a sharp intake of breath, he realized he'd already been the beast—to Patsy.

He bent over, his breathing coming quicker and quicker. His phone rang, and Cy seized onto that one thing as if it were a lifeline.

He couldn't see the name on the screen through the streams of panic racing through him, but he managed to get the call connected.

"Cy," Ames said. "Talk to me. What's wrong?"

How Ames knew something was wrong, Cy didn't know. He also couldn't get a deep enough breath to speak.

"I'm sending Colton over," Ames said. "Are you at home? Or the shop? Somewhere else?"

"Home," Cy managed to get out, his voice nothing like his own.

"Hang on," Ames said. "I'm going to text him right now."

Cy sucked at the air, and Ames started talking again. "Deeper, Cy. Take a long, deep breath with me, okay? Can you hear my voice? Just listen to my voice."

Cy did, training all of his focus on his brother, who'd known through his own twin sense that Cy had just lost everything by breaking up with Patsy.

CHAPTER 28

P atsy rolled over when her alarm went off, noticing that the sky beyond her window was still dark. A groan pulled through her chest and her sticky mouth, because while she needed to get up, she really needed more sleep too.

She hadn't slept well for a week, since Cy had said horrible things to her and driven away from the orchard, the truth of his words ringing in the air.

She *was* selfish. She hadn't tried—truly tried—to accept the motorcycle. And when he'd shown up with that folder that contained pages outlining how she could simply have the fifteen acres of apple trees back?

She hadn't even considered simply taking it.

Her impulse was to say no, hand the folder back, and politely ask him if there was anything else he needed. As if he were a client. A nuisance.

He'd been one-hundred percent right to break-up with her, but that didn't mean it didn't hurt.

Cy's absence in her life did hurt, all day, every day. It hurt when she came home at night, and the dull, aching pain of not being able to talk to him that day kept her awake for far too long at night.

She hadn't slept well in the seven days since he'd accused her of lying to herself. And he'd been right about that too.

She sat up, misery already swirling through her. She existed with it now, but it was heavy, and she'd do almost anything to find a way to get rid of it.

So she slid to the floor, her knees meeting the carpet of her bedroom as she started to sob. "Dear God," she started, and then her prayer moved into silence as she cried against her sheets. She begged for help, something she'd been doing for the past several months actually. Help to be strong enough for her father. Help to know how to approach Betty. Help with the orchard.

She'd never felt like such a failure, and the pain of that radiated through her in great waves. On and on it went, until Patsy had no energy left to even get off the floor, though her prayer had ended several minutes ago.

Eventually, Patsy did get off the floor. She somehow found the strength to get in the shower and get dressed. She made coffee and poured herself some, adding sugar as she checked her phone to see what time she was meeting with Richard White.

He was the buyer for a major applesauce company, and Patsy had been working to get in touch with him for two months. She'd spoken with him a couple of times this week, because one of the orchards Hammerstein had been buying from for the past couple of years had discovered worms in half of their crop.

Patsy shuddered just thinking about what that would do to her bottom line. Foxhill was already a small operation, barely operating in the black, and something like that would push her toward bankruptcy.

She had twenty minutes to be in the orchard, ready to speak with Richard. She should've flown from the house and gotten herself down the road and in position. Instead, she sipped her coffee and waited until she absolutely had to leave or she'd be late.

When she turned onto the piece of property where she'd been working the last couple of months, Richard's fancy corporate SUV was already parked. He was already out and walking along the edge of the trees.

Patsy's pulse kicked through a few beats, and she hurried toward him. "Good morning, Richard," she said smoothly. She couldn't remember if she'd brushed her teeth or put on makeup, but Richard smiled at her, so she must not look or smell too bad.

"Morning." They shook hands, both of them all smiles. "These look great."

"We have everything you need here," she said, tapping to open her phone. "I did these numbers last night, based on harvest projections." She handed him the device, and he studied the weights and bushels she'd put together. "The Snowsweets are beautiful this year."

"These are Honeygold," Richard said, taking a picture of her phone with his. "Right?"

"Yes, sir," she said. "Pick one and try it. We only use organic materials here. Hardly any pesticides, and nothing with the harmful chemicals, as always."

Richard reached up and plucked an apple from the tree. He handed her phone back, and Patsy was sure there wasn't a more satisfying sound than that of someone biting into a crisp, juicy apple. "Oh, wow," Richard said around the mouthful of fruit. "These *are* amazing."

Patsy just smiled. "We have thirty acres of trees," she said. "Plenty of Honeygold for your applesauce."

"But not enough Snowsweet," he said. "I need at least twice as many as what you have listed here for even a week of our juice production."

Patsy looked down the lane, toward the highway. She knew where more Snowsweet apples were—right across that road, in the north twenty that used to be part of the orchard.

"Who owns the orchard across the street?" Richard asked. "Those were Snowsweet—at least what I could see. Isn't that your orchard? Did you include those in the numbers?" He peered at his phone and took another bite of the Honeygold apple.

Patsy drew herself up as straight and as tall as she could. "We had to sell those acres," she said.

"Would it be possible to put me in touch with the new owner?" Richard looked up, hope shining in his eyes. "I'll take all of your Honeygolds and whatever Snowsweets you can get me. Maybe if I can talk to them, I'll get what I need for our Idaho stores."

"I can put you in touch with him," Patsy said coolly. Pure humiliation romped through her though, and she wasn't sure how much longer she could hide it. If she'd just accepted Cy's proposal for the acreage, she'd be able to close this deal right now. Richard wouldn't have to go to another orchard to get what he needed. He wouldn't have to doubt that Patsy and Foxhill Farm could provide what he needed.

"Great," Richard said, finishing his apple just as his phone rang. "Oh, excuse me. This is Neil."

Patsy nodded, because if Neil Hammerstein had been calling her, she'd have answered no matter what too. "I'll go get the paperwork ready."

Richard nodded as he said, "Hey, Neil," and Patsy left the two of them alone to chat. In her office-shed, she clicked on her computer and printed out the documents she'd need Richard to sign. He'd get a copy; she'd keep one; one would go in the files.

A sense of pride filled her as the printer whirred. She'd just sold two full crops of two varieties of apples in one meeting. She'd been working toward this day all summer, and a smile lifted the corners of her mouth. She couldn't even imagine Betty doing something like this.

True joy touched her heart, and she couldn't wait to tell Cy—her thoughts stalled. No, she couldn't wait to tell *her father* that she'd done exactly what she'd said she'd do— restore the orchard to their full glory and bring the farm back to profitable.

Cy lingered in the back of her mind, long after she and Richard had shaken hands, and long after she'd filed the paperwork, and long after she'd gone inside the farmhouse to celebrate the sale with her father.

She wanted to call him—she ached to call him—and tell him her good news. She could hear Cy's sexy, deep voice as he said, "You're amazing, Patsy," and she could smell the musky and mechanical scent that was uniquely his.

She reached up and touched her lips, feeling the gentle pressure of Cy's there when he'd kissed her the first time. A sigh came from her mouth, and she remembered the way he kissed her when he was feeling a bit more passionate. She felt the strands of his hair between her fingers, and the bumping thump of her pulse whenever the man so much as looked her way.

Patsy didn't even realize she'd started to cry until she sniffled and reached up to touch her eye, which itched. It wasn't itchy—tears were pouring down her face.

She leaned her head back and looked right up at the ceiling. "I miss him so much," she moaned. "What do I do?"

God didn't answer her, at least not in a way that Patsy understood. She didn't understand anything anymore, least of all herself.

"Why did I do this?" She bent over the desk now and cradled her head in her hands. "How did it come to this? How do I fix it? Can I get him back?"

She kept asking questions, and she wasn't sure if they were for herself or for the Lord, but they helped ground her and kept her thoughts moving.

Patsy had to keep things moving. Being stagnant was the kiss of death for a woman like her, and she knew eventually, she'd seize onto an idea that would be the answer.

"Please," she kept whispering. "What do I do?"

Later that evening, Patsy climbed the steps to the cabin where she used to live. She'd been in touch with Sophia, of course, but she'd been ignoring her best friend since Cy's departure from her life.

It was time to bring in the reinforcements. Sophia had been there for all the break-ups over the last four years, and Patsy needed her desperately now.

"Knock, knock," she said as she opened the door. She hadn't called ahead, but Sophia would be done at the lodge by now, as darkness had already fallen. Patsy didn't expect dinner, as it was past time for that, and Sophia didn't like to cook at home after she'd put together a meal for twenty-plus people at the lodge.

In fact, it had usually been Patsy who'd feed them in the evenings when Sophia finally got done in the kitchen at the lodge.

Tonight, though, the scent of something brown and delicious hung in the air, and Patsy stalled as she took in the living room in front of her.

A man sat on the couch while Sophia said something in the kitchen.

Patsy's hand flew to her mouth as a gasp pulled through her whole chest. "Cy?"

The man rose, and it was apparent it wasn't Cy. Foolishness hit Patsy in the chest, and her gaze flew to Sophia, who came out of the kitchen wiping her hands on a towel. Her eyes were wide too, and she glanced from Patsy to Ames.

"Patsy," she said, plenty of surprise in her voice. "I didn't know you were coming."

"I...I...." Patsy didn't know what to say. Her heart hammered way too hard for it to be over Ames Hammond. What in the world was wrong with her?

You're in love with Cy.

The thought was just there, and her heartbeat crashed like it agreed.

Go talk to him.

She shook her head as if Ames or Sophia had suggested it.

"Hello, Patsy," Ames said, taking off his cowboy hat. He shot a look at Sophia too, who seemed to get the message. She rushed forward and hugged Patsy, who couldn't hold back the rush of tears then.

"What's wrong?" Sophia asked, her voice right against Patsy's ear.

Patsy couldn't say, especially not with Ames here. Then, as if God had pulled back the curtain separating her and Him, she knew exactly what to do.

She pulled in a breath and stepped back. She said, "Cy broke up with me, and I'm devastated."

She looked past Sophia, who'd sucked in a breath with wide, shocked eyes, to Ames. She asked, "Do you know how to ride a motorcycle?"

"Yes," he said simply.

"Would you teach me?" she asked. "And help me figure out how to get Cy back?"

"Why?" Ames asked, his voice as sharp as his gaze. "So you can rip him apart again?"

Patsy pressed against a fresh set of tears. She couldn't imagine what Cy was going through, and she regretted keenly that she'd been the cause of it.

She shook her head, everything flapping in the wind now. "No," she said. "So I can tell him I'm in love with him, and I want him back, and beg him to forgive me."

Sophia linked her arm through Patsy's and said, "I'll help you, Patsy." They both looked at Ames, and he was so stoic and so dark. So much like Cy, and yet so different.

"Please," Patsy said, not above begging despite Ames's glower. "I'm dying without him."

That seemed to soften Ames, and he finally gave one nod. "Fine, I'll help." He took a step toward her as he stuffed that cowboy hat back on his head. "But if I even think for one *second* that you'll hurt him again, I will—"

"Ames," Sophia said, her voice sickly sweet but also firm. "Sweetheart, the timer is going off on those cheesesteaks. Will you please go check them?"

Ames glared at Patsy for another second as the word *sweetheart* rang in her ears. Then he walked into the kitchen, giving them twenty feet of privacy.

"Sweetheart?" Patsy asked dumbly, turning to look at Sophia. "And you made cheesesteaks after dinner at the lodge?" She felt like she was looking at a brand-new version of her best friend, and she didn't know the Sophia Cooke standing in front of her at all.

"Surprise," Sophia said weakly. "We really don't have time for this right now, though. Come sit down and eat with us, and we'll help you figure out a plan to get Cy back."

"Do you really think I can?" Patsy asked, glancing over to Ames. "Has he told you anything?"

"No," Sophia whispered. "I mean, he's here because he came to stay with Cy for a while. I guess it's pretty bad, and Ames didn't think he should be alone." She tugged on Patsy's hand. "Come on. His bark is just way louder than his bite, I promise."

Patsy wasn't so sure, because when Ames turned from setting a sheet pan on the stovetop, he still wore a dark, growly look in those oh-so-familiar eyes.

Do it for Cy, she thought, and she realized in that moment, she'd do anything—*anything*—to get him back into her life. Even lay all of her wrongdoings out on the table for his police officer twin to examine, judge, and criticize.

CHAPTER 29

Cy stared out the windshield at the familiar office building. The drive from his house to town got shorter every time Ames made it.

"Go on," his brother said. "You can go in alone today."

Cy nodded, everything he felt behind an invisible barrier. That way, it didn't infect his mind. His depression and anxiety and anger couldn't rear their ugly heads and say mean, hurtful things.

With all those things tucked safely away, he didn't hurt. That was a good thing, Dr. Montgomery kept telling him. But what she didn't understand was that Cy didn't feel anything. Nothing at all.

And that was *not* a good thing.

He got out of the truck anyway, because he'd committed to seeing his counselor every day for the first two weeks. He was only on day six, but it didn't matter.

Nothing really mattered. He'd talk to her. He and Ames would get something to eat on the way back to the house.

He'd throw a ball to Blue Velvet, barely feeling the chill in the air or the wind as it kissed his face and tried to chap his skin.

No big deal.

"Hey," he said to the secretary there. He supposed some men would find her beautiful, but to Cy, her dark hair was the wrong color.

"Good morning, Mister Hammond," Sabrina chirped. "I'll let her know you're here."

"Great," he said, though nothing in his tone suggested anything was great. He took a seat and stared at the wall across from him. He'd normally look at his phone while he waited. The first time he'd come with Ames, his foot had bounced a mile a minute, trying to keep up with his racing pulse and his frantic thoughts.

None of that happened anymore. Cy did like that effect of the medication he was on, but he suspected that nervous energy was just buzzing around somewhere behind that barrier he couldn't break through.

He wasn't as tired as he'd once been. He could sleep at night now. He didn't sit and obsess over little things anymore, and his mind didn't go in circles for hours.

Cy hated all of it, honestly. But the meds also made it so he wasn't a beast. They made it so he could laugh when things were funny and have real conversations with people without getting his feelings hurt or multiplying his doubts. They made it so he could focus when he needed to, and in so many ways, things were better in Cy's life.

He hadn't gone to therapy when Mikaela had ended their relationship, and he'd survived then too. Talking about his feelings and his actions didn't seem to be helping with the fact that he had an enormous hole in his heart.

A Patsy-shaped hole that wouldn't heal, no matter how many pills he swallowed or how many sessions he attended.

At least he was down to one per day. When Colton had found him in the back yard, he'd wanted to take Cy to the hospital. Cy had steadfastly refused, saying he was fine. He'd calmed down by then, though he was jittery and exhausted at the same time.

Colt had slept at Cy's that night, on a cot in the same bedroom. It wasn't until Ames showed up the next morning that Cy realized his brothers were worried about him taking his own life.

He honestly hadn't thought of doing that. It was more of a sense of anxiety and panic driving him to the edge of reason. From there…Cy didn't even know where to go. In California, he'd put on a helmet and ridden his motorcycle down the coastal highway until he ran out of gas. He'd slept on the beach and showered at a campground. He'd plugged in his phone at a coffeehouse and filled up his gas tank before heading north again.

He'd run away. In California, he could do that. He had an amazing shop manager, and no obligations. Here, he was still the shop manager, and he couldn't run from his responsibilities. He'd been an absolute ogre to Marissa the day after he'd broken up with Patsy, despite Ames never being more than a few feet from him.

He'd yelled at McCall…and maybe a client. Cy couldn't exactly remember. He hated the beast inside him, but the pills tamed it, so that was nice.

"Cy?" A hand touched his forearm and sent a shock-wave up to his shoulder.

He blinked and turned toward Dr. Montgomery. She never came out to the waiting room to get him, and he looked over to the door that led back to her office. Her assistant stood there, holding his folder, and she must've called for him and he hadn't heard her.

"Are you ready?" Dr. Montgomery didn't smile as she stood up and gestured toward the doorway.

"Yes," Cy said, going with her through the door and down the hall. She held the door to her office for him, and he glanced at her as he passed. "Sorry, I zoned out."

Dr. Montgomery remained silent until he'd sat down and she'd closed the door. She settled into a comfortable chair across from him and crossed her legs. "Does that happen a lot, Cy? You zoning out?"

"Yeah," he said, his head starting to throb. "I mean, a little bit."

"I think we should adjust your dosage then. We don't want you to be a zombie."

Hope pricked his heart. "We can do that?"

"Yes," she said with a quick smile. He'd never seen her with her hair down. She always wore it in a bun near the top of her head. Big earrings always dangled from her lobes. She always wore the same makeup, and a blouse with a skirt. Never a dress. Of course, this was only his sixth day with her, but he could tell she was organized and routine.

Like Patsy.

No matter what he did, Patsy was always right there in the back of his mind. She'd creep forward from time to time, like she just had, and Cy would have to figure out if he wanted to push her away or embrace the thought of her.

"So let's try thirty milligrams," Dr. Montgomery said. "Instead of the thirty-seven-point-five. I'll have Rhonda call it in right now." She tapped on her phone a few times and then put it back in her lap. She looked at him and said, "Tell me how your thoughtfulness exercise went yesterday."

Cy took a deep breath and tried to remember what he'd done. "Okay, well, I started out pretty good. I went through a specific situation, like we talked about. At the shop, we're building this custom bike for a guy who lives in Jackson Hole, right?"

He continued the story, and he outlined how he'd been thoughtful in his approach with McCall, the lead mechanic on the project. He'd been thoughtful about what to say to Marissa when she'd interrupted his meeting, as she often did.

"And I think it went well," Cy said. "I identified what was happening, how I felt about it, and I thoughtfully chose how to respond."

"Excellent," Dr. Montgomery said, her pen never ceasing in its motion. He'd asked her to see what she was writing, and she'd shown him. It was all just lines and swoops though, and she'd called it shorthand. She, apparently, could read it. Cy could not.

"Did you journal it?" she asked next, and Cy hated that he hadn't anticipated the question. The pills sometimes made his brain a little too slow.

"No," he admitted.

Dr. Montgomery nodded as if she didn't care one way or the other, but she did. Cy knew she did. She was simply exceptionally skilled at hiding how she really felt. He'd been like that once too, but it was a very heavy burden that he simply couldn't keep carrying.

"If you could type out your journal, would you do it?" She looked up from her notebook.

"Maybe," he said, shrugging. "I just don't get the point."

"The point is to make you slow down and analyze how you're feeling."

"I know how I'm feeling," he said, feeling everything sharpen around him. "I'm living behind waxed paper now. I don't *feel* anything."

"Cy—"

"Everything is so slow already, Doctor Montgomery. I don't need things to slow down." If anything, he wished they'd speed up again. He hated being trapped in moments of agony for such a long time. Thankfully, the meds also made it so what was agony was really just a dull ache to see Patsy, hold her hand, dance with her, and kiss her goodnight.

"We definitely need to adjust your medication," she said. "I want you to get this new prescription right after you leave today, and I don't want you taking any more of the pills you have, okay?"

"Okay," he said, looking at his hands. Whatever she said. Didn't matter.

"And I'm going to make a note that in three days, we need to talk about the changes, if any. We might need to step you down even more, and we can. It just has to happen pretty gradually."

"Okay," he said again, ready for this session to be over and it had barely begun.

Dr. Montgomery gave him another one of her tight, professional smiles. "All right, let's talk about your strategy for coping with stress…."

Cy needed to play this game with her, because if he had any hope of Ames going back to Colorado and getting the rest of his brothers to stop texting him and dropping by in the evenings, Cy had to figure out a way to find the joy in his life.

He knew it was there, somewhere. Hiding. Lurking just out of sight. He spoke about prayer and his faith, and he realized it had been a while since he'd had an open, honest, out-loud talk with the Lord.

He finished his session, got more homework, and made Ames drive through the pharmacy to get his new prescription. Back home, he said, "Come on, Blue," and the two of them took off into the trees that stretched toward the highway.

The scent of apples and wet earth accompanied them, and Blue Velvet enjoyed herself as she darted from object to object, her nose working overtime. Cy enjoyed how carefree she was, and how much joy she got from barking at a bird sitting in the tree. He smiled, and for that one moment, he experienced happiness.

He just needed to string a whole lot of moments together, and maybe then he'd be able to find a future where he wasn't angry or sad or anxious, but also not medicated so heavily he didn't know who he was anymore.

"Dear Lord," he started, his voice loud out in all the silent trees. "Did You know I would be like this? I'm sure You did. How do I overcome this? How do I find my own happiness?"

He took a few more steps, glad for a large enough space for his thoughts to bloom and grow. "I know I can overcome this," he continued. "I'm going to need Your help though. If You'll lead me, I'll do whatever You need me to do."

When the alarm on his phone sounded, Cy turned around and started back toward his house, whistling for Blue. "Come on, girl," he called. "We've got a meeting at the shop in a few minutes."

As he walked, he set another alarm, this one as a reminder for him to stop and say out loud one thing he was grateful for in that moment.

"I'm grateful for dogs," he said as he tapped save. Blue Velvet came trotting up beside him, and Cy bent down and scratched her head. A smile spread across his face, and Cy experienced a blip of real happiness before his medication buried it again.

A week passed, and Cy's dosage had been stepped down twice. He liked this new level he was at, and he'd told Dr. Montgomery as much. She was pleased, and Cy felt like the barrier between who he was now, and who he'd been when he'd literally sneered at Patsy about how selfish she was, was more like a piece of plastic wrap.

It moved when he pushed against it. He could see and hear through it. He wasn't nearly as angry or emotional as he'd been before, and he did like taking a few extra seconds to consider his words before he said them. He'd apologized to Marissa and McCall, and they'd both hugged him and said he was forgiven.

He wished he could go across the street to the Foxhill Farm, or down the highway and around the corner to the rental house where he'd once lived and apologize to Patsy. He needed her to forgive him, but Dr. Montgomery said she didn't think Cy was ready to see Patsy quite yet.

He'd asked her if he'd be ready one day, and she'd said, "Oh, sure. Soon, Cy."

Soon.

He put two pieces of metal together and lowered his eye guard. The welder sparked, and the metal heated together, and Cy pulled it out. He'd designed a sign for the farm in Ivory Peaks that featured the Hammond surname and the magnificent Rocky Mountain peaks.

He'd spent plenty of time in his welding shed, making gifts for his brothers as Christmas seemed to be right around the corner.

Time was one of those things that his anti-depressants skewed, and Cy didn't hate that either. It meant he lived by the alarms on his phone, and when it went off this time, he glanced at it to check the note he'd typed in.

Call Ames.

That was right.

Ames had left that morning, and he'd wanted Cy to call him that afternoon and tell him how he was doing. So Cy flipped up his visor and dialed his brother's number.

"Hey, little bro," Ames said, something like rushing water in the background.

"Where are you? Still driving?"

"No, I met Gray and Hunter at a creek a couple of hours north of home."

"Are you wearing waders?" Cy teased, and it felt good to be able to do that.

"Maybe," Ames said with a chuckle. "What are you doing?"

"I'm in the shop," Cy said, looking at the sign he'd started. Now that he looked at it, the pieces weren't at the right angle. "Making something for Mom and Dad for Christmas."

"Nice," Ames said.

Cy smiled at the happiness in Ames's voice. "Listen, Ames, I wanted to thank you for coming to stay with me for the past couple of weeks."

"Of course," Ames said.

"I was really out of it there for a few days, and I... appreciate it."

"Cy, you're my brother. More than that. You're my twin. I *know* you, and I'm just glad I could be there."

"Yeah." Cy took a breath. "I just want you to know I'm grateful. I love you, Ames." His throat closed, especially when Ames repeated the sentiment back to him.

"I was wondering," Cy said. "How you got the time off so fast." He heard someone shout in the background, and it sounded like Hunter. "And now you're fishing instead of going straight back to your desk."

"Teri Lynn's got it covered," Ames said coolly.

"And you've left everything to your partner...when?"

"You're ruining my last day off," Ames said. "I'm fishing right now."

"You're the one who wanted me to call you."

"And you did, and I'm glad you're doing well," Ames said, and Cy knew he was hiding something about his job. Saying he'd been pretty out of it was an understatement, and Cy was glad his mind wasn't as hazy as it had been last week.

"Who's coming tonight?" Cy asked.

"What?"

"You and Gray aren't in town anymore," Cy said, because it was September now, and Gray had taken his family back to Ivory Peaks for the school year. Hunter had just entered eighth grade, and Cy missed their little family that would be growing by one in just another month or so. "And I know you've set up a rotation so I won't have to be alone."

"Wes should be stopping by tonight," Ames said.

"I'm doing a lot better," Cy said. "I don't need a babysitter."

"I know," Ames said, but he didn't try to defend himself. He also didn't say he'd call Wes and tell him he didn't need to check on Cy. "What were you thinking about while welding?"

Cy didn't want to lie, but he didn't want to say either. "Patsy."

Ames sighed and said, "Cy."

"I'm fine, Ames."

"I just think you need some time," his brother said.

"I was thinking about the last time I kissed her," he said, his memories flowing back to that incident. "I'm hoping it wasn't really the last time."

"Cy."

"I'm allowed to talk about her," Cy said. "In fact, that's all you and Wes and Colton and everyone have been hounding me to do for the past two weeks. Heck, the past year."

"No," Ames said. "I wanted you to talk to a counselor to deal with your anxiety and get the help you needed *before* it got to the point where you were in the back yard, having a panic attack."

Guilt filled Cy, and he'd never felt like such a failure. "I'm sorry, Ames," he said, not for the first time. "I don't know how else to say it. I don't know how many more times you need to hear it. I'm sorry."

"I know you are," Ames said. "I don't need you to apologize again. I really don't."

"It helps me to talk about her," Cy said. "And you're

my only safe person, Ames." If he couldn't talk to Ames about Patsy, then what? He didn't even want to imagine what might happen to him them.

"I know that, and I'm glad to be that person, Cy."

"All right," Cy said. "I should go."

"You're not going to call her, are you?" Ames asked.

"Doctor Montgomery doesn't think it's a good idea." Cy heaved a sigh, suddenly keen to end this conversation. "All right, I have to go."

"Hey, real quick. Gray's already asking about Christmas. He'd love to have everyone down to the farm this year."

Cy didn't answer right away. His mind had gone back to last Christmas, when Elise and Gray had gotten married. His parents and Grams had come up to Coral Canyon, and they'd spent an amazing holiday at the lodge. He'd started his relationship with Patsy, and he wanted to go back to Whiskey Mountain Lodge, where the Whittakers had created such an atmosphere of love and acceptance. Family was whoever came through the door, and Cy had felt it.

"I'll talk to Colton," Cy finally said.

"We're not going to get Colt." Ames sighed and added, "I'll talk to Gray and make sure he's not too disappointed."

"You might get Colt," Cy said. "And Wes."

"Hey," Wes's voice sounded behind him, and Cy faced his oldest brother.

"Wes is actually here," Cy said. "I'll call you later."

"Yep."

Cy hung up, and smiled at Wes, who carried his ten-month-old in his arms. "Can I take him?" He reached for the chubby-cheeked boy, who babbled and came happily into Cy's arms. "Hey, Mikey." He grinned at the little boy, seeing so many Hammond genes in his dark hair and eyes. His hair curled like Bree's, and he was such a cute baby with Wes's big, brown eyes that always shone with happiness.

"I ordered fried chicken," Wes said. "Should be here in a few minutes."

"Great." Cy handed Michael back to Wes. "I need to wash my hands real quick, and then we can go to the house."

"Sounds good."

Cy stepped over to his shop sink, his heart pounding. As he turned and dried his hands, he said, "You don't have to stay long, Wes. I'm really okay."

"Oh, yeah, I know that," Wes said easily. "But we'll stay for a while if you don't mind."

"I don't mind." He tossed the towel down. "But why would you want to be hanging out here instead of at home?"

"Bree needs a little break," Wes said with a smile. "Mikey's teething, and she's booked a massage and a pedicure. So I've got a few hours to kill."

"Great," Cy said, taking his nephew again. "Let's go find Blue Velvet then, okay, Mikey? You want to see the doggie, right? Doggie?"

Michael just babbled, but Cy felt sure he heard the D-sound in there. Mikey definitely wanted to find Blue

Velvet. As the little boy gripped Cy's elbow, his heart filled with love until he thought it would burst.

He was glad he could feel it as keenly as he did, and he never wanted to be wrong for falling in love. He just needed to figure out if he should hold onto Patsy for a while longer…or if it was time to let her go.

CHAPTER 30

Patsy enjoyed the wind in her face as she rounded the last corner and crested the hill, the lodge where she'd spent so much of the last four years appearing in front of her. She flipped on her blinker, though she certainly didn't need it on this road.

But she wanted to be able to do everything on the motorcycle, and that included using the blinkers. A strange sense of power flowed through her as she chugged up to the curb and stopped the motorcycle.

"You look good on that thing," Beau said, smiling at her as she took off her helmet.

"Thanks," Patsy said. "I feel good on it." She gazed at the yellow machine, seeing all the details that Cy had put into it. "No pointers on that entrance to the parking lot? I almost felt like I needed to gun the gas."

"Yeah, but you didn't." Beau smiled at her. "So progress."

"Yeah," Patsy said, wondering how much more progress she needed to make before she made the five-minute ride to the shop down the lane lined with apple trees.

"Come review the contract, and then we'll go," Beau said, gesturing for her to follow him.

"Thanks for doing this, Beau," she said, falling into step beside him. Her boots felt too heavy, but Ames had insisted she get the thickest, sturdiest pair available. He told her to never ride without long pants, long sleeves, and a helmet.

She wasn't sure how, but he'd snuck over to her house every night since she'd begged him for help. He'd taught her how to start the motorcycle. How to get on. How to lean, turn, balance. All of it.

He'd left town a little over a week ago, but Beau Whittaker happened to be into motorcycles, and he'd caught Patsy practicing in the parking lot at the lodge on Ames's last night in town. He'd said he'd help, and he'd been riding with Patsy every night for the past eight evenings.

She didn't want to ride at night, but Beau said she should learn. Just like she learned to drive in less than optimal conditions, she should be able to ride her motor-cycle too. So she'd done what he said.

They'd gone up to Dog Valley to take Celia a loaf of the cinnamon bread she loved. They'd gone around town during rush hour. They'd even done a long stretch of highway driving as they rode to Jackson Hole and back last weekend.

Patsy was ready to go show Cy that not only did she love the gift he'd given her, but she loved him too.

"Of course," Beau said. "I haven't lawyered in a while, but it's a simple purchase contract." He went down the hall to the office, where he'd been working on her contract for the past few nights. "It's straight-forward." He picked up a folder. "Three pages. He has to initial all of them and sign this last one."

He handed her the folder, and Patsy flipped it open. She could read legalese quite well, as she'd managed plenty of things with policies. But tonight, her eyes couldn't seem to settle on the letters for long enough to form them into words.

"What does it say?"

"It says you're going to purchase fifteen acres of land, located at the address you gave me." He pointed to it. "You'll maintain it. The road through it will be maintained by the other party, and you won't do anything to compromise their ability to do that. The contract takes effect the moment it's signed. And the purchase price is—" Beau cleared his throat, though a huge smile sat on his face. "One kiss."

"It has to be a good kiss," Patsy said jokingly, though she wasn't joking at all. If Cy would accept a kiss from her, she'd take back the orchard he hadn't touched.

Easy.

Simple.

Her heartbeat rioted in her chest, testifying that there was nothing simple about what she was going to do.

Nothing.

She shivered, because the autumn weather had arrived in Coral Canyon, and it seemed to be permeating the lodge.

"I'm sure it'll be a good kiss," Beau said, smiling. He reached up and ran his hand down the sides of his beard. "I've seen him with you, Patsy. He'll forgive you."

Patsy looked up from the folder, hope shining through her now. "You think so?"

"I would, if a woman rode up on a motorcycle I built, apologized, and said I had to kiss her so she'd accept what I've wanted her to have all along."

"Yeah." Patsy looked down again. Ames had told her over and over that Cy wasn't the same man he'd been before. Patsy hadn't told anyone what he'd said to her, because those words still bounced around inside her, their sharp teeth shredding her a little bit more every day.

Ames had said he was softer now. Medicated. Able to think clearly.

She missed him so much. Sometimes, she simply lay in bed, thinking about him, wondering if he was asleep in that moment. If he was thinking about her. If he wanted her at all anymore.

She drew in a deep breath. "Should I sign it first?"

"Sure," Beau said, reaching for a pen. "Then he'll know you're serious. I mean, he'll already know that the moment you ease up on that bike." He grinned and handed her the pen.

Patsy initialed the three pages and signed her name at the bottom of the third one. "Thank you, Beau."

"Good luck, Patsy." He drew her into a hug. "We sure do miss you around here."

Nostalgia caught Patsy right behind the lungs. She breathed through it and stepped back before she said, "I miss it here more than I thought I would."

"You didn't like it here?" Beau looked shocked, his dark eyes swimming with questions.

"I loved it here," she said quickly. "I've just wanted the orchard for so long. I didn't think anything would be as good as managing that." She shrugged, not sure she wanted to admit her thoughts out loud. In the end, she said, "Turns out, it's just another job. One I feel personally attached to, with stakes I really want to win. But yeah. It's work."

Beau nodded, acceptance filling his expression. "I understand that. Well." He blew out his breath. "Go get your billionaire back, and then maybe it won't be so much work."

Patsy laughed with him, glad for the moment of respite. Then she zipped her jacket again. Put on her helmet. Tucked the folder into the single saddlebag on the side of the motorcycle.

She hummed down the canyon, her pulse picking up the vibrations from the vehicle beneath her. She did love riding this motorcycle, and she'd fantasized so many times about what it would be like to have Cy at her side.

She wanted him there so badly, she couldn't even name the desperation pulling through her. It was certainly stronger than mere desperation.

Before she knew it, she arrived at the new road Cy had

put in, and she drove under the canopy of the apple trees she loved so much.

But she knew now that she loved Cy more. She loved him more than her orchard. More than her motorcycle. More than her pride.

She wasn't sure what his hours were at the shop right now, but it was almost dark, and she assumed he'd be at home. So she went past the parking lot—which was empty, save for a couple of motorcycles—and to his house in the corner. His truck sat there, as did a blue motorcycle with a gray seat and two big saddlebags, one on each side.

A fleeting moment of panic suggested he might be leaving town, and Patsy thought perhaps she should just go on home. She had no right to be here.

She pushed against those feelings and parked her motorcycle. Surely Cy had heard her approach. The bike wasn't very quiet, and everything about the land and atmosphere out here was.

Sure enough, she'd removed her helmet and set it on the handlebars before she turned to the saddlebag containing the folder. She hadn't allowed herself to even look toward the house, but she could feel Cy's eyes on her.

Everything inside her warmed and buzzed, and Patsy forced herself to unzip the bag as if nothing was wrong. But tears already sat in her eyes, and she honestly didn't know what she'd do if he didn't forgive her.

Blue Velvet barked, and Patsy looked up to find the pretty dog bounding toward her, a ball already in her mouth.

Patsy started to laugh as the dog slowed to a trot, her

whole body waving back and forth as she approached. "Hey, girl," she said, reaching down to pat the dog. Blue went right between her legs, and Patsy continued to giggle as she looked up to find her master.

Cy stood at the bottom of the front steps, a completely passive look on his face, his arms folded.

Patsy swallowed, the smile slipping from her face as her giggles dried up. She gripped the folder like it was a shield and stepped toward him.

He looked amazing—exactly how she imagined him before she fell asleep at night. His hair had grown out in the past three weeks, and she wanted to run her fingers through it as she cut it. As she kissed him.

He wore a pair of jeans, a pair of boots, and a dark gray T-shirt with the word Hammond across the chest. She wasn't sure where someone would even get a shirt with their surname on it, but Cy obviously knew, and he wore it well.

"Hey," she said as she drew a little closer. She cleared her throat. "Do you have a minute to talk?"

"Yes," he said, and Patsy took that as a good sign. She wasn't sure if it was that one word or the fact that Cy unfolded his arms, but Patsy suddenly felt buoyed and strong.

Ames and Sophia had given her a ton of advice. So had Beau and Lily. Lead with the most important thing first. Kiss him first. Apologize first. Explain everything first.

None of it mattered.

When faced with him, Patsy only had one thing to say.

"I love you, Cy Hammond." Her voice broke on that

darn last name. She pressed her lips together and shook her head. She started spelling complicated words like *Mississippi* and *lieutenant* to force herself to focus.

She extended the folder toward him, but he didn't move to take it. "I love you so much that every moment without you is complete agony." She drew in a breath, already committed. "I'm sorry I didn't try. I'm sorry I was selfish. I'm sorry I didn't just let you shower me with gifts."

He held up one hand, his dark eyes firing things at her she couldn't interpret. He took the folder silently and opened it. He wasn't stupid, and he dealt with a lot of contracts and sales forms.

It didn't take him long to read the first paragraph, where everything was outlined. Her name as the buyer. His as the seller.

The contract between them that would literally be sealed with a kiss.

He looked up, something new in his expression now. To Patsy, it looked like hope. She felt it gathering way down deep in the soles of her feet.

"I love the motorcycle," she said, gesturing to it behind her. "And I love what you've done with the yard here, and I can't wait to see what you did inside with that accent wall you hadn't finished." She swallowed aware that he had still only said one word to her.

"Ames and Beau taught me a little bit about riding. I'm not as good as you, and the weather is almost getting too bad to ride, but I was hoping you'd do a few things for me."

He closed the folder and tucked it under his arm. "What are they?"

"Sell me the fifteen acres you're not using." She drew in a long breath. "Find a way to forgive me. Doesn't have to be right now. I know stuff like that takes time." Patsy knew better than most, in fact. She was still working on forgiving Betty, and every time she found another nest of snakes she had to sort through, her resentment for her sister came roaring right back.

"Give us a second chance," she continued. "And go riding with me." She looked down at her fingers as if she were in kindergarten and couldn't do simple math. "Four things."

He held up one finger. "Sell you the land I bought. Forgive you. Give us a second chance. Go riding." By the end, he had four fingers up.

"Yes." She lifted her chin while he lowered his. "I know it's a lot. I know that. I just…miss you so much, and I really don't want to try to figure out how to stop. I get it if I was too selfish. If you just can't. I'll do my—"

"Stop," he said, though his voice wasn't loud or demanding. He looked up at her, and in the next moment, he'd taken three steps and closed the distance between them. "I can do all of that," he whispered, taking her right into his arms as if she hadn't spent a moment out of them. "Because I love you, too, Patsy."

She melted into the strength and warmth of his arms, and nothing had ever felt so good. So much like coming home. She clung to him with every ounce of strength she had—mental and physical—and cried against his chest.

Thankfully, that didn't last very long, and she stepped back. Cy smiled tenderly at her and wiped her face for her. "I'm sorry too. I wasn't very nice to you. I'm different now."

"Ames mentioned some medication."

Something hot flashed in Cy's eyes. "Yes," was all he said. "I'm not as beastly anymore."

"I never minded your beast," she admitted.

"Oh, you did," he said. "There at the end. He was cruel."

Patsy shrugged, though his words had carved scars through her soul—but only because he'd been right.

"I'm sorry for that," he said. "I'm not going to be perfect. But I'm going to try to do the best I can, I can promise you that."

She nodded. "And I'll take any gift you want to give me."

He chuckled and cupped her face in his hands. "Let's get these orchards where they belong." With that, he leaned down and kissed her, and Patsy had never been more grateful for the gift of forgiveness than she was in that single second.

CHAPTER 31

Everything had settled in Cy the moment he saw Patsy. And kissing her? Cy once again didn't recognize himself at all. He was a completely new person while kissing her. She healed so much inside of him that was so broken.

"I love you," he whispered, and the best part was when she whispered it back.

Blue barked, and that got Cy to look away from the blonde who'd captured his attention so completely last Christmas. He looked out into the orchard where Blue was staring, but it was too dark to see anything.

"Come on," he called to the dog, glad when she came trotting over to them. "Get your ball, and let's go inside. Maybe Patsy's hungry." He looked at her, hardly able to believe she was here. He'd spoken to Ames earlier that afternoon, and Cy had outlined his plans to go talk to Patsy this weekend.

They'd talked through everything, and never in a million years had he imagined the woman of his dreams to come riding up on the motorcycle he'd built for her.

Wow, what a sight that had been.

She was so sexy, and so strong, and so perfect for him.

Cy opened his front door, glad he'd hired a housekeeper to keep the floor at least semi-clean. Annalise did an amazing job every Wednesday making the house smell less like grease and more like a real human lived there.

"Wow," Patsy said, glancing around. "The rugs are new. Those curtains are much better than those others you had." She turned toward him, her beautiful face glowing with light. Cy wanted to kiss her again, so he turned toward her, a smile passing through his whole soul. He touched his lips to hers sweetly, in complete awe that he even could.

"It was Ames who clued me in to the curtains," Cy said as he straightened. "They are better. I like them, *and* I actually put something in the oven a few minutes ago." He could smell the cornbread that would go perfectly with the chili Bree had dropped off forty minutes ago. Cy hadn't wanted to take it, but Patsy had been there in his mind, and he'd accepted the pot with the food in it.

Cy wasn't particularly skilled in the kitchen, but Ames had stocked his pantry with boxed mixes, and Cy could add eggs and water and oil to a mix. He wasn't completely useless.

"I love the windows here," Patsy said. "It's so bright. My house is so dark."

"It's just older," Cy said, threading his fingers through

hers and leading her further into the house. He loved the open concept of it, and that he had plenty of room to entertain—not that he did a lot of that. But he could. He could have the entire Hammond family over, and everyone would have a place to sit in the living room and at the dining table.

He took Patsy past that and into the kitchen. "Don't get too excited. I made a boxed cornbread mix. Bree brought over some chili."

"Sounds like perfect fall food," Patsy said, squeezing his hand. "Have…Has your family been bringing you a lot of food?"

Cy glanced at her, sure he heard something pinched in her voice. He didn't want to tell her about the babysitters, but if she'd been hanging out with Ames—and it sounded like she had been—she probably already knew.

"Yeah," he said. "Or they invite me over. Annie's daughter has been taking a culinary class, and she's been testing her new recipes. We've been tasting them." He faced the stove, which wasn't on. The pot just sat there. "Or Bree brings me something. I order in while Wes and I watch college football on TV. He brings Mikey, and that baby is the cutest thing ever."

Cy realized he was talking too much, but it felt good not to be talking about how he felt. Or about how his latest thoughtfulness exercise had gone. Or confirming for his mother that yes, he was taking vitamin D now that winter was approaching. Or trying to convince everyone that he was okay.

He *was* okay.

"I'm in therapy," he blurted when Patsy didn't say anything. "And I'm taking an anti-psychotic." He pulled his hand away and tucked both of his into his pockets. "And a variety of other vitamins with a lot of letters." He tossed a smile and a glance her way, but he didn't truly look at her. He didn't want to see the judgment.

"That's great, Cy." Patsy moved in front of him, and all of that judgment he expected to see, he couldn't find. "Do you like going to therapy?"

He shrugged and looked at the timer on the oven. Five minutes until it would go off. He could have this conversation for five minutes. "It's not terrible," he said. "I'm down to twice a week, and my therapist says after this week, I can just come in once a week. Then once a month. Then as needed." He inhaled deeply and exhaled all the air out.

"And the drugs?" Patsy ran one hand up his chest, which made every muscle in Cy's body tense. "How are they?"

Cy looked at her then—right into her eyes. Hers were so bright, and so blue, and so filled with nothing but compassion and acceptance.

"I know you didn't want them before," she said. "And I feel like I need to know, Cy."

"Of course you do," he said. "I hated them at first. The dose was too high. I was living behind this thick, frosted glass." Cy's memory flowed back, and he really didn't remember much of that first week. "Then we changed the dosage, and things got better. We changed it again, and I think we've found a good spot."

"What happens if you don't take them?"

"I don't know," he said. "I haven't forgotten to take them."

"You're not exactly the most routine person in the world," she said, smiling. "Are you telling me your type-A brother doesn't text you every morning about the pills?"

Cy chuckled and shook his head. "He doesn't. I set an alarm on my phone." He reached back and pulled it out of his pocket. "I have an alarm for everything now, Patsy. That way, I don't have to hold so much in my head. I don't have to think so hard about literally everything."

He handed her the phone, and Patsy just looked at the dark screen.

"I'm going to hire a shop manager," he said. "I need to be able to just get on a bike and get away sometimes, and I can't do that without someone to run the shop."

Regret crossed her face, and that was the last thing Cy wanted. "I'm sorry—"

"Don't," he said. "I didn't say that to make you feel guilty. It's just that I couldn't find anyone in March, but I have to look harder. There has to be someone who can run the shop."

"What about moving one of your existing people into the role?" she asked. "Marissa, for example. She's been with you a long time. She knows how the operation runs. She moved here to keep working for you." Patsy fell back a couple of steps, a certain level of anxiety in her eyes. "Why can't she manage the shop?"

"Marissa." Cy rolled the name around inside his mind. "Why haven't I thought of that before?"

"Probably because then you'd have to replace her, and well, she's irreplaceable."

The stars were definitely aligning. "But it would be easier to hire a secretary and have Marissa train her than hire a shop manager and have to train that person."

"Yeah." Patsy turned as the timer went off on the cornbread. "I'll get that."

Cy watched her work in his kitchen, opening a couple of drawers before she found the oven mitts. She bent and took the cornbread out, and Cy had a moment where he was back behind the waxed paper again.

This just didn't seem real. Was she really here?

She turned to face him, and Cy's reality came roaring back. His natural reaction when he looked at Patsy was to smile, and he found himself doing that. "Thanks. Did you eat already?"

"No," she said.

"All right, then," he said. "Let's do that, and then I can show you what I was planning to do to get you back."

Patsy had started to turn, but she stilled. "What? You were going to…? What were you going to do?"

"It's a surprise," Cy said with a smile, stepping into the kitchen with her and getting down a couple of bowls from the cupboard. "Spoons in the drawer on the right of the island there."

She opened that drawer and took out two spoons.

"Listen, I know we just got back together and all of that," Cy said, opening another drawer and taking out a ladle. As he filled one bowl with chili, he asked, "Do you want kids, Patsy?" He glanced over his shoulder to her, noting that she'd once again frozen.

He quickly turned back to the pot. "Because I'm in love with Mikey, and I want a whole bunch of little boys like him." He put down the full bowl and reached for the empty one.

"You can't guarantee you'll get boys, you know." She came up beside him and leaned into his bicep, and Cy paused too. The moment lengthened, and Cy wished he could get a picture of it to remind him of how wonderful it was to have Patsy here with him.

"I've heard," he said. "But I suppose girls would be okay too. I just don't know what to do with them."

"The same thing you do with boys."

Cy started laughing and finished filling the second bowl. He turned and put both of them on the counter. "That's not true, Pats. I have only brothers. Wes has a son. Gray has Hunter. All we know in the Hammond family is boys."

"You think a girl wouldn't like horseback riding? Or working around the ranch? Or taking over the family company and the penthouse on the top floor?"

"I'm not saying a girl wouldn't like that or do any of that," Cy said. "What I'm saying is I don't know anything about girls. They…scare me a little."

Patsy burst out laughing, and Cy sure did like that. The sound of it had been sorely missed in his life, and he hooked his arm around her waist. "That's why you have a wife," she said, still giggling. "Believe it or not, I'm a girl."

"Oh, I know it," Cy said, gazing down at her. The

moment sobered, and Cy couldn't keep the question contained. "And you think...me and you...you'll be my wife and I'll be your husband?"

Patsy nodded slowly. "I think that's the next step, Cy. When two people fall in love, and they want to build a life together."

"And that's what you want?"

"Yes," she said, not a moment of hesitation. "Is that what you want?"

"Yes," he said. "Absolutely. I'm sort of shocked. I just need to absorb it all."

"Let's eat while you absorb," she said. "And I can't wait to see what you were going to do."

Nerves ran through him, but they were fleeting and barely there. He could handle these low emotions, and he thanked the Lord for modern medicine. "I'll get the honey for the cornbread. You cut that up for us."

"Deal."

———

An hour later, Cy handed Patsy her helmet and said, "You think you can ride behind me?"

"Yeah, I think so," Patsy said. "I'm a little nervous. When it's just me, I can blame myself if I fall."

"I won't let us fall," Cy said as he walked toward his motorcycle. He threw his leg over and waited for Patsy to get settled behind him. "The key, sweetheart, is to press right into my back and just do what I do."

She snaked her hands around him, and Cy actually looked down to make sure she was real. "Like this?"

"Yes," he said, his voice sticking in his throat. "Like that."

"How far do we have to go?"

"Just into town," he said. "I've rented a welding shop off-site, so I can get out of the bike shop sometimes. Get away from the trees."

"You don't like the trees?"

"I love them," he said. "I just need a change of scenery from time to time. After a while, it feels like the whole world is only made of apple trees."

Patsy giggled, and Cy was glad he hadn't said something to upset her. Her whole world *was* apple trees. He normally didn't mind them, but he did need to get away sometimes.

He enjoyed the ride down the lane to the highway, and the curvy drive to town had never been so fun. He pulled in to a barely-there parking lot behind the library, where a row of shops was hidden in front of a stand of trees.

He'd rented the whole row, though there were four available. He just wanted to come here and be alone.

"These are air conditioned and heated," he said. "I rented them all. I keep an office here, and all my welding stuff, and I may have bought a recliner and a television so I can just zone out if I need to."

"An off-site man-cave," she said as she removed her helmet. "Do you come here often?"

"Not as often as I thought I would," he said. "Especially since I started taking the drugs." He left his helmet on the seat too and walked toward the shop, all of his senses on high-alert. Well, as high as they could get.

He stopped several paces away from the door. "Maybe this is too soon."

"Cy." Patsy's fingers slipped into his. She didn't say anything else, and he appreciated that she could say so much with only one word. Two letters. He heard so much more than just his name, and her confidence and support gave him the courage to continue toward the door.

He unlocked it, the familiar scent of wood, leather, and metal meeting him instantly. He needed his housekeeper to come here and freshen things up, but he also didn't want anyone else in his space. Even bringing Patsy here was hard for him.

He hadn't planned to give her the gift this way. He'd planned to erect the sign at the orchard and sit beside it until she returned.

"I just finished it," he said. "But I can change anything you don't like." He stepped over to the wall, where the huge Foxhill Farms sign hung. He'd finished the painting last night, and he loved it as much now as he had then.

"Oh, Cy." Patsy sucked in a breath and pressed one hand to her heart. "Look at it. It's perfect. It's absolutely perfect." She stepped right over to the sign, which had an elegant yet chunky font for the letters. He'd made the O in Foxhill and the A in Farms with apples, and he'd painted those bright red.

The fringed grass along the bottom of the sign added some color as well, as he'd done that in a dark green.

"I'm not sure if it's too Christmassy or what," Cy said quietly. "Maybe it needs something else."

"It doesn't," she said. "It's wonderful, even if it is Christmassy." She spun back to him, her eyes shining with unshed tears. "Besides, Christmas is my favorite holiday."

She flung herself into his arms and cried for the second time that night. This time, though, Cy was happy about the tears wetting his shirt.

"Love you, sweetheart," he said.

She tipped her head back and smiled at him through her tears. "I love you, too, Cy. And I love this sign."

"I'll get it up before the snow comes," he said.

"Oh, we have tons of time before that," she said.

"Do we?" he asked. "Because it's freezing."

"It'll rain a lot before it'll snow," she said. "So, let's plan to go riding tomorrow, okay?"

"Absolutely," Cy said, because he couldn't think of anything better.

CHAPTER 32

P atsy listened to Cy and her father talking in the other room, her focus half there and half on the turkey she'd just dressed. It needed to go in the oven, and she hefted it up to do just that.

She'd brought in the twenty pounds of potatoes from the garage, but they needed to be peeled and diced. Her siblings and their families should be arriving soon, but Patsy wasn't surprised Betty wasn't there to help.

Since Patsy had taken over the orchard, Betty had basically disappeared. She was busy with her teenagers, and her dramatic streak only amped up her pride. Patsy understood that, because she'd had to really take a bite out of her own pride in order to fix things with Cy.

They'd been back together for almost three months now, and Cy was a saint for spending Thanksgiving here at the orchard with her family. She'd told him it wouldn't be fun, but he'd said he'd be fine.

They were spending a week in Colorado starting the day after Christmas, and Patsy couldn't wait to spend more time with his parents and grandmother.

She set the timer for the turkey and turned to get out a potato peeler. Cy came into the kitchen and said, "I can do that. It might be the only thing I can do, so let me." He took the peeler from her, and Patsy smiled at him.

"It's going to be crazy."

"I like crazy," he said, leaning down to kiss her. "Remember?"

She shook her head and let him get to work peeling the potatoes. She hated doing it, so she felt like she was winning on all fronts. She put together a roll dough while Cy peeled, and working with him in the kitchen sent satisfaction straight through her.

She sometimes spent time with him in the shop too, and he was as amazing as she'd always known he was. Marissa ran the shop now, and Cy had found a new secretary, who was doing an amazing job.

Everything with him seemed made of light and sunshine, and she wondered how he'd operated so well before the medication. Cy had insisted that Patsy come to therapy sessions with him, because he wanted her to go into the future with him knowing exactly what she was getting.

She'd appreciated his concern for her, but even if she'd seen something to worry her, she'd also already received confirmation that she belonged with Cy. She loved him. Everything about him, even the imperfections, the mental illnesses, the anxiety. He loved her, despite her imperfections, and she'd never thought that would happen.

They sat in church each week, each of them clutching the other's hand as they healed, both spiritually and emotionally. Patsy had learned that church wasn't about listening to a sermon or doing the right thing. It felt like a hospital now, where the spiritually sick needed to go to make it through another week.

Every day she spent with Cy also built up her strength to face the tasks she had to complete on a daily basis.

Just as she covered the bowl that held the dough with a clean tea towel, the front door opened and noise entered in the form of teenagers. Very loud female teenagers. And Betty was just as loud as she trilled, "*Helllooo*, everyone." She came down the hall and into the kitchen, carrying a beautiful three-tiered cake on a decorative stand.

Her husband followed, carrying a few bags of bread.

"Thanks," Patsy said as she took the loaves from Cory. "Wendy, you're helping me with the stuffing."

"Sure thing, Aunt Patsy." Her niece came into the kitchen and opened the cupboard above the microwave to get down an apron.

"I hardly know what to do if I'm not stuck in the kitchen," Betty said, glancing at Patsy and Cy. "Joe's not here?"

"Not yet," Patsy said. "And Dad needs company." Being in the living room entertaining their father was just as much work as peeling potatoes and making sure the roll dough rose properly. Betty would find out as soon as she had a conversation with their father that took longer than five minutes.

Within that five minutes, though, Joe arrived with his two kids, one of whom was already crying. Cy glanced over to them as Joe tried to console his crying six-year-old daughter.

"Angie, it's time to stop." Joe seemed at the end of his rope already, and Patsy actually felt dangerously close to hers too.

"Michelle," Patsy said, and that was all it took to get her niece to go take Angie from her dad. She said something about taking the little girl upstairs to see if there were any dolls there, and that got Angie to calm down enough to go upstairs.

"I could give them rides on my motorcycle," Cy said out of the corner of his mouth.

"Save it for later," Patsy whispered back. "We have a long way to go."

She was right, and she knew she was right, and she hated that she was right. She hoped she could survive the next six hours with her family—and that Cy could too.

She shouldn't have been worried, because Cy could charm snakes and scorpions and even piranhas. He swooped in and saved the day with Joe's son when he fell and hurt his ankle. He told Betty's two youngest daughters what the teenage boys they liked were thinking, and that sent them into fits of giggles. All three of them, with Betty narrowing her eyes from across the room.

He took her father his pills right on time, thanks to that alarm on his watch. He made sure he got down the hall safely when he needed to use the restroom. He took him whatever he wanted to drink, even when Betty protested against the soda.

"I can have one soda a year, Betty," Dad had said, and Patsy swore the entire Earth had stopped revolving for a few seconds. Her father had never stood up to Betty, but he'd popped the top on that soda can and drank the whole thing.

Patsy had muttered to Cy that he really could only have one, and Cy had steered their father toward water and fruit punch after that. Easily.

He played cards with all the nieces and nephews, all seven of them exploding into a roar and laughter as Laura threw down her hand and won the game. Patsy stood on the sidelines, wondering how everything Cy touched turned to gold.

Betty said, "He's great, Patsy," and that was the closest she'd ever come to complimenting Patsy.

"Isn't he?"

"Is he going to ask you to marry him?"

"I sure hope so," Patsy said. "Should I ask him?"

"No, sweetie," Betty said, watching as her oldest daughter taunted everyone though she'd won. "He's got a plan, that one, and it's going to be amazing. Wait for him."

Patsy had only nodded, her steady pulse matching the steady stream of prayer moving through her mind.

Thank you for leading me to him, she thought. *Thank you, thank you, thank you.*

———

A MONTH LATER, PATSY HAD HER BAG PACKED FOR Colorado. They were joining the celebration up at Whiskey Mountain Lodge on Christmas Eve. The next morning, Cy wanted her to come to his house for an intimate Christmas Day celebration, and then they were flying to Colorado with Wes, Bree, Michael, Colton, and Annie.

Cy's mother was making a Christmas Day dinner, and Patsy was excited to get out of Wyoming. She hadn't left in years, and though Colorado was just one state south, it felt like an exciting trip.

"Patsy's here," Beau bellowed the moment Patsy walked in behind Cy, and several women's voices filled the air. Sophia was the first to greet her, and she gripped Patsy tightly as they hugged.

Patsy had asked her about Ames several times over the past few months, but Sophia had been evasive and vague. Patsy had finally driven up to the cabin they'd used to share, because it was too cold and wet to ride a motorcycle safely. She'd waited in the cabin until Sophia came home from the lodge, and she'd demanded to know what was going on.

Sophia had finally admitted that she didn't want to "do the long distance thing" like Elise and Gray, and that she and Ames were "still friends."

Patsy let go of her friend but held her shoulders as they separated. "How are you?" In their few inches, she had some privacy.

"Good," Sophia chirped, which meant less-than-good. So Patsy would keep texting her and asking her to come down the canyon to lunch. Sophia never would, even on the weekends. So Patsy resolved right then and there to bring lunch up to the lodge on the weekends. She could borrow Cy's truck if the weather was bad.

No matter what, she wasn't going to leave Sophia in the dust. She already knew her friend felt like that as it was. She tried to glance around for Ames, but then she remembered he hadn't come. Why would he, for just one night?

There's no reason, he'd told Cy, and that had further cemented Sophia's story that they weren't seeing each other anymore.

Patsy got swept away by Elise, who had come with Gray and Hunter—and their new baby.

"Oh," Patsy said as she laid eyes on the infant for the first time—at least in the flesh. Elise had sent plenty of pictures and several videos over the past two months. "Can I?" Patsy reached for the tiny, sleeping bundle of pure joy.

The little girl gurgled during the exchange, and then she snuggled right into Patsy's chest. Her heart grew five sizes in the time it took to breathe, and she couldn't even look away from the baby's angelic face to tell Elise how perfect she was.

"Hello, baby Jane," she whispered, Cy's hand on her back warm and heavy. She glanced at him. "Look at her, Cy." She looked back at Jane's face. "How can you say you don't want one of these?"

"You don't?" Gray asked. "Cy, I thought you wanted kids."

"He wants boys," Patsy murmured so as to not wake

the baby. Which was ridiculous, given the amount of noise filling the huge, two-story vaulted ceilings in this giant room.

"Only boys?" Gray repeated. "I don't get why. We're loud and obnoxious."

"And you smell bad," Elise said.

"Hey," Gray said.

"What?" she asked. "Have you *been* in your son's room? It's disgusting."

"He's fourteen," Gray said. "They're a special breed. We grow out of it, you know."

"Do you?" Elise asked, leaning into her husband's side. "Because I think we just had a conversation about who should pick up who's socks the other day."

Gray blinked at her and then looked at Cy. Even Patsy looked up from Jane to see his reaction. "All right," he said. "Better start praying for girls, Cy. She's right. We're disgusting."

They laughed, and Patsy joined in. Patsy wouldn't give up the baby to just anyone, but she did pass her to Bree when she and Wes arrived. It was okay, because Mikey adored Cy, and the boy wouldn't leave his side. He'd just learned to walk, and he wanted to go everywhere with his uncle.

Patsy took the opportunity to go around to all the stockings and drop in trinkets. Cy had made horseshoe keychains for the older boys and men in that welding shop of his. He'd told her he'd started working on "finer things" only a week or so after they'd gotten back together, and he'd learned how to make keychains.

For the younger boys, Patsy had brought sticky hands —exactly what she knew their parents hated. But they'd last the day, and then they could go in the trash. All the children under six years old got those, and any women above that got an apple charm.

Cy had tried to make them, but the work was too delicate and the design too small. So Patsy had bought them. She thought of the gifts she had for Cy at home, and a sudden wave of panic hit her. What if they weren't good enough? How could she ever get him something as good as what he'd gotten her?

She pushed the doubts aside and finished with the presents. She stayed out of the way while final preparations were made, and then Andrew got up and called everyone to attention

"Welcome to the lodge," he said. One thing about Andrew—he didn't say much if he didn't have to. "We're glad to have old friends back with us this year." He looked at Elise, then Patsy, and finally Bree. "And we welcome our new members of the family."

Patsy cut her eyes to the two new women loitering near the doorway. They looked like someone had smacked them with two-by-fours. She knew the feeling, because a family celebration like this couldn't be adequately described. It had to be experienced.

"I'm not one for big speeches," he said. "I think I can speak for all the Whittakers when I say that the Lord has been good to us this year. We're blessed beyond measure, and though not everything has gone exactly right, we're still here. It's an amazing gift to be able to learn new things. An amazing blessing to be able to fail and take something from it."

He paused for a moment, and Patsy simply watched him. She'd always liked Andrew, who was a bit more serious than the other brothers. He knew how to have fun too, but he carried a lot of responsibility, even now. She had been gone from the lodge for a while, and she didn't know of all the things he spoke about.

But she felt the love of God in that moment, and she reached for Cy's hand. He squeezed hers, and she inched her feet closer to him, needing and craving the nearness of him. If someone would've told her she'd be snuggling up to the long-haired man last Christmas, she'd have laughed.

Of course, she hadn't expected to be managing the orchard either.

God really was good, and Patsy had plenty to be grateful for.

"Our tree lighting this year is going to be done by—"

"Andy, you forgot the snowman building contest." His wife got up and touched his arm, their toddler following her.

"Oh, right. The snowman building contest," Andrew said, speaking into the mic, which came over the PA system so everyone could hear. He grinned out at everyone. "We had an amazing snowman building contest this morning, and the winner is none other than Team Minecraft, which is Ronnie—"

Patsy couldn't hear the other names, because three boys started cheering as they came forward. Ronnie, Graham's son. Stockton, Eli's son. And Charlie, Beau's son, who was much younger than the other two. Still they all high-fived and stood at the front of the crowd with huge grins on their faces.

Patsy clapped along with everyone else, because she knew those boys and she loved them. Beside her, Cy's phone rang, and he said, "I have to take this. It's my vet." He stepped past her, and Patsy worried that he'd miss the tree lighting. She told herself it was a ten-second thing.

But it meant a lot to the people here at the lodge—to Patsy. She knew what it was like to have to put some things above others, and she supposed one of Cy's vets was very important to him.

"All right," Andrew said. "All right. You boys go sit down. Celia's shooting daggers from the kitchen."

"I am not," Celia called from the doorway, and several people laughed. She loved all the children at the lodge as if they were her own grandchildren, and though Patsy wasn't close to grandma age, she loved the Whittaker children too, just like she adored her nieces and nephews.

Andrew chuckled and hesitated for another moment, still looking toward that doorway. Patsy swung her attention that way too, and Andrew cleared his throat. "Okay, I think we're finally ready to light the tree. Then we'll do stockings and move into the newly remodeled dining room for what is sure to be the best Christmas Eve dinner of our lives."

"Oh, boy," Patsy heard Graham say, but no one objected. Patsy had eaten Celia's cooking, and it was amazing.

"Okay, so this year, the tree will be lit—"

A screeching sound came over the speakers, like feedback from a microphone. Andrew looked up as his hand lowered the mic.

"Sorry, uh, sorry," someone said over the speaker system. Patsy straightened from the where she'd been leaning against the wall. That was Cy's voice. She looked up too, and a few people murmured in the brief silence.

"Hey, so I just have a real quick question before the tree lighting," he said, his voice a bit tinny and mechanical. "Patsy, I accidentally asked you out for the first time over this speaker system. It was kind of a disaster, but one of the best things I've ever done."

She met Sophia's eyes, so many thoughts running through her mind. The weight of most eyes was on her, and Patsy wasn't sure if she should go into the hallway where the speaker was or stay in the living room.

Then Cy said, "This year has been one of the best and one of the worst of my life, and I want a whole lot more of them. With you. So if you could come meet me in the hall, I have a very important question to ask you."

Patsy took a step, but it felt like her feet had been glued to the floor. She nearly fell down, but she reached out and pressed her palm against the wall. She tried again, and this time, her legs worked. She passed the people sitting in chairs and met Celia's eyes.

She wore excitement and love in her expression, and Patsy calmed right down.

She stepped through the doorway and then around the corner, and Cy was already down on his knees. Both of them.

He held up a black velvet box and cracked the lid open. "Patsy, I love you with my whole heart. In fact, I fall in love with you a little bit more every day, which makes no sense, because I thought I was in as deep as I could go."

He drew in a breath, his eyes flickering over Patsy's shoulder. Someone touched her, and she turned to find Sophia there. Elise and Bree crowded into the space, with their husbands. Annie and Colton came, and so did everyone else. They all formed a crowd behind her, with Cy in front of them all, down on those knees and so utterly perfect.

"Oh, wow," he said. "Okay, so I should've known this would be a group event."

"Just focus right here," Patsy said, taking a small step forward in the hallway that had suddenly gotten so small.

Cy's eyes came back to her, and she watched as he zeroed in on Patsy. "Patsy, I love you. I want to be your husband and have all those boys we've talked about."

"She has the babies," Wes said.

"Hey," Colton said. "Leave him alone. He's *proposing*."

"Both of you be quiet," Gray hissed.

"Will you marry me?" Cy asked.

Patsy smiled, joy filling her from top to bottom. "Yes," she said, loud and strong and sure. "Yes, absolutely, I'll marry you."

Cy grinned too, and he braced one hand against the wall to stand. He groaned as he got to his feet. "Wow, I'm old." He chuckled as he removed the ring from the box and slid it on her finger.

"I love you," Patsy said, throwing her arms around her fiancé's neck. "I love you so much."

He bent down and kissed her while the crowd at the lodge clapped and cheered. She giggled and pressed her forehead against Cy's.

"I love you, Pats," he said. "I can't wait to marry you."

"I can't wait either." Patsy closed her eyes and breathed with Cy. Then she kissed him again, experiencing the best Christmas of her life.

Read on for a sneak peek of **HER COWBOY BILLIONAIRE BAD BOY** featuring Cy's twin, Ames, and whether or not he'll try a second chance relationship with Sophia.

SNEAK PEEK! HER COWBOY BILLIONAIRE BAD BOY CHAPTER ONE

A mes Hammond pulled into the park-and-wait lot at the Denver airport, already ready to be out of the eight-passenger SUV he'd rented. He put the vehicle in park, thinking maybe he'd buy something like this for his next car. He'd always liked driving a pickup truck or his police cruiser, but maybe he should start to switch things up.

He'd been making a lot of changes in the past several months. Why not extend that to what he drove?

The temperature in Colorado would not allow him to stay outside for long, but he'd been driving for two hours, and the trip back to the farm in Ivory Peaks would take just as long. He tucked his hands in his parka pockets, his mind on the people flying in from Wyoming.

Three of his brothers and their significant others, along with baby Michael. Thus, Ames needed the eight-passenger vehicle to get them all from the airport to the farm. Gray had flown to Coral Canyon a couple of days ago, and he, Elise, Hunter and their new baby had parked at the airport, so they'd drive themselves back to the farm. Gray had promised Ames he'd pay for the SUV and bring everyone back to the airport in several days.

Ames had accepted, though he didn't need the money. He had plenty of money. "You're going to have to tell them," he muttered to himself, his breath steaming in front of him. He shivered, because it *was* cold, and he didn't want to make any announcements on this Christmas Day.

He drew in a deep breath, the cold air making his lungs turn brittle. Still, he inhaled and inhaled until he felt like he would pop. Then he held all that chilly air in his lungs for a moment and finally blew it all out.

He turned around, his muscles humming with the short walk, and hurried back to the SUV. He got the vehicle started again and pressed the button for the seat heaters.

The flight should be arriving any moment, and Ames kept his eyes on the big screen with the flight numbers. He swiped on his phone and checked the text Cy had sent with the number on it. Glancing up, he found the number on the screen, and the big, bright words PICK UP NOW were flashing.

He didn't even have time to flip the SUV into drive before Cy called. The phone rang on his device for half a ring and then transferred to the Bluetooth system and came through the speakers.

"Hello?" Ames asked. "Can you hear me?" He put his phone in the cup holder and flipped the car into Drive.

"Yeah," Cy said, and his voice sounded among a ton of other noise. "We just arrived at baggage claim, so we'll probably be a few minutes." He didn't sound super happy, but Ames knew better than to ask his twin what was happening while Cy was in a crowd. He wouldn't say anyway, and he'd just end up more frustrated.

"Okay," Ames said, pressing on the brake. "How about you text me when you're almost ready? It's not very warm."

"It's twenty degrees warmer here than Coral Canyon," Cy said. "I'll text you."

"Great." The call ended, and Ames stayed in his parking spot. He needed to get excited to see everyone. Once he pulled up to the curb and saw them, the joy would come. He just hated the anticipation of it. He didn't want anyone looking at him and making a judgment, which they'd all do once he made his announcement.

He and Gray had worked really hard to get the whole family to come to Ivory Peaks for the holidays, as Coral Canyon seemed to exist inside a magical bubble of Christmas charm and holiday tinsel.

Ames had experienced it last year, and he sure had enjoyed going up the canyon to Whiskey Mountain Lodge a few months ago. While Cy worked in the shop and had others around him, Ames would make the drive and spend afternoons with Sophia. And later, if Colton or Wes could come sit with Cy, Ames would return to the cabin in the corner of the back yard and sit with Sophia or go teach Patsy to ride her motorcycle.

He'd really liked Sophia. He liked holding her hand.

He liked talking to her. He liked kissing her. He simply didn't like where she lived. She didn't like where he lived. Neither of them were willing to relocate or sustain a long-distance relationship, and when Ames had finally left Coral Canyon to return to Colorado, he'd left Sophia in his rear-view mirror too.

Don't be so salty, ran through his mind, in his mother's voice. She'd told him that so many times growing up that Ames had the words imprinted on his soul.

Ames took another deep breath and decided to just go to the pick-up zone. There would be airport personnel there, making sure no one pulled up and parked, but Ames didn't care. He was feeling salty, and he'd argue with the crossing guard if he had to.

"He's not a crossing guard," Ames told himself. "Be nice." He had to be nice for the duration of the next week, and he was determined to do it.

He just wished he wasn't the only brother without a woman to spend Christmas and New Year's with. His thoughts went straight back to Sophia, but he refused to so much as look at her social media.

He'd made his decision. She'd made hers.

He eased around the corner and into the lane that led to the pick-up zone on the bottom of the Denver airport. There were five levels here, and at least it was covered so there wasn't snow piled everywhere. They'd had quite a few storms in the past week, and without Gray and Hunter, it was all Ames and his father could do to keep the road to the farmhouse clear and the path out to the barns and stables walkable.

Ames stopped against the curb, tapped on his phone screen, and listened to Cy's line ringing. He kept glancing in the rear-view mirror, expecting the man wearing the orange traffic vest to notice Ames had been there longer than five seconds. But he was helping someone with their luggage, and Cy answered in the next moment.

"We're on the way out now," his brother said.

"I'm outside door twelve," Ames said.

"I see you," Cy said. "Red SUV?"

"Yep." Ames got out and let his brother hang up. He opened the back gate so the traffic guy would know Ames's people were coming. He turned, and his face split into a grin when he saw a carbon copy of himself coming toward him.

Well, Cy wore his hair longer than Ames ever had, but everything else was the same.

"Ames." Cy laughed as he abandoned his suitcase a couple of steps away and embraced Ames. They laughed together, each pounding the other on the back. Ames moved to Patsy and lifted her right up off her feet as they hugged. He'd been so angry with her this past fall, but she made Cy happier than anyone else ever had. She'd made things right between them, and she loved his brother with her whole heart.

Ames set her down and looked at her, half a dozen unspoken questions streaming between them. He'd told her she could text or call him anytime she didn't know what to do with Cy. If she needed help dealing with him.

Cy was an amazing man, but he struggled with some mental issues that Ames could feel, even from hundreds of miles away. But he'd waited for Patsy to text before he'd just barged into their relationship. And she'd only reached out to him a few times.

She nodded at him now, and Ames moved on to Wes and then Colton. Everyone loaded their luggage in the back of the SUV, and then the jostling for seats started.

"Let's put Michael in the back," Bree said. "And Patsy and I will ride back there." She looked at Wes. "That leaves Annie, Colt, and Wes for the middle. Cy can ride up front with Ames."

"It's a plan," Wes said, ducking into the SUV to get the car seat buckled in where it needed to go. Ames marveled at the change in his brothers. The past few years had brought a lot of changes to the Hammond family, and Ames sure did like seeing the little dark-haired boy on Bree's hip who looked so much like Wes.

Elise and Gray's daughter was only a couple of months old, and she was so much lighter than Michael. That came from Elise's nearly-white features, and Jane had been born bald, but she had some wisps of blonde hair coming in. Her eyes showed some evidence of Gray, because they were a dark brown that almost didn't fit among all of her pink skin.

With everyone situated in the SUV, Ames got behind the wheel and adjusted the air that was blowing. "This thing has four temperature zones," he said, feeling the extra weight in the vehicle as he eased away from the curb. "So settle in. We've got a two-hour drive."

Knobs got adjusted and conversations started, and Ames focused on getting on the freeway and away from the airport. He talked easily with Cy about how the proposal had gone. Ames had been on speaker phone, but he hadn't been there in person. Cy had said it wasn't a big deal, and he wasn't acting like it was either.

He talked about it for a while, and he seemed so happy.

"So what's going on with you?" he finally asked.

"Nothing," Ames said, and that was so true it wasn't even funny. His voice still sounded false, though.

"Sure," Cy said dryly.

"I'm telling everyone at the same time," Ames said, throwing his brother a glance.

"Are you kidding me?" Cy practically hissed. "I always get to know before everyone else."

"Well, Gray already knows," Ames said. "So that's not true this time." His fingers clenched around the wheel, because he hadn't told Cy first the way he normally would have.

"What is going on?" Cy demanded.

"Nothing," Ames said again, glaring openly at him now.

"We're all here then," Cy said. "If Gray already knows."

"Cy," Ames said, but his twin was already turning around.

"Listen up, guys," he called to everyone else in the car. "Quiet down. Shh. Ames has something to tell us."

The chatter in the back of the car stopped, so Ames's voice sounded really loud when he said, "No, I don't."

"You said you were going to tell us all at the same time," Cy said. "So tell us."

"Gray's not here," Wes said.

"Gray already knows," Cy said, glaring holes into the side of Ames's head. He folded his arms. "So tell us, Ames."

Ames looked in the rear-view mirror and found everyone looking at him and waiting. His chest pinched, and he wanted to stride away. Put some distance between himself and this situation.

But he'd put this off for long enough. It wasn't like he could keep this secret with everyone here, and he wanted them to know.

He did.

"I quit my job," he said. "Months ago. Maybe four or five."

The silence in the SUV was suddenly far too loud and unbelievably heavy. Ames shifted in his seat and glanced at Cy. "Happy now?"

"No," Cy said, the word barely audible.

"You quit your job?" Wes said. "At the police station?"

"Yes," Ames said.

"Four or five months ago?" Colton asked.

"Before I came to Coral Canyon in the fall," Ames said. "So yes."

"Why?" Cy asked. "You love being a cop."

Ames looked out his side window, because he couldn't answer this question. He hadn't been able to when Gray had asked, nor when his parents had wanted to know. His boss had been stunned, as had his partner.

Heck, most of the time, Ames would wake up in the

morning in a state of pure panic, thinking he was late for work.

"I don't know," he said. "It just felt like the right thing to do."

"You went to Texas, right?" Wes asked.

"It didn't feel right," Ames said, hating the words. But he knew no one would question his decisions if he said they just felt right or didn't feel right.

"You should come to Coral Canyon," Colton said.

"No," Ames said, practically growling the word. "I'm not looking for job recommendations or life advice. Okay? I'm fine. I'm doing fine."

He focused out the windshield as it started to snow again, and he flipped on the windshield wipers.

He wasn't doing all that fine, but Gray needed help around the farm, and Ames had plenty of time to do that now. They ran at the gym together after dropping Hunter off at school, and Ames managed to fill his afternoons and evenings with…something.

Quitting his job on the Littleton force *had* felt like the right thing to do. He couldn't meet a woman as a cop, and he really just wanted to find someone he could fall in love with. They could start a family, and his life would be filled with good things again.

"What about private security?" Cy asked. "You've always wanted to do that."

Thankfully, his phone rang, and Ames kept both hands on the wheel as he glanced at the screen where the call came up.

Sophia's name appeared there, and Ames sucked in a very audible breath.

"I thought you two broke up," Patsy said from the back seat, and Cy wore a look of intense interest on his face.

"We did," Ames said, reaching to press the red icon that would end the call.

Cy's hand shot out and blocked Ames's, and Ames had half a second to growl before Cy tapped the green icon to connect the two lines.

"Hello?" he said, actually making his voice a touch deeper so he'd sound more like Ames.

"Cy," Ames said. "I'm going to kill you."

His brother just grinned at him, and then noise started coming through the line.

"Hang up," Ames said.

"Sophia?" Cy said instead, and Ames grabbed for his phone as her voice came over the speakers for everyone to hear. He jabbed at the button that would disconnect the phone from the Bluetooth, and he glared at his brother as he put the phone to his ear.

"Hey," he said, but Sophia clearly wasn't talking to him. She was talking though.

"...put the cups over there, Stockton. We'll call everyone into the kitchen once Celia finishes with that cake."

Scuffling came through the line, and Ames knew she'd dialed him by accident.

A pocket dial.

How embarrassing.

Darkness crowded into his mind and soul, and he became very aware of how quiet the SUV still was.

He'd just admitted to something crazy and humiliating. He wasn't going to tell his brothers Sophia had called him on accident.

"Yes," he said, as if she'd asked him something. "Merry Christmas to you too."

"Thatta boy," Cy said, and when Ames looked at him, he wore such a happy smile.

Guilt pulled every muscle tight in Ames's body, but he'd committed to this charade and he'd have to see it through now.

"That's right," Ames said. "I just picked them up. We're on our way to the farm now."

Another scuffle, and then Sophia said, "Ames? Are you there?"

SNEAK PEEK! HER COWBOY BILLIONAIRE BAD BOY CHAPTER TWO

Sophia Cooke pulled the phone away from her ear, and sure enough, she'd called Ames Hammond. And the call was still connected.

"Yes," he said, and she hurried to put the phone back to her ear. "I'm here."

"I guess I called you," she said, trying to figure out why her heartbeat was sprinting through her whole body. She glanced at Bailey and Stockton, who'd been helping her set up the hot bar for that afternoon's movie event.

There would be coffee, tea, and hot chocolate, and Sophia had bought some flavored syrups and creams to go with everything.

She ducked out of the kitchen—the hub of activity at the lodge—and moved down the much quieter hall toward Patsy's old office.

Julianne Wallace had taken Patsy's job, and therefore, she'd taken over the office too. She liked scented candles and lots of knickknacks, so the office wasn't the same at all anymore.

"How's your Christmas?"

"A lot of driving," he said. "What are you up to?"

"The afternoon movie is starting in a few minutes," she said. "So I was putting together the hot bar with the teenagers."

"Ah, the hot bar," he said, and his voice strummed something inside her that no one else ever had. They'd spent three amazing weeks together, but Sophia couldn't let those twenty days dictate her whole life.

Ames obviously hadn't.

He hadn't called or texted her once since he'd left Coral Canyon in September. *Of course he hasn't*, she told herself. They'd agreed that they weren't dating, and they could text if they wanted to.

She hadn't reached out to him either. She'd coached herself relentlessly to allow him to be the one to make the first move post-break-up, and he hadn't.

She blinked, realizing the conversation had stalled completely. "Sorry," she said. "I'm a little swamped."

"I'll let you go then," he said. "I've got everyone in the car with me, and I'm driving, so."

"Ames," she practically shouted.

"Yeah?"

"Can I…maybe you'll be free to…call me later?"

Heavy silence came through the line, and Sophia pressed her eyes closed as she pressed her back into the wall behind her. "Never—"

"Sure," he said at the same time. "I'll text you first to see if you're still swamped."

"Okay," she said.

"Okay."

She didn't hang up, and neither did he. Finally, the line beeped, and Sophia pulled the device away from her ear to see Ames's handsome face on the screen. He wasn't smiling in the picture, because everything about Ames was so straight and proper. So laced up tight. So right at the speed limit.

In fact, she couldn't believe he'd answered the phone while he'd been driving at all. That was completely out of character for him.

A sigh passed her lips, and she was aware of what it held. Longing and bliss. The kind of sound she used to make after he'd kissed her goodnight for the final time, settled that cowboy hat on his head, and ducked out the door of the cabin.

She'd liked Ames Hammond very much. She still did, if she were being honest with herself. A hint of humiliation hummed through her though. She wasn't going to be yet another female to fall to the charms of the Hammond brothers, though. She'd watched all of her friends do that, each of them falling in love one by one while she got left behind.

Sophia gave herself a mental shake. She was happy here in Coral Canyon. This was the first place she'd ever truly made real friends and found that happiness, and she wasn't going to give it up for just anyone.

"There you are," Julianne said as she entered the office.

"Celia was just asking where you went. I think she might get on the PA system to find you." She picked up a piece of paper from the desk, a smile on her face. "The cake is ready, and I guess that means it's movie time."

"It does," Sophia said, glad her voice came out normal. Julianne was a very nice woman, and she was the same age as Sophia. She lived with Melinda, the new event coordinator, in the cabin where Elise and Bree had once lived.

Sophia's heart shrank, though she wasn't sure why. She still got to see Bree all the time. She lived here in Coral Canyon. Elise did too, at least in the summertime.

Sure enough, the speaker system that ran through the lodge crackled to life, and Celia's voice said, "The cake is ready, and the kids are telling me the hot bar is too. Let's gather in the kitchen for our celebration."

The Whittakers got together every Christmas season. Since Sophia had no family in town, and no desire to go visit her anyone in her family, she stayed at the lodge with them.

She'd enjoyed their family traditions. She loved participating in the good-natured contests they had. Yes, she had to work, because it was a big job to feed thirty people, but she didn't mind. If she weren't cooking, Sophia wouldn't even know what to do with herself.

She'd always adored cooking, even when her father had warned her against the idea of becoming a chef. *You'll have to work long hours,* he'd told her. *You can't have a family and be a chef.*

Turned out, she didn't have a family yet. She knew she

was a great disappointment to him, but Sophia couldn't make a man fall in love with her. If she could, she would've done so with Jake Cyprus, the quarterback Sophia had spent the better part of her teenage years crushing on.

She followed Julianne down the hall to the kitchen, others streaming in from downstairs and the living room. The Whittakers had expanded the kitchen and dining room so the gathering area was twice as big now. The guests loved it, and it definitely fit the whole family better than the table for twelve had.

Sophia stayed on the fringes of the family, but she didn't mind. She was loved and accepted here; she knew that.

Celia made a big deal about presenting the triplets with the immaculate cake she'd made. A thread of jealously moved through Sophia. She'd gone to culinary school, and she certainly had a chocolate cake recipe memorized. Celia had never gone to culinary school, and she still made a better cake and better meals than Sophia.

A sense of failure moved through her though she cheered when the triplets managed to get their candles blown out. It wasn't their birthday for another month or so, but their parents were taking them on an extended vacation, and they'd wanted to celebrate at the lodge this Christmas.

She stepped forward to help with plates and forks, trying to strike up a conversation with a couple of the children. But she'd never been all that great with kids, and they seemed to sense her awkwardness. In the end, she found herself with a delicious-looking piece of chocolate cake on a plate, alone.

She looked around at everything going on in the lodge. The dozens of conversations. The laughter. The cowboy hats. The teenagers and children.

And then there was her.

Even Julianne sat next to some of the younger children, happily helping them make bibs out of a couple of napkins she'd unfolded.

Sophia hadn't felt this level of isolation for a long, long time, and she wished she could erase it. She wished she could go back in time and fix some of the bridges she'd burned. Or at least not light those matches.

She turned away from the dining room and headed outside. Down the sidewalk that the Whittaker brothers were religious about clearing for her, and across the back yard, Sophia marched toward her cabin.

Once up the steps and inside, her heartbeat felt like it was trying to flee from her body. She hadn't felt like this in a while.

"Since the day Ames found you on that trail."

She had the sudden urge to call Patsy, but her best friend was gone to Colorado.

Still, her fingers fumbled as she tried to set down her cake and pull out her phone at the same time. She managed to do both without dumping the cake on the floor, and she sent a text to Patsy.

How was the flight? Are you nervous to go to the farm?

She knew Patsy was nervous about meeting Cy's parents as his official fiancée. She'd met them in group settings before, but this was different, and they both knew it

You called Ames?

Sophia took a long breath, something steadying inside her. She didn't want to say it was an accident, because what if it hadn't been? What if somehow, the Lord had allowed that pocket dial to happen?

"It's just because his name starts with an A," she told herself, dismissing the feeling of divine intervention.

But it kept creeping back, and Sophia looked down at her phone again, trying to figure out how to answer Patsy.

You don't have to tell me, came in. *Forget I asked. The flight was great. Not terribly long, and Cy had all these treats.*

Sophia smiled, because Patsy didn't leave Coral Canyon very often. She'd grown up here, and been raised here, and she wanted to say here and raise her family on her generational orchard.

Sophia thought that sounded like a fairy tale. To stay in one place for longer than a year or two, to always have somewhere to belong, to have a place that brought peace to her soul.

She'd never had that, and she'd spent plenty of years bitter about it.

"I'm not bitter," she whispered to herself and to reassure God that she wasn't ungrateful for what He'd done for her. "Thank you for bringing me here and for letting me stay for so long."

She'd been in Coral Canyon and at Whiskey Mountain Lodge for almost five years now, and she didn't want to leave.

What kind of treats? she asked Patsy, because that mattered. As she started an easy, non-important conversation with her best friend, Sophia left her chocolate cake on the side table and settled on the couch.

Every once in a while, when Patsy wouldn't answer for a few minutes, Sophia looked up from her phone, her thoughts centering on one person only.

Ames Hammond.

She'd been so resistant to a relationship with him, because he'd been very clear that he wasn't going to relocate to Coral Canyon. She'd told him about herself, including that she hadn't enjoyed moving often. Even now, her dad and step-mother moved all the time, always searching for the next place to be. Sophia didn't even know where her father lived right now, as she hadn't spoken to him in years.

Sophia had found her place, and it was right here. She looked around the living room. Yes, it was small. But it was hers, and she'd felt the first inklings of God's love here, and she didn't want to leave the cabin, the lodge, or Coral Canyon.

With that between them, her relationship with Ames had become about companionship. Friends. They could probably be friends, if either of them made an effort to speak to the other.

"Maybe I can still be friends with him," she murmured to herself.

Text him then.

The thought appeared in her mind, and Sophia knew exactly who it had come from and what to do with it.

She backed out of her texting conversation with Patsy and started a new one with Ames. *Hey*, she started, trying to think of what else to say. *I sure do miss talking to you. Today was an accident, but I liked hearing your voice. Maybe we could be friends?*

She read the words over and over again, trying to decide if they were too needy. Too desperate. Too cold. Too much of anything.

In the end, she decided they were fine, and she sent them flying the five hundred miles between Coral Canyon, Wyoming and Ivory Peaks, Colorado.

She drew in a deep breath, feeling strong and sure. The ball was in his court, and Ames was very good at bouncing it back. He was surely still driving, and Sophia would just have to employ her patience until he wasn't surrounded by his family and he could text back.

She could do that….

She could.

———

Oh, I can't wait to see what happens when he calls back…
You can read **HER COWBOY BILLIONAIRE BAD BOY**
in paperback.

Keep scrolling to view series starters from three of my
other series!

BRUSH CREEK COWBOYS
ROMANCE SERIES

Go up the canyon to Brush Creek Ranch, where a community of retired rodeo cowboys are looking for love...

Brush Creek Cowboy (Book 1): Former rodeo champion and cowboy Walker Thompson trains horses at Brush Creek Horse Ranch, where he lives a simple life in his cabin with his ten-year-old son. A widower of six years, he's worked with Tess Wagner, a widow who came to Brush Creek to escape the turmoil of her life to give her seven-year-old son a slower pace of life. But Tess's breast cancer is back...

Walker will have to decide if he'd rather spend even a short time with Tess than not have her in his life at all. Tess wants to feel God's love and power, **but can she discover and accept God's will in order to find her happy ending?**

FULLER FAMILY IN BRUSH CREEK ROMANCE SERIES

Join the Fuller Family in Brush Creek for heartwarming and inspirational romance series set in a picturesque small town.

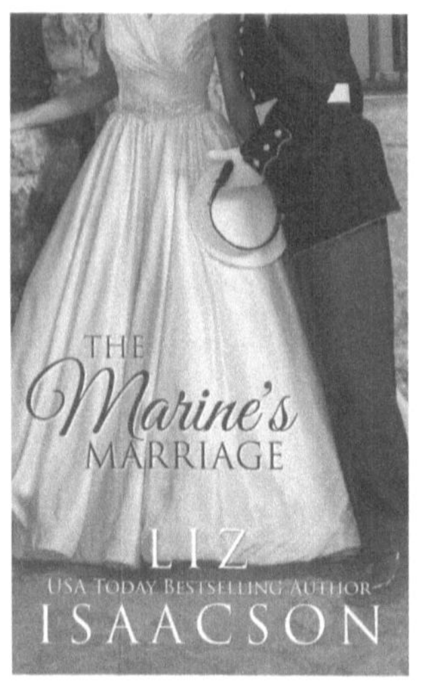

The Marine's Marriage: (Book 1): Tate Benson can't believe he's come to Nowhere, Utah, to fix up a house that hasn't been inhabited in years. But he has. Because he's retired from the Marines and looking to start a life as a police officer in small-town Brush Creek. Wren Fuller has her hands full most days running her family's company. When Tate calls and demands a maid for that morning, she decides to have the calls forwarded to her cell and go help him out. She didn't know he was moving in next door, and she's completely unprepared for his handsomeness, his kind heart, and his wounded soul. **Can Tate and Wren weather a relationship when they're also next-door neighbors?**

ABOUT LIZ

Liz Isaacson writes inspirational romance, usually set in Texas, or Wyoming, or anywhere else horses and cowboys exist. She lives in Utah, where she writes full-time, takes her two dogs to the park everyday, and eats a lot of veggies while writing. Find her on her website, along with all of her pen names, at feelgoodfictionbooks.com